A TERRIBLE BEAUTY

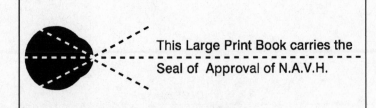

This Large Print Book carries the
Seal of Approval of N.A.V.H.

A LADY EMILY MYSTERY

A TERRIBLE BEAUTY

TASHA ALEXANDER

WHEELER PUBLISHING
A part of Gale, Cengage Learning

GALE
CENGAGE Learning·

Farmington Hills, Mich • San Francisco • New York • Waterville, Maine
Meriden, Conn • Mason, Ohio • Chicago

GALE
CENGAGE Learning·

Copyright © 2016 by Tasha Alexander.
Wheeler Publishing, a part of Gale, Cengage Learning.

Wheeler Publishing Large Print Hardcover.
The text of this Large Print edition is unabridged.
Other aspects of the book may vary from the original edition.
Set in 16 pt. Plantin.

Library of Congress CIP DATA on file. Cataloguing in publication for this book is available from the Library of Congress
LCCN 2016042848
ISBN-13: 978-1-4104-9613-3 (hardcover)
ISBN-10: 1-4104-9613-9 (hardcover)

Published in 2017 by arrangement with St. Martin's Press, LLC

Printed in Mexico
1 2 3 4 5 6 7 21 20 19 18 17

For my father, who, when I was little, told me a Greek myth every morning on the way to school, instilling in me forever a love of all things classical.

For my mother, who combines Aphrodite's beauty with Athena's wisdom.

ACKNOWLEDGMENTS

Myriad thanks to . . .

Charlie Spicer, genius editor who always pushes me to be a better writer.

Andy Martin, Melissa Hastings, Paul Hochman, Sarah Melnyk, April Osborn, Tom Robinson, David Rotstein, Annie Kronenberg, and Anne Hawkins. A truly wonderful team.

Tom Cherwin, copyeditor extraordinaire.

Don Huff, for making beautiful maps.

Joe Konrath, who told me years ago that Philip had to come back.

Vasso Kavala, Apollonia van Bergen, Malia Zaidi, and Karin Gruedl, whose extensive knowledge of German ensured Fritz speaks his native language correctly.

David Thomas, for inside information on Cambridge student life.

Edward Gutting, phenomenal classicist, for checking my ancient Greek. Any lingering mistakes are my own.

As always, my writer pals and dear friends, who make every single day brighter: Brett Battles, Rob Browne, Bill Cameron, Christina Chen, Kristy Claiborne, Jon Clinch, Charlie Cumming, Zarina Docken, Jamie Freveletti, Chris Gortner, Tracy Grant, Nick Hawkins, Robert Hicks, Elizabeth Letts, Carrie Medders, Javier Ramirez, Deanna Raybourn, Missy Rightley, Renee Rosen, and Lauren Willig.

Xander Tyska, whose breadth of knowledge across so many subjects constantly impresses and amazes me. Best research assistant ever.

My parents, always.

Andrew, because he is quite simply the best.

Ah, no wonder
the men of Troy and Argives
under arms have suffered
years of agony all for her,
for such a woman.
Beauty, terrible beauty!
— *The Iliad,* Homer,
TRANSLATED BY ROBERT FAGLES

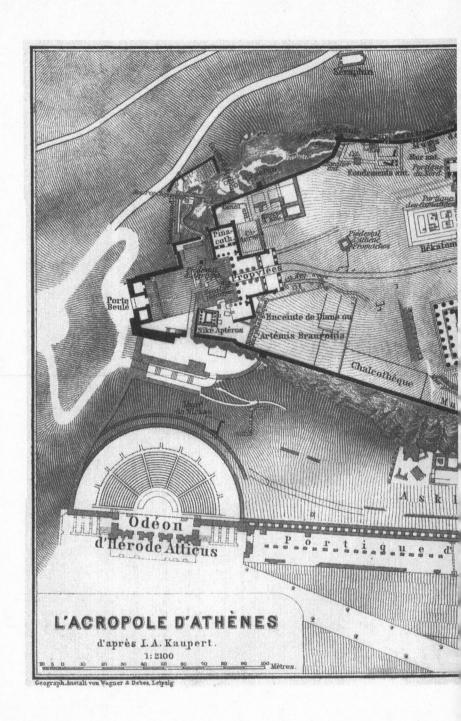

L'ACROPOLE D'ATHÈNES

d'après I. A. Kaupert.

1 : 2100

20 5 0   10   20   30   40   50   60   70   80   90   100 Mètres.

Geograph. Anstalt von Wagner & Debes, Leipzig

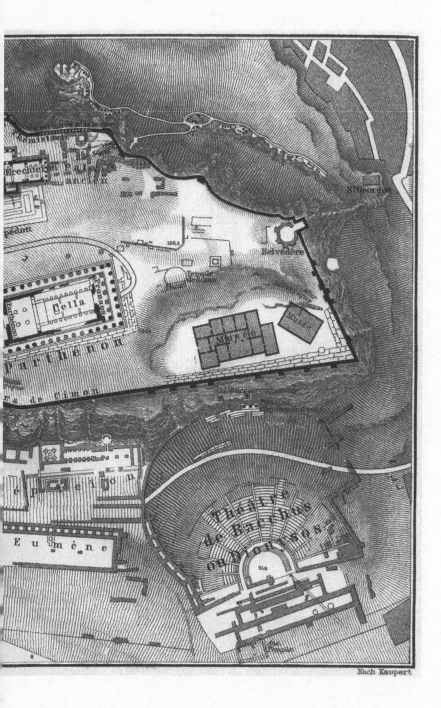

Kemnion

Erechtheion Ele... ancien

...gédon

Cella

Parthénon

...s de Cimon

É... pe... de... n

Eumène

St Géorgios

Belvédère

156,2

Musée

MUS... O

Théâtre de Bacchus ou Dionysos

91,4

Nach Kaupert

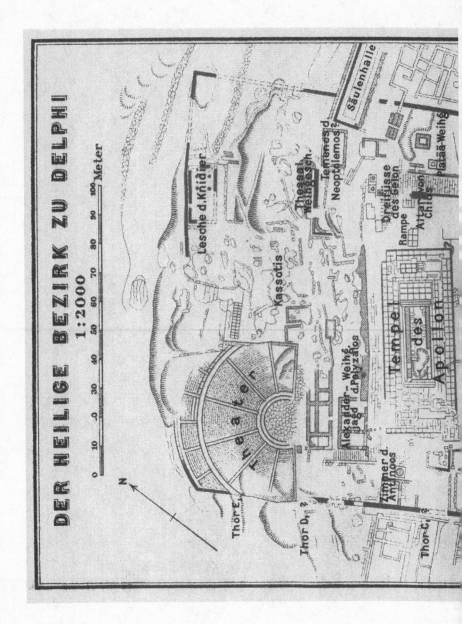

DER HEILIGE BEZIRK ZU DELPHI
1:2000

Meter

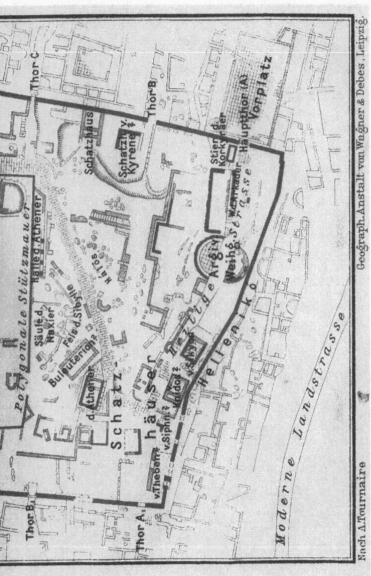

Thor C

Polygonale Stützmauer

Halle d.Athener

Schatzhaus

Säule d. Naxier

Schatzh. v. Kyrene ?

Thor B

Feis d.Sibylle

Buleuterion?

Halos

d.Athener

Stier d. Korkyräer

S c h a t z - h ä u s e r

Wagenlenker

Häupthor (A)

Vorplatz

Thor B

Thor A.

v.Theben?

Thez thige Argiv

Weihg. d.

v.Siphn.? Knidos ?

Halle d.

H e l l e n i k o

Stienfr.

Moderne Landstrasse

Nach A.Tournaire

Geograph.Anstalt von Wagner & Debes , Leipzig.

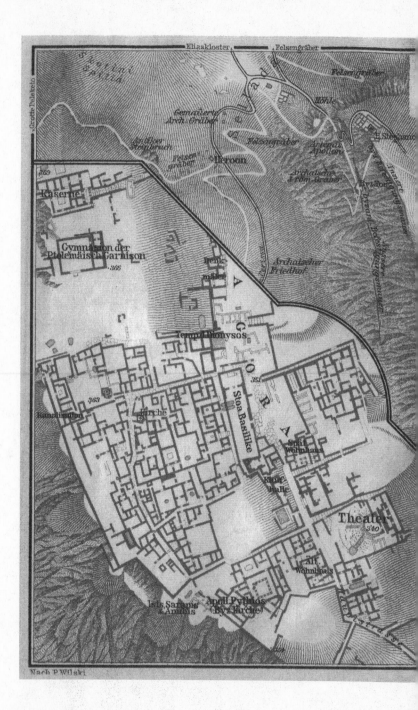

Eliaskloster — Felsengräber

Felsengräber

Höhle

Gemauerte
Arch. Gräber

Antikes
Steinbruch

Felsengräber

Felsen-
gräber

Daoon

Archaische
u. röm. Gräber

Kaserne

Gymnasion der
Ptolemäischen Garnison
366

Denk-
mäler

Archaischer
Friedhof

Templ Dionysos

AGORA

351

Kanalisation

363

Kirche

Stoa Basilike

Stoa
Wohnhaus

Rund-
halle

Theater
340

Alt
Wohnhaus

Isis Sarapis
& Anubis

Apoll Pythios
Byz. Kirche

Nach P. Wilski

ANTIKE STADT
THERA
1:5000

Meter
1 *Artemissäule*
2 *Heiligtum der Ptolemäer*
3 *Thesauros*

THERASIA

THERA (SANTORIN)
1:250000

INNERE STADT
1:2000
Meter

Geograph. Anstalt v. Wagner & Debes, Leipzig.

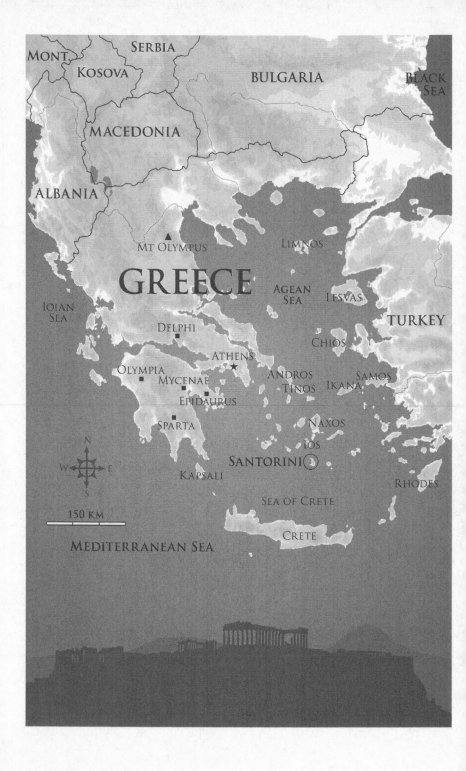

ISLAND OF SANTORINI

■ OIA

ISL.
THIRASIA

■ IMEROVIGILI

■ THIRA

ISL. NEA
KAMENI

▲
VOLCANO

ISL. PALIA
KAAMENI

KAMARI ■

ANCIENT THERA ■
MESA VOUNO ■
PERISSA ■

■ AKROTIRI

N
W—E
S

3 KM

PROLOGUE:
LONDON
DECEMBER, 1888

I looked at the profusion of mourning jewelry spread across my dressing table and sighed. A commotion coming from the corridor warned me of my mother's approach, so I selected a cameo brooch and a pair of small dangling earrings.

"Please remove the rest, Meg," I said to my maid, who was hovering behind me. "If Mother had her way I'd be wearing all the jet in Whitby. Has Miss Cavendish arrived?"

"She has, madam, but I'm afraid Lady Bromley won't let her come up," Meg said. "She does not want you to be further upset."

"You can assure her I am not in any danger of becoming more upset." I pressed my lips together and leaned toward the mirror in order to better fasten the earrings into place. Had my mother even the slightest awareness of anything beyond her own thoughts, she would have noticed that I was less upset than I ought to have been; indeed,

I should have been traumatized. Only a few months ago, I had been a bride. Now I was a widow, swathed in crape, my handsome young husband having died on safari in Africa. A pain shot through my head, and I rubbed my temples. He had been handsome, hadn't he?

The door to the room opened and my mother bustled in, a vision of mourning perfection. If anyone might have been able to coax jet into sparkling, it was Lady Catherine Bromley. "We must leave for the church almost at once. Why are you not yet ready?"

"I want to see Ivy. Please let her come up," I said.

"Your friend has no business upsetting you," my mother replied. "I sent her home. You will see her after we return from the cemetery —" She stopped and scowled at me. "Have you been crying?"

"No." I clipped the brooch onto my bodice.

"Very good. I realize that a widow — especially one so young as you — is often unable to avoid showing signs of tender emotions on the occasion of her husband's death." She frowned and picked up the bonnet she had selected for me to wear. "One must maintain one's dignity at a funeral.

Weeping would be unseemly."

"There is no danger I shall weep," I said.

"I have never been more proud of you, Emily," she said. "Well, perhaps on your wedding day, but I always thought you could do better than a viscount. You should have had a duke." This was the closest my mother had come to complimenting me in as long as I could remember. She motioned for me to stand, which I did. She did not attempt to hide the fact that she was appraising my appearance, no doubt already considering strategies to get me a duke the second time around — after, of course, an appropriate interval of mourning. Resisting the urge to tell her I would never marry again, I smoothed my skirt and pulled on a pair of black gloves so new I had to fight to get my hands into them. My gown was horrifyingly elegant in its cut, but decorated only with dull jet beads, perfectly capturing the incompatible extremes required by fashionable mourning. I draped a heavy, silk-lined mantle around my shoulders and my mother tied my bonnet under my chin. Its veils reached almost to the floor. "Fortunately, crape hides nearly everything, so you need not fear should a few tears escape," she said.

She ought not have worried.

I heard hardly a word spoken during the service at St. Margaret's, although I am assured the sermon was particularly poignant. Not much fans the flames of rhetorical inspiration more than the death of a young man. The smell of incense, which ordinarily conjured in me images of exotic biblical lands, today struck me as acrid and harsh. I did not raise my eyes from the ground, even when the eight pallbearers rose to carry Philip's coffin to the waiting hearse. My mother ushered me into the aisle behind them, and I felt my sister-in-law clasp my gloved hand. I could not bear to look at her.

I did not speak in the carriage during the procession from the church to the cemetery at Kensal Green. My mother, always at her finest when she had a captive audience, barraged me: I must keep the mirrors draped and must keep the curtains closed, though it would be acceptable to restart the clocks by the end of the week. When would my black-bordered stationery arrive? Had I ordered enough widows' weeds to get me through the winter? Wasn't it a pity to be stuck in mourning just when fashions had adopted a style so suited to showing off my figure? My father, next to her, pulled back the curtain with the tip of his walking stick and leaned toward the window. I knew he was not listening, and I did not so much as nod in reply to her. We both knew Mother's monologues allowed no room for the thoughts or opinions of others.

I wondered how many carriages formed the procession behind the hearse. So far as I was concerned, I might as well be the one in the coffin. Never before had I questioned my rash decision to accept Philip, the Viscount Ashton, when he proposed. At the time, my mother's constant hounding about the need to make a brilliant match had become unbearable and I determined that Philip, who seemed to like me well enough, would make as good a husband as anyone. I knew almost nothing about him when he asked for my hand, and had learned little more by the time he died in faraway Africa. I had succeeded in escaping from the prison I felt my childhood home had become, but I had never anticipated being trapped in another so soon. Marriage ought to have brought freedom; instead, it left me a widow. For two years I would be forced to mourn for a man who'd had so little interest in me he'd cut short our wedding trip to go on safari.

His time in Africa had proved the happiest of my life. I could come and go as I pleased without a chaperone, read what I wished, and have my friends over to dine whenever I wanted. For that brief time, the world had opened up to me, only for it all to be dashed in an instant. When my father, full of concern and kindness, had come to me at the house in Berkeley Square, taken my hands in his, and told me of Philip's death, I felt nothing. When the dressmaker came the next morning, the unrelenting black of his fabrics suffocated me. When Ivy, my dearest friend, came to me that afternoon, I could not cry with her. She wept instead, devastated by the idea that one could so quickly become a widow. This was not what young debutantes were promised during glittering balls and parties. Everyone around me waited, eager for visible signs of the despair they knew I must be feeling, but despair remained a stranger to me.

The carriage stopped. I closed my eyes and listened to the sound of rain pounding on the roof.

"There is no need for you to do this, Emily," my mother said. "It is not required. Her Majesty was too consumed by grief to attend her dear husband's funeral —"

"No," I said, stopping her. "I must go."

"It is somewhat unseemly, my dear. Ladies should not —"

This time my father interrupted. "Let her do what she must, Catherine."

He rapped on the door. A footman opened it and then helped my parents alight, but my father insisted on taking my hand as I stepped down. He squeezed it, and then patted my cheek through the layers of veils.

"It will be all right, Emily. I will help you through this." The kindness in his voice at last broke through the numbing stupor in which I had been trapped, and I felt a sob catch in my throat. He led me to the graveside, where I stood in front of the flower-covered coffin, the smell of lilies nearly overpowering me. My boots sank in the cold, wet ground, and I looked at the faces of the pallbearers, their expressions serious and somber. I recognized just one of them, Mr. Hargreaves, and he only because he had stood as best man at my wedding. I tried to conjure the details of that day, but found I recalled almost nothing, and shifted my attention back to the coffin. I could hardly picture the man inside — I remembered neither his voice nor his mannerisms — and this realization unleashed in me a flood of emotion.

It was not grief, it was guilt. Surrounding me were those who loved Philip, who mourned him, whose lives would be the poorer because of his death. Yet I, the one who ought to have felt the loss most keenly, had not known him at all, and was left to do my best to appear grieved. I was a fraud, a charlatan, a heartless woman who had not loved her husband. Two years of forced mourning, out of society, would not be punishment enough for my shortcomings. Nothing could ever erase my darkest sin — the relief that had filled me when my father had left me alone after delivering his bleak news. I had not been eagerly awaiting Philip's return; I had been dreading it, unsure of what our life together would be and loath to give up the freedom I had enjoyed while on my own in London. Now I would never have to adjust to his expectations, never have to learn to live with him, never have to play the role of obedient wife.

I hardly noticed when the vicar stopped speaking and the mourners began to return to their carriages. The rain was lashing against me, my umbrella proving to be of little use, and my soaked veils hung heavily, tugging at my bonnet. My mother was speaking to my sister-in-law; my father crossed over to the pallbearers. Philip's mother, devastated by the loss of her only son, had not come to the service. She was in no condition to leave her dower house. I ought to have shared her feelings. Instead I was grateful I would not see her today. She would recognize the depth of my offense, my failure as a wife.

I felt a hand on my arm. "There now, Em, that's finished." Jeremy Sheffield, the Duke of Bainbridge, a close family friend, and playmate of my youth stood before me, rain funneling from the brim of his tall hat. "Wretched business. What a fool Ashton was. I say no loss to anyone. Scold me if you will, but a gentleman ought not desert his bride in favor of a safari. Got what he deserved for abandoning you so soon after the wedding. Now what are you to do with yourself? You're too young to be locked up at home wearing black. Wasn't thinking of that, was he? Wretched business. Wretched."

My mother, not having heard a word he said, sidled up to him and took his arm. "My dear boy, you must stand by our girl now. She will need old friends more than ever in these dark days. Do promise you shall not abandon her."

The coffin had not yet been lowered into the ground, and already she had begun her campaign to see me married again.

Spring, 1899
1

The words on the envelope began to blur as I stared at them in disbelief.

The Viscountess Ashton.

The rest of the address was correct, down to the number of our house in Park Lane, but the name — the name — nearly stopped my breathing. More than a decade ago, I had married Philip, Viscount Ashton, only to be left a widow in the space of a few months. I had given up the title of viscountess when I married again, four and a half years later.

Davis, my butler, who had handed me the day's mail on a silver tray, remained standing in front of my desk in the library. He did not speak and, as always, his countenance appeared impassive, but I suspected him of sharing my curiosity as to the contents of the letter.

"Is Mr. Hargreaves home?" I asked.

"No, madam, he is still at his club."

I fingered the silver letter opener in my hand. One envelope ought not invoke such a pressing sense of ominous foreboding. "Very strange to be called 'viscountess' again after all this time. Surely there's none among my acquaintances who is unaware I am no longer the Viscountess Ashton."

"I could not comment, madam."

"Oh, Davis, don't be so serious," I said, trying to sound cheerful. I sliced open the creamy white paper and pulled out what was inside. "Look, it is nothing but a photograph from Greece. The Parthenon. Someone must have sent it as a joke. There is neither note nor signature."

"Port, madam?" Davis asked. He knew me too well.

Memories of my first husband always filled me with mixed emotions. Our marriage had not been an arranged one, but neither had it been a love match, at least not on my part. I had accepted his proposal because I viewed becoming a wife as an inevitable, if unwelcome, step in my life. On the day he asked for my hand, living with him seemed preferable to staying any longer in my mother's house. He was kind and decent, a respectable gentleman, and I expected we would be happy enough, whatever that meant.

Nearly two years after he died, I found a journal — one volume out of the many he had kept from the time he was a schoolboy — and reading it made me feel as if I knew him better than I had when he was alive. On its pages I learned he had entered into our union with an attitude far different from mine: For reasons beyond my comprehension, he fancied himself in love with me. Since then, I have always felt a keen guilt at not having recognized this while he was alive, despite the fact that his death, only a few months after our wedding, had precluded me from ever getting to know him well.

My youth and inexperience might have rendered it impossible for me to recognize his feelings, but that is no excuse. The journal revealed the man he was, and I appreciated and loved that man, even though my feelings came far too late. Philip gave me a gift that enriched my life in ways I would never have thought possible. He fired in me, through his writings, a desire for intellectual pursuits, a longing to study Ancient Greek, to read Homer, and to travel to the land of Alexander the Great and gaze upon the monuments of Pericles' Athens.

What began as an attempt to emulate his interests grew into a deep intellectual passion, and over the years I had gained a reputation as a careful scholar. I translated both *The Iliad* and *The Odyssey,* and had written several well-received monographs on vase painting in Hellenistic Athens. Philip had left me a villa on Santorini that he'd had built as a gentleman's retreat, using traditional Cycladic methods, and from the moment I first set eyes on its brightly whitewashed walls, curved archways, and bright blue shutters, I recognized it as a place in which my soul would always rest easy. I spent as much time as I could manage to in its comfortable confines.

I owed a great debt to Philip. I would never have become the woman I am now if it were not for him. Furthermore, had I not married him, it is unlikely I would have made the acquaintance of his closest friend, Colin Hargreaves. Thrown together by circumstances two and a half years after Philip's death, we fell in love. After two more years passed, we married, both of us conscious of Philip's role in our happiness; but all those raw emotions conjured up by his death had long since smoothed away.

Until now. This envelope had, for me, brought them all back to the surface.

I accepted the port Davis brought me and tried to clear my mind, focusing on all the things I needed to accomplish during the fortnight I would be in London before we departed for Greece with two of our dearest friends, Jeremy Sheffield and Margaret Michaels. Margaret and I had organized the trip in an attempt to distract Jeremy from his multitudinous woes. The previous year, his engagement to Amity Wells had scandalized *le beau monde.* England's best had objected to his choice of an American heiress as his future bride, but this had paled next to the furor caused by her subsequent actions, which left him heartbroken and humiliated. He soldiered through the next season as best he could, maintaining an admirably stiff upper lip in the face of an onslaught of gossip, but he had no interest in dealing with more of the same this year.

Margaret and I had easily convinced him a holiday abroad was what he required, but the details of our itinerary proved far more difficult to agree upon. Margaret, a devoted Latinist, and I, a lover of all things Ancient Greek, clashed over what would better soothe our friend's soul. She wanted him to stand in the Forum in Rome and mourn Caesar. I wanted him to seek solace in the beauty of the Acropolis in Athens. In the end, I won the argument, but only because Jeremy intervened, insisting upon Greece because he knew we would include in our travels several weeks at my villa on Santorini, where we would find no expatriate society, no preening young ladies, and, best of all, no hope of useful occupation.

I did not require an entire fortnight in London to organize the journey, but I had other reasons to be in town. My husband, one of the queen's most trusted agents, is frequently called upon to investigate matters that might prove embarrassing to members of the royal family or the aristocracy. Together, not always in conjunction with his work for the palace, we have brought at least ten heinous murderers to justice. Over the years, my own detectival instincts and skills have been honed, and I beg the reader's forgiveness if it is immodest to admit I am quite good at my work. My talents, however, did not often interest Her Majesty; she nearly always required only Colin's services. He had just returned from St. Petersburg, where he had spent six weeks working, and we wanted some time in town with our twin boys, Henry and Richard, and our ward, Tom, all of whom had now passed their third birthdays.

I heard the door open, and looked up to see my husband. "You appear almost dour," he said, crossing to me and sitting on the edge of my desk. "Davis tells me the mail disturbed you."

"Davis speaks most freely to you," I said. "I do wish he would offer me the same courtesy." I handed him the envelope.

"The Viscountess Ashton," he said. "I almost forgot you were once called that." He barely glanced at the picture of the Parthenon before returning it to my desk.

"Do you not find it slightly unnerving that someone has anonymously sent this?"

He shrugged. "Not in the least. You do draw controversy, my dear. Between your scholarly pursuits, your campaigns for social justice, and your refusal to behave like a good little wife, you manage to scandalize society at least once every six weeks. No doubt some ill-mannered person who thinks himself very important sent this to remind you of your aristocratic connections. Poor bloke doesn't realize he's taken entirely the wrong tack."

"It is possible, I suppose."

"Come now, this can't be troubling you so much, can it? I thought we were done with all that."

"We are," I said. "Yet there are times I think of Philip and feel a twinge of guilt."

"That, my dear, is one of the many reasons I adore you. You have an extremely sensitive soul. It is a most fetching quality." He moved very close to me and traced the neckline of my bodice with his finger. "Although at the moment, I am afraid I am inspired to act in ways one might not consider entirely 'sensitive.' Would you object to me locking the door?"

I did not object. His subsequent actions pushed all thoughts of the mysterious envelope and Philip out of my head. I might not have considered it again, had the spectre of my late spouse not surfaced the next day, when we had taken the boys to the zoo. Colin, wanting to spend as much time as possible with them before we left for Greece, had insisted we wrangle them without the aide of Nanny, the elderly but still-spry woman who had raised him and was now entrusted with the care of this latest generation of Hargreaveses. Tom and Richard held Colin's hands, dutifully following any instructions he gave them as we strolled through the park, but Henry tugged at mine, dragging me from enclosure to enclosure, until at last he stood still, mesmerized by an exhibit of silkworms in the insect house. Tom and Richard, less enthralled with the tiny creatures, pleaded to go back outside. Colin obliged them, leaving Henry to study the remaining terrariums. He reached his little hand out to the glass, careful not to touch it, and traced the path of an aquatic beetle in the tank before him. I bent over to look more closely myself, but was shocked upright when I heard a voice call out.

"Ashton! Philip Ashton, as I live and breathe!"

Hearing this name spoken aloud squeezed the breath out of me.

I spun around on my heel to see a rotund gentleman vigorously shaking the hand of an even more rotund gentleman, neither of whom fit the description of the Viscount Ashton to whom I had briefly been united in matrimony. Still, it unnerved me to hear his name. I shook off the discomfort. I did not see the gentlemen again, but while waiting outside the camel house so the boys might have a ride on one of the ungainly beasts, I heard someone call out *Ashton! Philip Ashton!*

Colin raised an eyebrow as he studied my face. "That's an odd look."

"It is nothing, I assure you," I said, and explained what had happened. "I am a bit unnerved to hear the name twice in one day."

"Unnerving indeed." Our eyes met and he gave me a knowing smile. In the early days of our courtship, we had both struggled with the painful knowledge that our attachment could never have occurred without Philip's death. The dead are beyond betrayal in matters of love, but that had not precluded a host of emotions from rearing their, if not ugly, certainly complicated heads. One does not expect to fall in love with one's dead husband's best friend. We had come to terms with all that long ago, yet I could see in Colin's dark eyes a hint of the grief he still felt at the loss of someone so dear to him. I was reaching out to touch his arm when Henry burst into tears and flung himself to the ground.

"Cruel, vicious man!" he cried, beating his little fists into the grass next to the pavement. Henry had a vocabulary beyond that of either of his brothers and most of his peers. He also had a penchant for dramatically stating his opinions for maximum effect.

I crossed my arms. "Up, Henry, now."

"Cruel man making camel unhappy." I had to agree with my son that the camel did not appear happy, but the keeper leading it around a smallish circle while visitors rode on it hardly seemed cruel. If anything, he looked bored.

"He isn't hurting the camel, Henry," I

said. "The rope is only so he doesn't run away."

"I want camel to run away." Henry had stopped pounding the ground and drew himself back up to his feet, his clothing now covered with dust. Nanny would not be pleased. I took him firmly by the hand.

"Camels do not do well on their own in London," I said. "And little gentlemen who cannot behave do not get rides."

"Don't want a ride," Henry said, the tears pooling in his eyes betraying the lie. Colin dropped Richard's and Tom's hands and picked up his ill-mannered son.

"You are good to worry about the camel, Henry," he said, turning so the boy could better see into the enclosure. "But he is quite all right and looks a rather happy chap to me. Camels don't have the same expressions as us, do they, so their faces can be rather difficult to read."

I sighed. "Colin . . ."

"I am not indulging him, Emily, I am teaching him. Now then, Henry, did you know camels live in the desert?"

"I am not a baby, Papa," Henry said. "Even Richard knows about deserts." Henry, born four minutes before his brother, considered Richard intolerably young.

The queue inched forward, and it became clear that I would be in charge of managing Richard and Tom, as my husband was now thoroughly embroiled in a discussion of the care, maintenance, and emotional well-being of camels. Henry would get no ride — we could not allow that after he had caused a scene — but I did not doubt he far preferred what he viewed as a serious discussion with his father to bumping along on the platform strapped to the poor beast in question. As I handed the other boys up to the keeper, who secured them for their ride, I caught a glimpse of a lean gentleman with a striking shade of sandy hair, the precise color of Philip's. Shocked, I stepped away from the queue to get a better look, but the man had disappeared.

When we returned from the zoo (Nanny was quite severe with Henry upon our return — he had ruined his jumper), I retired to the library to consult the itinerary for our trip. There, on my desk, I saw a slim leather-bound book: Philip's journal, which I kept stored, wrapped in tissue paper, in a box tucked away in my dressing room. Not even Colin knew of its location.

Philip had filled volume after volume of diaries, but I had kept only the single one I found in the house I had shared with him in Berkeley Square. The rest I left for his family — his nephew might enjoy reading them, and if not, some future viscount might find them diverting, or at least worthy of a place in the family history. This volume, though, cut too deeply into my heart to part with. I always intended that I would see it eventually returned to the Ashtons, but for now, I kept in my possession the words he had written while courting me.

I had not looked at the journal in years. Yet now here it was, carefully placed in the middle of my desk, next to the envelope addressed to *The Viscountess Ashton* and turned to the entry he had made the day of our engagement. There was no question of this being accidental — a heavy leather book weight held the ivory pages in place — leaving me to wonder who had chosen to open the book of my past.

PHILIP
CAIRO, 1891

He had recounted the story with such frequency that he no longer needed to pay attention to the words he was speaking; it had become second nature. He always started at the same place, back when the fever had passed, but he had not yet regained his former strength. Kimathi, the Masai guide who had saved him from death, had done an admirable job in speeding his recovery, but Ashton could still not reconcile himself with the manner in which his fortunes had taken such a radical turn. Initially, he would tell people very few details — only that he had been on safari with friends, that he had, at long last, got the elephant he had so craved, and that he had collapsed soon after having indulged in some celebratory champagne.

Kimathi painted a fuller story, one so outrageous and unlikely that Ashton had been loath to accept it, but the guide, who had proved loyal time and time again, insisted he had saved the Englishman from murderous hands by spiriting him off under the cover of night to the remote camp of the tribe with whom Kimathi's sister had lived from the time of her marriage.

Ashton told his eager listeners — they were always eager — that for months he had known nothing more than this. So far as he could make out, he had been unconscious for weeks. He understood their language, but the Masai did not subscribe to anything like the concept of the English calendar. After he awoke to find himself in a primitive tent, a heavy beard covering his face, his mind had remained clouded with fever for at least another month. It was not until his body had recovered enough for him to start going out with the tribe's hunters that he began asking questions no one could answer. No one, that is, until Kimathi returned from his own domicile. Ashton smiled as he realized the inanity of his word choice. *Domicile* and *Masai* did not go together in any ordinary sense.

Kimathi had visited Ashton erratically after having first brought him to his sister. The Masai were nomadic, and it was no short journey across seemingly endless plains for Kimathi to see his friend. When at last they sat together in front of the fire in the center of the camp, the warriors circled behind, as if protecting them from some unseen spirit. Kimathi told him what he had seen that fateful night: One of the white men in the hunting party had put something into Ashton's drink, something that had nearly killed him. The other Englishmen, Kimathi said, believed their friend had a fever, and they all went away, worrying it was contagious. Only Hargreaves had remained behind, nursing his friend through illness and — so Hargreaves thought — death.

Kimathi knew better, though. He knew this was not sickness, but poison, and he knew the sleep it brought mimicked death. He also knew that the man who had administered it had come back to the camp when Hargreaves was asleep, to see if Ashton had succumbed to his evil deed. This frightened Kimathi. He could see devils in this white man, and he knew that only he could protect Ashton.

Everyone who witnessed the tragic scene believed Ashton to be dead. Even the newspapers had reported as much. His breath appeared to have stopped, and any trace of a heartbeat was too faint for anyone to detect. Kimathi stood by as Hargreaves bathed his friend's body and dressed it before lowering it into a hastily built coffin. And then, while the Englishman dealt with the necessary arrangements to return the coffin to Ashton's family, Kimathi replaced it with a second one, built hastily as well under the cover of night, and occupied by the corpse of an elderly Masai man from Kimathi's tribe who had died the day before.

The Masai do not bury their dead, but instead leave them out for predators. No one would have objected to Kimathi's having moved the remains — bodies did not matter; the essence of the person was gone. Only great chiefs were buried, so, if anything, this man was receiving an unexpected honor. Kimathi did not think this would offend his god, Enkai, who was all of the earth and the sky and whatever else Kimathi might never see. He worried the body was too slim and added a few rocks to the wooden box, wanting to ensure that the weight would not arouse suspicion. He had wrapped it securely in blankets, and could only hope no one would try to remove them if they did have cause to open the coffin. But even if it were opened, this would not matter once Kimathi had got his friend to safety; no one would have any idea where to look for him. He removed the lid from the wooden box occupied by the Englishman, attached it to a makeshift sledge, and dragged it for a day and a night until he reached the tribe of his sister's husband.

Now that Ashton had his strength back, he knew he ought to set off for home, but the days he spent with the Masai ran one into the other, and he found leaving more difficult than he could have anticipated. He had grown accustomed to life in the camp, and the tribe had begun to accept him as one of their own. He hunted with them, and the thrill of this proved superior to any prior experience in his life.

In the past, his safaris had been decidedly tourist affairs, even though, at the time, he had believed passionately he was the least European of the European hunters on the Dark Continent. How wrong he had been! Now he stalked his prey without the Western trappings of comfort he had previously required. Now he had no cook, no servants, no one to tend to his game after it had fallen. Life presented him with fewer complications here, and his experience was far richer than any he'd had in England, or even when he had traveled.

While honing the tip of his spear in camp one day, he looked up and called a greeting to a young woman who had just recently given birth to her first child, the infant now snuggled tight against her chest. The image stirred something in him, and he began to think about Kallista — Emily, his wife — and to consider how long he had been gone. Now that he had regained his health, he had no reason to delay his trip home, and he admitted, with a degree of reluctance he found nearly inconceivable, that he could not live the rest of his life with the Masai. He had to return to England.

The next time Kimathi came to see him, they agreed he would start his journey when the moon was full again. When he left, Kimathi walked with him, the days blending into weeks, to the nearest European outpost, where Ashton persuaded a group of Germans en route to Cairo to let him join their party. The viscount promised remuneration as soon as they arrived in the Egyptian capital. Kimathi wept when they parted, but Ashton promised to return, determined they would hunt together again.

Much as he had relished his time with the Masai, being back in the company of educated men quenched a thirst he had forgot he had. He had lost so much of what mattered to him during his time in Africa — his study of Greek, his writing, his antiquities, his wife — and when he'd learned three years had passed since that fateful day of his last safari, he'd begun to worry that going back to his old life might not be a simple endeavor.

When they reached Cairo, the Germans refused to let Ashton give them anything in return for their hospitality, which proved fortunate for the Englishman. He never suspected he would have trouble securing a room at Shepheard's Hotel, believing the manager would be sure to recognize him from previous visits. His assumption was foolish. The clerk at the desk, after consulting with the manager, told him that Philip, the Viscount Ashton, had perished in East Africa on safari years ago. His demise had been reported in all the papers and the management of Shepheard's did not look kindly on those adopting false identities. Ashton demanded to speak to the manager himself, and the man, who did admit he looked familiar, stated firmly that he could not give him a room on credit if Ashton could not somehow prove his identity.

He met the same resistance at the bank. Unable to access his funds, Ashton stormed into the office of the British consul, where he was treated with politeness and a great deal of pity before they ushered him out with the address of a physician they hoped might be able to treat his disorder.

How foolish to have believed his appearance alone would make the world recognize he was still alive! He had nothing that proved his story. He had almost no possessions: just the clothing given to him by the Germans. He had no books, no letters, no objects of sentimental value, not even the photograph taken of his lovely wife on their wedding day.

That, he had left in France.

2

The benefit of hindsight suggests I perhaps ought to have given the journal more consideration than I did. As things stood, however, I decided Margaret must have left it as a joke. She had gone up to Oxford that morning to see her husband in what we both knew would be a vain attempt to convince him to join our trip to Greece. Very little could induce Mr. Michaels (Margaret steadfastly refused to call him by his Christian name, Horatio, as she insisted — rightly — that it did not suit him) to leave his life at the university. Sometimes, she claimed, he would go days speaking nothing but Latin, much to the dismay of his students.

The previous evening, she and I had sat up late in the library with a very fine bottle of port. The conversation naturally veered to our trip, and as a result, to the villa, and as a result of that, to the man who had built it. Margaret, whom I had not met until two years after Philip died, knew only slightly less about him than I did. I had always welcomed her American bluntness when we discussed him, even, on this occasion, when she had declared that if he were anything but a fool he would have constructed in Italy a perfect reproduction of a Pompeian villa instead of burdening me with a house she called a Cycladic nightmare. She loved the villa, but loved more making overly dramatic statements that offered support for whatever agenda suited her in the moment.

Leaving the journal open was just the sort of thing Margaret would find harmless and amusing. I remembered that she alone knew where I kept it — she had watched me wrap it in tissue and store it away — and teased me occasionally about it. I closed the volume without so much as reading a word, returned it to my dressing room, and gave it no further thought until weeks later, when I was standing on the deck of the steamer taking us from Brindisi to Corfu.

The bright sky, a deep, crystalline blue prevalent in the Mediterranean, pulsed with beauty. The calm sea had let us slip into an easy rhythm on board, and the sun warmed us pleasantly against the occasional stiff breeze. Colin, who had deliberately left in London the smoke-colored spectacles I had purchased for him, leaned over the railing squinting, his dark hair tousled by the wind, his straw boater firmly in his hands rather than on his head. Jeremy and Margaret, leaning together conspiratorially, were sitting on a nearby bench evaluating the perceived merits of our fellow passengers.

When a strong gust of wind caught my parasol, I turned around so that its delicate ribs would not be broken. As I moved, I saw a gentleman on the deck above the one on which we were standing. He was tall and slim, with an elegant slouch worthy of Jeremy's best. His hat covered most of his hair, but I could see it was sandy-colored, and everything about him reminded me so violently of Philip that I gasped.

"What is it?" Colin asked, turning away from the water to look at me. "You appear most unwell. Are you seasick?"

"Do you see him? That gentleman there?" I pointed, but it was too late. "Never mind, he's gone."

"Was it someone with whom we are acquainted or merely an individual with a taste in hats that you find shocking?" he joked.

"Neither," I said. "He . . . he could have

been Philip's twin. It took me by surprise is all."

Colin studied the passengers on both decks as best he could from where we stood, but saw no one who fit the description. "You are bound to think of him when we are on the way to his house in Greece. Do not let it make you sullen."

Two days later — after another boat and a long and dusty train ride — we settled happily into rooms at my favorite hotel in Athens, the Grand Bretagne in the Place de la Constitution, just across from the king's palace. The square brimmed with orange trees and oleander, forming a pretty little park in the center of the city. For every European tourist one saw, there were a handful of Greeks, some in ordinary dress, but many in traditional garb, the colors and styles lending an exotic flair to the scene and reminding one how removed the place was from the rest of the Continent.

Very little of Athens resembled the other capitals of Europe, first because of the scale of the city. It did not sprawl like the arrondissements of Paris or encompass the wide variety of neighborhoods to be found in London. The population of the British capital had totaled more than three million by the middle of our century, whereas the

Athenians now, in 1899, numbered little more than a hundred thousand. More important, ancient monuments dominated Athens in a way not duplicated anywhere else in the world. Margaret might argue that Rome had more than its share of ruins, but I give those only a small measure of credit, as I find them inferior to what the Greeks had constructed centuries before.

As anyone with even the barest knowledge of ancient history would guess, Athens is anchored by the Acropolis, standing proud atop a limestone promontory, surrounded below by the streets of the Plaka, a jumble of houses, shops, and cafés. Beyond this, one found the more familiar type of European streets built during the period when the architects Stamatis Kleanthis and Eduard Schaubert, both neoclassicists, had sought to improve the layout of the quickly growing town. Their attempts and those of Leo von Klenze established a certain sense of order, but the contemporary parts of the city interested me very little. I wanted ruins.

And ruins were to be had nearly everywhere one looked in Athens. Aside from the Acropolis, one could visit the Agora, the old marketplace of the ancient city, where Socrates had met with his students, and where still stands the Temple of Hephaestus, the best remaining example of what is to my mind the loveliest style of buildings, the Doric peripteral temple. The nearby Roman Agora is worth a visit as well, but no one can claim surprise to learn I prefer the other, older market. Whenever in Athens, I also required a quick visit to the Olympieion, called *staes Kolónnaes,* or *at the columns,* by the Greeks and *a work of despotic grandeur* by Aristotle. I loved to stand in the midst of what had once been a magnificent temple to the Olympian Zeus, a structure that had taken more than five centuries to be completed: the perils of political unrest in the ancient world. Of the hundred and four original columns, only fifteen remain, yet the site retains an impressive power.

"That's quite enough, Em," Jeremy said. "If I hear you wax rhapsodic about one more column I shall pack up at once and make my way to Paris or Baden-Baden or someplace no one will try to educate me." Our carriage clattered over cobbled streets en route to the Acropolis. My preferred means of attacking Athens always included a moonlight trip to the monument, and the first thing I had done after arriving in the city was to contact the Ministry of Religion and Education to get the required *per-*

messo. Jeremy pulled a face. "I refuse to be educated. Do not try to succeed where Oxford failed."

After we reached the base of the Acropolis, we hiked to the top of the plateau, Colin and Jeremy carrying lanterns for illumination. When we reached the final turn, just below the charming Temple of Athena Nike, and mounted the steep stone stairs leading to the Propylaea, following the path of the ancients who had made the identical trek during the Panathenaic processions of centuries past, Margaret blew out a loud breath.

"Whenever I catch my first glimpse of the Parthenon, I know the Greeks were superior to the Romans, but I will never admit this in any other circumstance." The moon hung heavy in the sky above, its silvery light bathing the marble buildings in a mystical glow. We continued along a narrow ramp, through the columns of the Propylaea, all of us awestruck the moment the Parthenon filled the space before us.

"This is what man can accomplish at his best," Colin said.

"Even I can't think of anything cynical to say." Jeremy tilted his head and studied the noble edifice. Mesmerized, we stood, conscious of nothing but a beauty so perfect as to be at once incomprehensible and utterly engaging. The powerful elegance of the Parthenon and, in the distant moonlight, the Caryatids on the porch of the Erechtheion reached deep into the soul, satisfying some primal need for hope and harmony and meaning.

The spell was broken by a rowdy group of young men who started cheering on one of their party as he tried to shimmy up a column on the front of the Parthenon. I scowled and stepped forward, ready to intervene, but was spared having to do so when the would-be climber fell to the ground, laughing.

"Tallyho!" Margaret cried, and made her way along the wide pavement that opened up on the far side of the Propylaea. Colin followed, but as they walked toward the Parthenon, I took Jeremy by the arm and pulled him past it, in the direction of the Erechtheion.

"Keeping me from the best part, are you, Em?"

"Hardly," I said. "The Erechtheion was the most sacred building on the Acropolis. It is where Athena and Poseidon battled for the right to be patron of the city. It is my favorite spot on earth." We skirted past the Parthenon, along a rock-strewn pavement with broken pieces of columns and statues on both sides.

"They are lovely ladies," Jeremy said, tipping his hat as we approached the Caryatids.

"Stunning, aren't they?" I pointed to the second from the end on the left. "She is a copy. Elgin took the original."

"And thank goodness for that," Jeremy said. "If he hadn't, would any of us care that the rest are here?"

"Of course we would. She should be with her sisters."

"Would you like me to have her removed from the British Museum and returned to the Greeks?"

"Yes, please." I smiled as we made our way into the temple, through the Ionic columns supporting the east portico, and entered Athena's sanctuary. Most of the ceiling was gone, as were most of the floors, but one could still get a sense of how the building had once appeared. "I recall there being a den for snakes somewhere in here, but I do not know the precise location. I can tell you with confidence a statue of the goddess, not as large or imposing as the one in the Parthenon, stood in this spot, fashioned from olive wood — appropriately, as it was the olive tree that won Athena the city. She was the patron, you know, after defeating Poseidon for the honor. If you look here" — I led him down a wide staircase to a narrow chasm in the ground — "you will see the mark left by Poseidon's failed attempt to impress the citizens. He struck his trident on the ground and a spring burst out, but the water was salty, like the sea, and the Athenians found it not nearly so useful as the olive tree Athena had given them. You can see it on the outside of the building."

"Surely not the same magical tree?" Jeremy teased, the flickering light of his lantern making his eyes seem to dance.

"No, this would be a descendent of a second magical tree. The Persians destroyed the first when they razed the Acropolis ten years after their defeat at the Battle of Marathon in the fifth century B.C. Two days later, a new shoot had already grown."

"Had it, now?"

"I thought you weren't being cynical," I said.

"I am not being cynical. I am merely expressing what I view as a healthy inquiry into the ancient methods of planting trees. Magic, it would appear, proves more effective than most gardening techniques." He pulled a small penknife from his pocket and started scratching at the wall.

"You are not going to leave graffiti."

"Of course I am. It is a time-honored tradition that goes back, well, probably to your dear friend Pericles. I won't stand for that Byron chap having left his name more places than I have mine."

"This I cannot watch," I said. "It is a despicable thing to do! I shall meet you outside by the olive tree." I climbed the staircase — a modern addition no doubt added for the safety of visitors and archaeologists alike — and made my way to the North Portico, on the opposite side of the building from the famous Caryatids. Much though I adored the ancient maidens, this less showy porch had long resonated with me. I stepped onto it and looked down at the lights of the city beneath me, framed by the temple's fluted columns. Under the cover of night, with none of the trappings of modern conveniences, it was almost as if I were gazing down on the ancient world, sharing the view with Pericles.

I sighed. In fact, nothing looked as it had to Pericles. Even the Acropolis, with its gleaming marble, had been altered irrevocably. Long gone were the bright colors of ancient paint that coated the buildings, the monumental sculptures — some destroyed during wars, some taken home by

Lord Elgin — and even Poseidon's spring. Yet this did not disappoint me. Would the Acropolis stun us with its beauty were it still in its pristine, original form? Or did the very fact that it survived in ruins instill it with a sort of romanticism, a painful nostalgia, awakening in our souls a longing for all that we cannot have?

I returned to the path and continued to circle the building, a marvelous feeling engulfing me. Truly, there was something about this place, something that —

A tall figure moved toward me from the darkness behind Athena's olive tree, navigating the rocky debris with a nimbleness suggesting familiarity with the site. His linen suit nearly matched the hue of the Erechtheion's marble, and his sandy hair was bleached by the moonlight almost to white. His gaze made me tremble, and he spoke only two words before turning and disappearing into a shadow:

"Tê kallistê."

PHILIP
MUNICH, 1891

Ashton's story haunted the Germans who had so graciously transported him from the depths of the African bush to the relative civility of Cairo. When they saw him again, on the streets some weeks later, despondent and on the verge of falling ill, they took him back into their fold. In the early days of their acquaintance, Ashton had formed an instant connection with Fritz Reiner, a young archaeologist who shared his passion for classical studies, and now Reiner invited him to travel with him to his home in Germany. What other option did he have?

When they arrived in Munich, Reiner's mother took one look at Ashton and declared him to be under her protection. She would see to it that he regained all of his strength and his place in the world. Regaining strength, apparently, meant regular consumption of strong German beer, sausages, and potatoes, but Ashton found he objected to none of it. Slowly, he lost all pallor of illness. But nothing stopped the nightmares plaguing his sleep. They, Ashton knew, would cease only when he was back home, comfortably settled with his wife. He considered going to Berlin, to meet with the British ambassador, but Reiner convinced him not to bother.

"You will meet the same resistance you did in Cairo, my friend," he said. "You need to go where people recognize you. Not the manager of a hotel or some useless civil servant or bank employee — the people who know and love you. The minute your family sees you, this whole dreadful business of needing proof will evaporate."

"I realize what you say is both wise and correct," Ashton said, "but I am full of fear. I have been gone so long. What will they think? I ought never have stayed in Africa for so long."

"You were not of sound mind, my friend — first the poison and then the fever addled your brain. But now you are recovered and ready to return to your former life — the life that never should have been taken away from you."

Ashton pushed his palm hard against his forehead. "Kallista, my wife. How will she ever be able to find it in her heart to forgive me?"

"It will be like a dream to her," Reiner said. "No more dreary widowhood. You will be giving back to her all of the hopes for her future she was forced to abandon the day she learned of your death."

"What if she has remarried?"

"So soon?"

"It has been nearly three years."

The two gentlemen sat silent for a moment.

"It is possible, I suppose," Reiner said. "We could make discreet inquiries with someone in London, perhaps?"

"Hargreaves would be the man for that," Ashton said.

"Send him a telegram?" Reiner suggested.

"Yes," Ashton said. "I shall do so without delay. His reply will tell me how best to proceed." He did not wish to reveal his return to Hargreaves quite yet, so signed it from an old mutual acquaintance of theirs from Eton. That done, he steeled himself for his friend's response.

3

Tê kallistê.

To the fairest.

The shadowy figure had spoken the same words written on the golden apple dropped by Eris, or Discord, at a wedding to which she had not been invited. Athena, Hera, and Aphrodite all claimed it, each believing herself the most worthy of the sentiment. Zeus stayed out of the argument, and chose a shepherd — Paris — to adjudicate. Paris gave the apple to Aphrodite, in exchange for a promise that he could have the most beautiful woman in the world for his wife. Unfortunately, as Helen was already married to Menelaus, the king of Sparta, Paris and Helen's subsequent elopement gave rise to the Trojan War.

To me, the phrase held nearly the power it had for Paris. It formed the basis for the name Philip had bestowed on me: Kallista. He never, in his journal, referred to me by my given name, only by Kallista. When I first read it, the word held no significance to me, but on the day a keeper at the British Museum told me Paris's story, I realized Philip's choice of nickname suggested he thought I was beautiful. He had never told me, and this insight into his thoughts affected me profoundly, making me wish I had known him better when he was alive.

By the time I managed to shake myself from the stupor caused by that simple Greek phrase, I could find no trace of the man who had uttered it, and was still mulling over the words when Jeremy found me sitting, motionless, on the fallen section of a column outside the Erechtheion. He dropped down next to me and playfully squeezed my shoulder.

"Now don't be so glum, Em. I am not deserving of this much censure for one small bit of graffiti."

"You are deserving of far more censure than you shall ever get," I said, "but that is not what is troubling me at present." I described for him the appearance of the mysterious stranger. "Although I cannot, in faith, call him a stranger."

"What are you saying, Em? That Philip has come back to haunt you?"

"I should feel less unsettled if I thought I

had seen a ghost. This was no apparition, Jeremy. It was a living and breathing man."

"Then where did he go?"

"I don't know."

"Em, I am not in such dire need of distraction that you must sink to this. My broken heart will mend without an apparition of your dead husband."

"I wish I were inventing it to distract you, but nothing could be further from the truth."

"You are still exhausted from traveling — the train to Athens was a horror I hope never to experience again — and no one sleeps well the first few nights in a hotel."

"You believe I am seeing things?" I asked.

"Yes." He rose to stand in front of me and held out his hand to help me to my feet. "Greece and Ashton are linked inextricably in your mind. Combine that with fatigue, and voilà — your dead husband re-animated."

"I might agree with you if I hadn't thought I saw him on the boat as well."

"Hardly surprising on a trip to Greece. Philip was so obsessed with the place I'm surprised his ghost didn't wear a toga."

"Romans wore togas, Jeremy, not the Greeks."

"Romans, Greeks, who could be bothered

to tell the difference? Forget about it all, Em. What we need now is the champagne I've been lugging in this wretched basket. Come, let's go find your tedious living spouse and that dreadful American. We don't need a ghost."

"You're a beast," I said.

"Thank you ever so much for noticing," he said, leaning in close. "And, Em, I wouldn't mention your ghostly visitor to Hargreaves."

"Why ever not?"

"You know he and I don't get on — I never could tolerate a Cambridge man — but I have done my best to stop actively disliking him over the past few years, strictly for your sake. Ashton was his best friend. Dragging up memories will only cause him pain."

"I never thought I would see you so concerned about Colin. The two of you have been getting on so well of late I'm almost afraid you will transfer all of your affections from me to him. Life would hardly be worth living."

"Ah, Em, if only you took me more seriously." He pulled my arm through his. "You break my heart."

"You are a dreadful tease," I said.

Champagne by moonlight at the Acropolis

cures nearly any ill, and by the time we had spread a blanket in the center of the Parthenon and opened the first bottle, I had all but forgot Philip. There were several other small parties visiting the site that evening, and we struck up conversation with the local guide, Alcibiades, one of them had hired. He regaled us with tales from mythology, and joined in when, regretting that I had not brought a copy of something to read aloud from, I began to recite a passage from Sophocles' *Oedipus at Colonus.*

"Last and grandest praise I sing / To Athens, nurse of men, / For her great pride and for the splendor / Destiny has conferred on her. / Land from which fine horses spring!"

Alcibiades finished for me. *"Land of the sea and the sea-farer! / Upon whose lovely littoral / The god of the sea moves, the son of Time."*

"Enough! Enough!" Jeremy made a show of covering his ears with his hands. "No poetry! I much preferred your stories, sir. You must not allow her to force more poetry on me."

"Are you traveling to any of the islands?" Alcibiades asked.

"Just Santorini," Jeremy said.

"Well, then, be sure to answer to the Gorgona correctly if she questions you while you're on the boat."

"The Gorgona?" Jeremy asked. "Is she the one with snakes in her hair?"

"That's Medusa, a gorgon," I said. "The Gorgona is Alexander the Great's sister."

"Yes," Alcibiades continued. "One day, Alexander, after a quest of great difficulty, came to possess a flask of water that, if drunk, would bestow immortality. When he reached home, exhausted, he gave it to his sister to look after while he slept."

"I am quite onto the way these myths work," Jeremy said, pouring himself more champagne. "First mistake is not drinking the bloody water the moment you get it."

"A valid point," Alcibiades said. "While her brother was sleeping, she was carrying the flask to a place she thought it would be safe, but she tripped and spilled it. When Alexander awoke and learned what had transpired, he cursed her, condemning her to live for eternity as a mermaid."

"If he could give her eternal life, why couldn't he give it to himself?" Jeremy asked, refilling everyone's champagne.

"It doesn't work that way, old chap," Colin said. "There are many technical difficulties in these myths that require the modern gentleman to ignore common sense in order to fully appreciate them."

"I find it charming," I said. "Even the greatest heroes make mistakes. It reminds us of our humanity."

"The Gorgona, neither fish nor human — trapped in a state that kept her separate from both the creatures of the sea and those of the earth — was struck by a guilt so deep and so overwhelming that to this day she still stops ships in the Aegean to inquire after her brother." Alcibiades graced me with a sage smile.

Margaret interrupted. "Presumably one must be very careful to give the correct answer to her question."

"But of course, madam," he said. "She will ask, *Is Alexander the king alive?* You must reply, *He lives and reigns and conquers the world!*"

"If you tell her Alexander is dead," I said, "she will start keening and chanting songs of mourning that churn up the sea until the waves have destroyed your ship and everyone on board drowns. But if you know what to say —"

Jeremy leapt to his feet. "He lives and reigns and conquers the world!"

Alcibiades nodded. "Then she watches over your journey and teaches you the beautiful songs of the sea."

"Bit inane, don't you think?" Jeremy

asked. "Even I know Alexander is long dead. This sister sounds rather daft."

"Don't say so out loud," I said, laughing. "You must tell her what she wants to hear. 'He lives and reigns and conquers the world!' "

Soon we were raising our glasses and toasting the great Alexander, chanting the phrase again and again — *He lives and reigns and conquers the world!* — until we had all collapsed in mirth.

Our spirits damped temporarily when the sour gentleman who had hired our new friend as his guide urged him back to his group. We thanked Alcibiades for entertaining us and waved as he sullenly followed his employer toward the Propylaea.

"Perhaps those words are all Alexander needs to live forever," Margaret said, lying on her back and looking up at the stars glistening in the sky. "Say it often enough and they become true. Maybe that is how one defeats death, by never being forgotten."

"Dead is dead," Colin said. "He may be remembered, but that is not the same as being alive."

"I don't know that I agree, Hargreaves," Jeremy said. "It might be preferable to slogging through the rest of eternity. On the other hand, if dead is dead, then I need not worry about offending your spirit when I marry Em the day after you depart this world."

Colin shifted uncomfortably and looked away. "Might want to wait a decent interval."

Jeremy glanced at me and shrugged. "If it will make you feel better, of course. But if dead is dead . . ."

"You couldn't convince her to marry you if you had a thousand years at your disposal, Bainbridge." Colin stretched out on the blanket. "That said, I almost wish I did believe in ghosts, so that I could watch the farce that would be your unwelcome courtship."

"I would help our darling duke," Margaret said, "by composing Latin odes to Emily's beauty and grace."

"Don't encourage him," I said, swatting her arm.

"Margaret, you want me to accept your offer only so you can then poke fun at me for not realizing Latin odes would put her off me altogether the instant she heard they were not in Greek," Jeremy said. "I am not so ignorant as you like to think."

"Well, then I shall compose Greek poetry for you to recite to her, but you will have to learn the ancient language better than you did at school to ensure you are saying what you actually mean."

"Oh, yes," I said, laughing. "Please do that, but don't let him learn Greek. It would be much more diverting to hear him reciting words whose meaning he can't understand. You will prove a malicious Cyrano."

"The prospect of courting you, Em, grows less and less appealing," Jeremy said. "Another good thing ruined. At any rate, I owe your husband a debt. It was he, after all, who pointed out that Amity left me with a bulletproof excuse for avoiding marriage for the foreseeable future. The least I can do for him is promise to leave you to your lonely widowhood. Spent, I imagine, reciting dreadful Greek poetry."

Now we were all laughing again, although I must own to being not altogether amused by the direction the conversation had taken. I could see from Colin's expression that the guilt he had felt at having married his best friend's widow, even after a decent interval, had resurfaced. Not that he regretted our marriage, just that he wished, as did I, that our love had not been born from loss. I decided to follow Jeremy's advice and did not mention to my husband that I thought I had seen Philip. Why cause the dear man any unnecessary pain?

We passed several more pleasant days in Athens before setting off for Delphi. We took the train to Corinth and then a steamer to Itéa, where we hired a dragoman and horses, the means of transit upon which one must rely when traveling in the interior of the country. As we were all excellent horsemen — and -women — this proved no obstacle. We did not require the dragoman's services as a translator, but welcomed his guidance as to route and would rely on him to find us suitable accommodations in the nearby village when we reached Delphi.

The site was fewer than nine miles from Itéa, and our chosen route took us away from the carriage road and onto a narrower path that had been traveled since antiquity. At least I chose to believe it had; I cannot be entirely confident in the accuracy of my claim, and apologize to the reader for the enthusiasm that consumes me when traveling in Greece. While there, I like to believe I am always following in the footsteps of the ancients and imagine that the path under my boots might previously have been trod by Agamemnon or Pericles or one of the great ancient playwrights. Sometimes one must give in to romanticism.

As the path grew steeper, our pace slowed. Eventually we approached the ruins of the ancient Temple of Apollo, from whence the Delphic Oracle had made her prophecies. Craggy Mount Parnassus rose up behind it, its rough surface and dramatic angles giving it the appearance of only just having been thrust from the fiery core of the earth. Leaving the horses with our dragoman, we walked along the road taken by ancient supplicants, passing the ruins of various city treasuries, and winding up the side of the mountain to the temple, where a scant six of its original fifteen Doric columns remained. Only one still reached its original height.

We paced the floor of the structure, wondering where, exactly, the inner sanctum of the oracle had been — only she, the Pythia, was allowed into the adyton, where she would enter into a trance before speaking Apollo's words. After thorough exploration of the area — I remain convinced the adyton was beneath the main level of the temple — we continued on to visit the theatre and the stadion, both used during the Pythian Games, held every four years to honor Apollo, who, when four days old, had gone to Delphi and slayed Python, the beast who had wreaked havoc on the surrounding environs for years and tormented Apollo's mother, Leto. While Colin and Margaret ran the length of the stadion's track, he graciously letting her cross the ancient marble finish line first, Jeremy and I stood in the stands on the side nearer to the edge of the mountain, looking at the expansive view before us.

"You can see why the ancients believed this was the center of the world, can't you?" I asked. In the valley below, olive groves shimmered silver all the way to the sea visible in the far-off distance. Violet-blue mountains rose, rolling above them, not nearly so jagged as Mount Parnassus. "Standing here, it feels impossible to believe there is anywhere more important."

"It is stunning," Jeremy said. "But I must say, Em, I'm awfully glad you weren't in charge of planning my ill-fated engagement party. You'd have brought us here and it would have been the simplest thing ever for Amity to fling me to my death. She wouldn't have had to try to shoot me."

"You don't think Apollo would have protected you?"

He shrugged and lit a cigarette. "Hard to say. Difficult to rely on the old gods."

"Are you all right?" I asked. He looked

tired and drawn and lacked all of his usual spark.

"I despise her — obviously — but I miss her, too. We did have good times, you know."

I scowled. "You had good times when she wasn't trying to murder you. I know you have many shortcomings, Jeremy, but not so many that you deserve such a fate. Someday, you will meet your match, and she will erase forever any warm memories you have of Amity Wells."

"I assure you I never look back on the time with fondness, only with shame. I wonder that I could have been such a fool."

"Love can keep us from seeing even obvious truths," I said. "And Amity had a knack for keeping her true nature hidden."

"I am well cured of her now." Smoke curled from his lips. "And what about you? Here we are, in the most sacred of ancient spaces, and you have not seen your dead husband even once, have you?"

I laughed. "No, I have not."

"Sounds to me like he's a rather lazy ghost, put off by the notion of climbing mountains. I'd say you're well rid of him, Em."

PHILIP
MUNICH, 1891

The telegram to Hargreaves, which Ashton had sent requesting an immediate response, did not garner the reply he had wished. His friend's butler wired to say that his master, currently working abroad, would not receive the message until he returned to England. The butler had no way of reaching him.

"The time has come to stop being a coward," Ashton said, accepting the strong beer Reiner pushed across the table to him. Ashton adored the city's beer gardens, with their heavy steins and hearty food; the Augustiner-Keller in Arnulfstrasse had become their second home in Munich. "We must go to London. I cannot bear to be away from Kallista a moment longer. You will adore her the moment you see her. She is a vision of loveliness and feminine perfection."

"Her father must be a scholar to have chosen such a name," Reiner said.

" 'Emily' is her given name. I alone call her Kallista, as I find it a far more appropriate moniker."

" 'Kallista.' Most beautiful. She sounds more like a dream than reality," Reiner said, a grin on his face. "Are you sure she is not a creation of your fever?"

"If so, I would never want to be well again."

The next day, they boarded a train for Paris, where they tarried for a fortnight, Ashton's anxiety at seeing his wife growing as he came closer to England. Eventually, he could delay no longer. He comforted himself with the knowledge that even if she had lost her love for him, she was still legally his wife. He was confident he could win back her affections once they were living together again. Before setting foot on the train that would speed them to Calais, he combed jewelry stores until he found the perfect gift for his bride: a brooch depicting a single rose, exquisitely carved from ivory. For their wedding, he had given her a similar piece, an elaborate profusion of flowers rather than a solitary stem. This second gift would mark the new beginning of their life together.

No part of Ashton's journey had been easy, but he determined to be undaunted by this final leg. The channel tossed the ferry with such vehemence that hardly a passenger on board was not sick the entire trip to Dover, but Ashton stood on the deck, despite the warnings from crew members that he would be safer inside. Had he not already proved himself a survivor? He clenched the rail and strained his eyes, desperate for that first glance of the White Cliffs. When at last he stepped onto English soil, he collapsed on the ground and wept. He was home.

4

Delphi proved as mesmerizing as ever, worth far more than the half day Baedeker's suggests devoting to it. I could have spent weeks exploring every inch of the ruins — and had done so in years past — but recognized Jeremy would not enjoy the activity so much as I. So we returned to Athens, made leisurely visits to the museums, dined with other travelers in the Grand Bretagne, and shopped. Jeremy, we discovered, loved to haggle with local traders. He acquired three pairs of *tsarouhi* shoes — complete with woolen pom-poms — despite the insistence even of the seller that no one outside remote rural areas wore them anymore.

"They shall prove remarkably useful for fancy dress," Jeremy said, pleased with his purchase. "You ought to throw a ball for me, Em. A masquerade. The theme can be folk costumes."

He became rather attached to the idea.

Colin told me in no uncertain terms that he would not allow it, and if I insisted, he would come dressed as a Red Indian, wearing only a breechcloth and a feather headdress. If anything, this encouraged me rather than putting me off the notion, and as a result, he refused to discuss the topic any further.

The time had come to leave the mainland and make our way to my island villa. We left the port of Piraeus on a day bright with sunshine. Colin, as was his custom, had hired a sailing yacht and its crew to bring us to Santorini. The trip would take longer than if we booked tickets on a steamer, but we had no reason to rush, and there are few activities more pleasant and relaxing than cruising on the Aegean. Each evening, we dined beneath the stars on the deck and afterward would sit out for hours over whisky (for Margaret and the gentlemen) and port (for me). Whenever we approached anything that could be considered rocky — be it island, islet, or an actual rock jutting up from the sea — Margaret and I would leap up and start to sing the Sirens' song:

Come here, thou, worthy of a world of
    praise,
That dost so high the Grecian glory raise.

Ulysses! Stay thy ship, and that song heare
That none past ever but it bent his eare,
But left him ravishd and instructed more
By us than any ever heard before.

This display generally led Colin to threaten flinging us off the boat. I credit this not to our lack of singing ability, but to the loss of the song's original melody over the many centuries since Odysseus returned from Troy. I am certain had he heard the original version, my husband would have been charmed. Margaret returned his threat with one of her own, swearing she would tie him to a mast if he did not show better appreciation for our endeavors.

Despite our best efforts, Jeremy and I had started to burn in the hot sun, and Margaret, in addition to turning quite pink, had a sprinkle of freckles across her nose that would have horrified my mother. Colin, whose skin never burned, but rather turned a deep golden shade, looked more and more like the inspiration for a Praxiteles sculpture with each passing day. His dark curls, permanently tousled by the ocean breeze, tumbled over his forehead, and when he stood on the prow of the ship, pointing to identify the islands in the distance, the sunset coloring the sky around him, I was so moved by his beauty I was forced to push dinner back three-quarters of an hour and to request his immediate assistance in our cabin.

The last morning of our voyage saw the steep cliffs of Santorini — Thera, as it was called in ancient days — rising from the ocean, puzzle-piece white and blue and buildings clinging impossibly to their sides. Because it was still spring, lush greenery covered the dark volcanic rock of the island, with yellow, white, and pink wildflowers dotting the view. We pulled into the port below the small capital city of Fira, where a well-tended group of donkeys stood ready to transport us and our baggage up the six hundred steps to the top. Mrs. Katevatis, whom I had hired as a cook on my first visit to the island, had taken on so many additional duties at the villa after her husband died some years ago that to call her "housekeeper" would not begin to encompass all she did for me. Her twenty-year-old son, Adelphos, who had tutored me in modern Greek, was in charge of the donkeys, and took exquisite care of them. From ancient times, these beasts of burden were the only reliable way to move supplies and people on the island. The jovial sound of their bells welcomed us to our Greek home.

I kissed Adelphos on both cheeks. "Αγαπητέ μου αγόρι, είναι τόσο καλό που ϛε βλέπω," I said in my best modern Greek — which, I must confess, is more dreadful than my worst Ancient Greek. "My dear boy, it is so good to see you."

"You are lucky to arrive today, Lady Kallista," he replied, using the nickname bestowed on me by Philip and used now only by my friend Cécile du Lac and Adelphos; I had not yet been able to persuade him to stop using my title. "We had terrible storms last night. You will want to get to the villa as quickly as possible. My mother is eager to speak with you."

The sun blazed down on us as the donkeys made their way slowly up to town. Once we had reached Fira, I planned, as was my habit, to abandon the beasts to Adelphos and walk the rest of the way. The house, in the village of Imerovigli, abutted the cliff path that connected the two towns, skirting the edge of the island nearly nine hundred feet above the sea and providing spectacular views with every step. Jeremy balked, insisting he wanted a bath and a whisky, and Adelphos took my friend's side, imploring me to succumb to his request. His mother was waiting anxiously, he reminded me, and speed was of the essence.

Speed had never before entered into any conversation in which I had taken part in on the island. If anything, on Santorini things required so much longer to be accomplished it would not have been unreasonable for one to draw the conclusion there was a mandate forbidding haste. The languid pace endeared the place to me, and Adelphos' desire to rush struck all the wrong chords.

"Is something wrong?" I asked. "Was the villa damaged in the storm?"

"Oh, no Lady Kallista, the villa, it is unharmed. It is simply my mother. She —"

Misunderstanding his words to mean that his mother was ill, I urged my donkey along the path without letting Adelphos complete his sentence, and worried the entire way to the house. Margaret, who had been with me on the island many times before, did her best to distract me, flinging her final salve as we approached the house.

"I do love this place," she said.

"You have been complaining about it nonstop all morning," I said. "What about wishing Vesuvius could have been relocated so that it had destroyed Imerovigli instead of Pompeii? And what about the Cycladic nightmare?"

"I was only goading you." She glared at

me, but her eyes danced with amusement. "You are quite entertaining when all riled up."

The villa, like the other houses along the cliff path, all but spilled onto it. Unlike a prim and neat English home, this structure consisted of a series of rectangles and arches built one on top of the other, its walls gleaming with fresh whitewash, its shutters, doors, and all bits of roof that weren't flat painted bright blue. The main section, in the center, had a flat roof we used as a terrace, and the bedrooms — all of which faced the sea — had balconies of their own. I had renovated a few years prior and decorated them each in a manner reflecting a different historical period: Classical, Mycenaean, Etruscan, Archaic, et cetera. Philip had kept his collection of Impressionist paintings in the house. Their colors and use of light blended exquisitely with the natural beauty of the location; I had kept them there and continued to add to their number. From the windows, the incomparable view stretched across the caldera to the remains of the volcano that had radically changed the topology of the island long before the age of Pericles and to the two small islets, Palea and Nea Kameni, that had once been part of a larger whole.

Outside the front door, Mrs. Katevatis stood, ready to greet us, with the rest of our staff. At a glance, I could see the flush of health on her cheeks and felt a flood of relief, but nonetheless I hurried to embrace her.

"You are well?" I asked. "Adelphos wanted us to hurry. I was worried."

"I am well," she said, kissing my cheeks. "I am glad you have arrived. There is . . . we have had . . . I hardly know what to say, Lady Emily."

"What is it?" Colin asked as he stepped forward.

"Oh, Nico! You are more handsome than ever!" She was the sole person on earth my husband let use any diminutive of his full name other than Colin. Only his father, who had died long before I met the son, had ever called him Nicholas. Colin kissed her on both cheeks and murmured a greeting in Greek.

"What is it you need to tell me, Mrs. Katevatis?" I asked. She recognized the anxiety in my voice and took me by the hands.

"The Viscount Ashton is here."

Philip
London, 1891

Ashton had never felt more alive than when he arrived back in London. Spring was turning to summer and the city brimmed with activity. He had never much cared about the social season before, but now welcomed it, as its arrival meant Kallista would be in residence at their house in Berkeley Square. Discreet inquiries told him his sister had not moved his young nephew, the new viscount, into the family home, preferring instead to let her widowed sister-in-law remain. He did not want anyone to see him before his wife did — he could not wait to see her expression when she realized he had come home. He could already see the surprise in her bright eyes, the flush that would spread across her smooth cheeks, and the way she would bite her lower lip, just as he often pictured her having done when he had proposed to her.

Or so he told himself, over and over. In

truth, his anxiety about their reunion had not subsided. Twice he had started for the house, but both times fear consumed him and he fled. Reiner had taken rooms for them near the British Museum, Ashton vowing to reimburse him for expenses the moment he had access to his accounts. They went to the Reading Room at the British Library and pored over the newspaper stories recounting his disappearance and alleged death. He then turned to coverage of the subsequent trial of Andrew Palmer, the man eventually convicted of killing him. No one else had suspected foul play, but Kallista, suspicious, had pursued the case herself, desperate to find justice for her late husband. She had impressed even *The Times* with the clever scheme she employed to trick Palmer into confessing to the crime. It took the better part of a day to read through every sordid detail reported by the press.

"Andrew's father, Lord Palmer, was like a second father to me," Ashton said. "I must go to him; his son, profligate though he may be, was not guilty of murder."

"It is too late to rescind his sentence," Reiner said. "Would it not cause the poor man even more grief to know that his son was wrongly executed?"

"He will know the truth eventually, regardless of what I do. I feel I owe him the decency of calling on him and speaking to him myself."

"Before you go to your wife? You have been insistent that she see you before anyone else."

"Yes, but Lord Palmer will keep my visit confidential. And it is likely he would hear of my return from another source after I see her; once I move back home, the gossip is sure to spread like wildfire."

"You are delaying again," Reiner said. Ashton shook his head. His plan, however, proved impossible to carry out. When they reached Lord Palmer's house, they were told the family had moved more than a year ago and left no forwarding address.

"I do hope the old man is holding up," Ashton said with a sigh. "Losing Andrew will have been a blow to him."

"A blow that, for the moment, you must put aside," Reiner said. "Your wife should not be kept waiting any longer."

They hailed a hansom cab, alighting from it in Berkeley Square, opposite the house. It felt good to be back on the familiar paths of the park, pavements Ashton had trod from the time he was a small boy, holding his nanny's hand when they returned from a walk to see the ducks in St. James's Park, a favorite excursion of his until he grew too old to fully appreciate the charms of water fowl.

The sun was sinking in the sky, and the evening had grown chilly. Yellow light glowed from the windows of the house. The curtains in the library were not yet drawn, and he could see the tall walnut shelves inside, lining the walls, filled with the books he and his father and his grandfather before had added to the family collection. He recalled the first time his grandfather had brought him into the room and given him a copy of *The Iliad* in the original Greek. The old man had pressed the leather-bound book into his hands and told him the pages contained the stories of the greatest heroes ever to have lived. At eight years old, Philip could not yet read the ancient language, but he determined to learn it as quickly as possible when he arrived at Eton in the autumn. This, of course, had been precisely his grandfather's goal.

His vision blurred as he relived the pleasant memory, but a flutter of movement beyond the window brought him back to the present. Could it be her? Was Kallista in the library? He stepped closer, still in the park, and wished he had a spyglass, ridiculous though it was to be peeking into one's own home. Surely it was a maid, come to tend to the curtains and the fire. Kallista would be in a drawing room.

He slunk back and leaned against a tree, continuing to watch the house. Reiner elbowed him. "You can't wait forever," he said.

Ashton pulled himself up straight, brushed the front of his overcoat with his hands, and took a deep breath. "I ought not be this nervous."

The door to the house opened. Ashton warmed at the thought of seeing his butler, Davis, after so many years. Instead, an immaculately dressed gentleman held the door himself and stepped outside, followed to the threshold by a slim figure in an ice blue gown. Ashton bit the inside of his cheek; it was her, his Kallista. She had a soft shawl draped around her, but must have felt the chill of the damp air. She shouldn't be standing so near the open door.

"Why, that's Hargreaves," he said, smiling. "To find them both at once is a blessing." He nodded to Reiner. "This will be a reunion to be remembered."

He stepped forward, then stopped, paralyzed by the scene before them — his wife being kissed by Hargreaves, full on the lips.

5

"The Viscount Ashton? The boy?" Colin asked, referring to Philip's young nephew, who had inherited the estate.

"No," Mrs. Katevatis said, "the other one — the one who was your friend."

"Lord Philip Ashton?" Colin asked, the color in his face heightening. I had never seen him look so stunned. I did not react in similar fashion. My mother insists — rather emphatically, if not quite hysterically — that respectable wives should have the decency to faint when about to be confronted by a spouse long thought to be dead. It should surprise no one of my acquaintance to learn I failed her on that account. My knees did not so much as sway at Mrs. Katevatis's news. While I would like to credit my strong constitution, my dislike of affectation, and the generally imperturbable quality of my character, it would be somewhat dishonest to do so. This is not, as Colin suggests, a result of my having an incorrect grasp of the definition of *imperturbable,* a term he insists suits him far better than me. Rather, it was due to having been barraged with thoughts of Philip even before we left England.

After receiving the mysterious envelope addressed to *The Viscountess Ashton,* finding Philip's journal on my desk, hearing his name spoken aloud in the London Zoo, and twice having thought I saw him since leaving Britain, I was all but primed for his appearance.

"Yes, Nico. He arrived last night with a friend. There had been an accident of some sort —"

And then, as if he had never been gone all these years, a figure stepped into the doorway, interrupting her. "I imagine it would be best if I took things from here, Mrs. Katevatis, ευχαριστώ . . . Thank you."

My feet felt as if they had been encased in lead while some evil force drained all the blood from my body. He stood not quite so tall as I remembered, but I recognized his sandy hair. There had been a time when I could not recall whether his eyes were blue or gray, and I had asked Colin to remind me, but now, seeing their pale cornflower again, they were instantly familiar. His nose

96

was not quite as I recalled, but those eyes were unmistakable. My jaw went slack, and I felt myself start to sway. I have always prided myself on not fainting, but if ever an occasion called for it, it was this. However, I did not succumb and was already steadying myself when Colin reached out to assist me just as Philip — but it could not be Philip! — stepped forward, his arms stretched before him.

"Er — I — perhaps —" Colin stumbled over the words. I could not remember when I had last heard my husband reduced to incoherent inanities.

"Quite," the man replied with a grin. "I could not have said it better myself."

"I require no assistance," I said, backing away from both of them. "I merely —"

"Whisky," Margaret said. "At once." She put a firm arm around my shoulder and pushed me into the house.

Most of the interior of the villa adhered to Cycladic tradition, except for the main sitting room, just to the left of the entrance, where Philip had ordered enormous windows to be placed in the thick walls. Colin, who had been with his friend during much of the construction, had told me Philip did not care that this would make the room warmer in the summer. He wanted the view and would suffer any resulting heat. Margaret and I sat across from these windows on a long, wooden settee I had covered with plump, brightly embroidered cushions made by one of the village women. My friend stayed close and kept her arm around me. The gentlemen followed a moment later, but none of them sat. Colin paced — his usual reaction to stressful situations — Jeremy leaned against the wall perpendicular to the windows, and the newcomer, standing in front of me, clutched his hands behind his back and breathed out a long sigh.

"I have anticipated this for so long and rehearsed the scene in my head countless times, yet now that it has arrived . . ."

"Whisky, Jeremy. Now," Margaret ordered. Jeremy sprung to life and filled five glasses from the decanter on a narrow side table and distributed them to us all. The newcomer raised his.

"Hargreaves." He focused cold eyes on my husband. "Kallista." The sound of him speaking the name — a name he had never called me to my face during our short marriage; a name I learned about only after his death while reading his journal — was too much. I burst into tears, flung my whisky aside, and flew out of the room. Colin followed on my heels, but I turned and stopped him.

"No. Let me go. I must be alone." I ran from the house and along the cliff path, thinking for a moment I would go to Oia, a town larger than Fira and preferred by wealthy ships' captains. The walk would take at least two hours. I toyed with the idea of booking passage on a ship at the port there. I wanted to get as far from Santorini as possible — I could go to Russia, perhaps — and never return. I had made it no further than half a mile from the villa when I halted, lowered myself onto a convenient rock, looked over the caldera, and dropped my head in my hands, sobbing. Eventually, I felt a strong hand on my shoulder and looked up, expecting to see Colin.

"They didn't think I should be the one to come, but I saw no other option," the apparition of my dead husband — he could not be real, could he? — said. "I never meant to cause you such grief, after having already caused you such grief all those years ago."

I recoiled from his touch and rose to my feet. "Please, sir, I —"

"Kallista, my love, my heart, I know this comes as a terrible shock, and I am all too well aware of the difficulties facing us, but at the moment I cannot think of any of that. It has been more than a decade since I have seen your lovely face, and now as I gaze upon you I consider myself the luckiest of men."

I could not speak. Tears spilled from my eyes and I ran again, this time back to the house. He followed, but at a respectable distance, and when I crossed the threshold, I flung myself into Colin's arms. He pulled me close. I breathed his scent in deep — cinnamon and tobacco and a hint of shaving lotion — and buried my face in his chest, the strong muscles tense.

"We will get through this together, Emily," he whispered into my hair. "One way or another."

A sense of calm returned to me. I sniffed and wiped my eyes. "I should like that whisky now." Jeremy poured me a fresh glass, the one I had previously discarded having disappeared. I sat down next to Margaret and looked directly into the newcomer's blue eyes. "You cannot expect us to believe you are who you claim. Philip Ashton died in December 1888, more than a decade ago."

"I realize you all believe that," he said, looking only at me. "Perhaps it was foolish of me to think those closest to me would recognize me at once after all these years. Time has not been kind to me." His features, which I remembered as refined, no longer appeared to be those of a gentleman. A thin scar marred his chin and his skin was rough and lined.

"Time does not change the shape of one's nose," I said.

"No, but having it broken repeatedly does."

I stared at the floor, not looking up until Colin spoke.

"If you are who you claim, it should be simple enough to prove. Time cannot have erased the scar on your leg."

The intruder — for that is how I thought of him — grimaced, and his face flushed. "I should prefer not to reveal it in front of ladies."

"I do not think a glimpse of calf will send them reeling," Colin said. The man turned a deeper shade of red, but bent over and pulled up his right trouser leg, revealing a jagged red line six inches below his knee. My husband's brow furrowed. "Can you explain how you got it?"

"Do you not recall the first time I hunted with a spear? You refused to join me and went for a trek instead, did you not? The Masai circle their prey and send one warrior toward it, to provoke the beast. He has faith that his compatriots will strike before the animal attacks him. The young man next to me had not the stomach for it, and dropped his spear, terrified. It struck me before hitting the ground."

Colin nodded, but did not speak. He studied the man claiming to be his long-lost friend and blew out a sigh. "I . . . I do not know what to say."

"Is that what you remember happening?" I asked.

"As he said, I was not there, but his story is identical to the one I heard when I returned to camp."

"If what you say is true, you must have a spectacular story to share with us," I said, raising an eyebrow as I spoke. This brought a grin to the newcomer's face.

"Forgive me. I know levity is inappropriate, but you have not changed a bit," he said. "I realize many explanations are in order, but first I must beg you to allow me to recount what brought me here, now. I swear, Kallista — how many years I have waited to call you that name to your face; what a fool I was not to have done so on our wedding day — I never meant to disturb your domestic bliss. I have come to terms with your new life, but my feelings on the subject do not merit discussion at present."

"I cannot say I agree with that, sir," Margaret said.

"I assure you we will come to the topic eventually," he said. "For now, though, I must explain to you why I am here and why there is a dead man in the Mycenaean bedroom. I do love that you've done all the rooms up with appropriate antiquities, Kallista, although I am a bit sad to see you've flung out all the chintz furniture. My mother selected the fabric for me." He pointed to a painting on the wall. "I could not be more delighted to see Renoir's portrait of you. I always wondered how it had turned out and am glad you hung it here. Did you know I asked him to paint it from a photograph taken of you on our wedding day? I stopped at his studio en route to that fateful safari."

Colin cleared his throat. "It would, perhaps, be best if you got on with it, Ashton."

"Quite right as always, old boy. I have been working on an archaeological dig not far from here for the past three years. You are familiar with it, I understand? Ancient Thera?"

"Yes," I said. "I have visited more times than I can count." Fira, the modern capital of the island, built centuries later than its ancient counterpart, was more of a village than a city, although its small museum and a handful of municipal buildings gave it a gravity that surpassed that of Oia, the largest town on the island. Ancient Thera occupied the top of a mountain plateau, a long and dusty ride from Fira.

"I am well aware of that fact," he said, smiling. "I endeavored to make myself scarce whenever you came to explore the site. Professor Hiller von Gaertringen, the eminent archaeologist, was kind enough to offer me a position on his staff after receiving the recommendation of a dear friend of mine, Fritz Reiner, whom you will see soon enough. Last night, a terrible storm hit our camp, and one of my colleagues, Gerhard Bohn, fell outside his tent and slid partway down the mountain. You know how steep the slopes are."

"I do," I said.

Colonists from Sparta founded the ancient town of Thera in the eighth century B.C., almost a thousand years after a catastrophic volcanic eruption destroyed the civilization previously occupying the island. They chose as their location the plateau high atop Mesa Vouno, towering above the beaches on the eastern side of the island and the cliffs to the west. One reached it by means of the most wicked road I had ever seen, turning back and forth on itself sharply for two miles up the side of the mountain. The archaeologists had built a small camp at the end of the road on a flat section of land. The ancient city was a pleasant — if steep — hike the remainder of the way up the hill.

"I know it as well," Colin said. "Surely Bohn's tent wasn't near the edge."

"No, not at all. I do not know what led him to go outside during the storm. All I can say with certainty is that when I went to find him so we might all have a drink, he was gone. A quick search of the camp turned up nothing, so I started to look further afield. There is a beauty in storms, and all of us had stood watching the lightning longer than we ought when it first began. I surmised Bohn went back outside and wandered a greater distance than he realized, captivated by the dramatic weather, and slipped. The rain had made the rocks slick. I found him, unconscious, not far from our camp."

"So you brought him here?" I asked.

He ran his long fingers through his sandy hair with a movement so similar to the one I had seen Colin make countless times that I sat up straighter, taken aback. They had been friends since their earliest school days, but I had not expected them to share mannerisms.

"I did. I knew it would be safe in the storm, and I wanted to summon the doctor in Oia, as there is neither an Englishnor German-speaking one in Fira. Bohn was in no shape to be carried as far as that, but I had hoped . . ." His voice trailed.

"The doctor did not arrive in time?" I asked.

"It took me ages to reach Oia on horseback in the storm — I hope you do not mind I borrowed one of your steeds; it was faster than our donkeys — and longer still for the two of us to return here. We were too late."

"I am very sorry for your loss," I said, almost automatically.

Colin had taken to pacing again. "You have been here, on this island, for multiple archaeological seasons, yet you never once came to us?"

"What would be the point?" the man said, turning his empty glass in his hand. "Look at the chaos my appearance has already caused. I had hoped to avoid any such disruption."

No one spoke for several minutes until finally Margaret heaved a sigh. "All right, I will ask what no one else will. Aren't you supposed to be dead, Lord Ashton? And if, as current appearances suggest, you are not, what on earth happened in Africa, and why didn't you come back sooner?"

"These Americans, Hargreaves, truly I don't know what to make of them." He poured himself another whisky. "I realize it is far too early in the day for such a quantity of spirits, but the occasion does merit them."

Jeremy took the decanter from him and refilled his own glass. "Right, Ashton, that's enough blundering about. Answer Margaret's questions."

"I apologize, Mrs. Michaels, for not attacking the subject more directly. I fell ill in Africa, as you all know, due to poison added to my champagne on the night that should have been the most triumphant of my life."

"After you got your elephant," I said.

"Yes." He stood taller, pride brightening your face. "Hargreaves must have told you. I only wish I could have delivered the news to you myself."

"Colin did inform me, but I have also been subjected to the poor beast, stuffed and mounted in Ashton Hall."

"You do not approve?" he asked.

"I have always deplored hunting." I met his surprised stare.

He raised his eyebrows and turned to

Colin. "At any rate, Hargreaves, I am most grateful for the care you took of me when I collapsed. You could not have known then that the poison administered caused a coma so deep it is often — as it was in my case — mistaken for death. You remember Kimathi, our guide?"

"Of course," Colin said.

"He saw what happened, and when you thought I was dead and placed me in the coffin, he was waiting to switch my body with that of one of his fellow tribesmen. My would-be murderer, Andrew Palmer, returned after the others had left camp, to ensure I had succumbed to his poison, and Kimathi feared he would come back again to finish the job. So he carried me to the tribe of his sister's husband, and they cared for me during the long months it took me to recover. After that, my health was not good for some time, and I twice fell ill with fever. When, eventually, I regained the strength to travel, I had a great distance to cover before I reached even the most remote signs of civilization."

"Bloody hell." Colin dropped his face into his hands. "How could I have made such an error? I swear, Ashton, I was certain —"

"Do not abuse yourself," he said. "You had no way of knowing. Even Kimathi feared the poison had killed me, and he was acquainted with its use and symptoms."

"So you walked across Africa, Lord Ashton?" Margaret asked, crossing her arms. "How industrious of you."

"I cannot fault you for your doubt, Mrs. Michaels," he said. "It is an incredible narrative. Truth, as they say —"

"Yes, yes, stranger than fiction," Margaret said. "Do continue."

"Kimathi stayed with me until we came upon a party of German archaeologists who were returning from a dig in the Sudan. They took me to Cairo, where everyone believed me to be dead, leaving me in the unfortunate circumstance of being unable to access any funds. Reiner, with whom I had grown close during the journey, saw me some weeks later, desperate and on the verge of illness. He took me home with him. After a few months in Munich, I had regained nearly all of my strength, and set off for London."

"When was this?" Colin asked.

"Late in the spring of 1891," he said. "It might, perhaps, be preferable if I continued the story without your friends present."

"Absolutely not," Margaret said. "If you think I will leave Emily even for a moment —"

"It is quite all right," I said. "There is nothing Margaret and Jeremy cannot hear."

"Reiner and I came to Berkeley Square, where we saw you, Hargreaves, leaving the house. I shall never forget the scene. Kallista was wearing a pale blue dress and you kissed her on the threshold." I felt my face turn what must have been a shocking shade of vermilion as he spoke.

"I assure you —" Colin began.

He raised a hand to stop him. "At the time, I was livid; you can imagine. But that was long ago, and I have since recovered from the blow. You both thought I was dead, and it had been nearly three years, long enough for Kallista to be out of mourning. Though you will forgive me, my love, for having wished you might not have been ready to start afresh quite so soon."

I rose from my seat. "Sir, I cannot apologize for any of my actions. I have behaved honorably, and had no reason to think you were alive."

"We both know that is not quite true," he said. "I understand you — with the assistance of Mrs. Michaels and some other friends — undertook the investigation of my death, and that during the course of it, did entertain the notion that I might still be alive."

"We did," I said, "but our hopes were based on deliberately misleading and erroneous information."

"And I told her I saw you die." Colin's voice was soft.

"And she trusted you, as she should have," he said. "I blame neither of you. You acted as anyone would have given the information at hand."

"Lord Ashton — if that is truly who you are — would you satisfy me on one more count?" Margaret asked. "I understand your anger at what you claim to have seen at Berkeley Square, but why did you not come forward and confront your friend?"

"At first, my rage was too great. Then I felt humiliated and wanted to slink off into nothingness. My best friend and my wife, together? Can you imagine what that sort of betrayal feels like, even if one knows it is not really a betrayal? I watched the two of you — forgive me — from a distance over the following months, and I could see the love you shared. After all the pain I had already caused Kallista by leaving her a widow so soon after our marriage, how could I intervene and take away the happy life she had cobbled together from the despair she must have felt when she thought I had died?"

Truly, I felt horrible. The awful guilt that had haunted me after Philip's death — if I may still call it that — crept back, twisting itself around my insides. I hadn't grieved when I heard the news. I had hardly known the man, and despite his claims of loving me, he hadn't bothered to stay with me for long — he had left for Africa almost as soon as we returned from our wedding trip. Relief rather than despair had filled me when he died, because I had no idea what life with him would have been like. His death brought me a freedom unlike anything I could have imagined, and relishing that freedom came with a strong measure of torment.

But I had come to terms with all these emotions years ago. How could they return now?

Ashton's first urge was to knock Hargreaves soundly in the jaw and send him sprawling to the ground, but remembering something about discretion and valor, he resisted the urge. Hargreaves had never seemed the sort of man to take advantage of a lady, but what else could he think had occurred? Then he saw Kallista reach up and touch his friend's lips, ever so gently, with her delicate little hand.

This sent Ashton back into a rage. He'd never have expected Kallista would have engaged in such wildly inappropriate behavior, especially in public.

"This is what I come home to?" He turned to Reiner, his face blotched red. "He is — was — my best friend!"

Reiner, nodding, took Ashton firmly by the arm and led him back across the square, away from the house. "There is, I do not doubt, much about this situation we cannot at present understand. Is there no one other than Hargreaves and your wife to whom we can turn for an explanation?"

"I would not have myself further humiliated," Ashton said. "I cannot stay here."

"Shall we go to your sister?"

"So she can learn that the life she thinks is now hers, a life in which her son, my nephew, has already inherited my title and estate, is no longer to be? I am not convinced anyone from my past will welcome my return." He bit his lip. "There is nothing for me here. Not anymore."

In the span of a single moment, the world he'd once inhabited had lost all of the appeal it had ever possessed. His duty no longer was to wife and family, tenants and estate. None of them had any need for him; his presence could only cause them disruption. Without them and the responsibilities of his former position, he had no purpose.

Slowly, it occurred to him that for the first time in his life, he could go anywhere, do anything. Never before had he had such freedom. He would require money, of course, but that did not discourage him. He would seek employment, away from England, and make something of himself, become someone who mattered because of more than a title. He let Reiner steer him into a pub, and together they drank until the memory of his best friend kissing his wife ebbed to a dull, aching pain.

By the end of the week, he had decided, with only a bit of influence from Reiner, to pursue a career in archaeology. Antiquities had always been a passion of his, and the scholarly life appealed to him. He would return to Munich with Reiner, who would help him secure a position on a dig. His friend, delighted with this plan, promised a gushing recommendation, and went so far as to immediately get in touch with his employer, who was already at work in Turkey. After a quick exchange of telegrams, Philip, the Viscount Ashton, was set to earn his living for the first time in his life.

The decision had not caused him too much pain, although he owned it felt unsettling to no longer have the comfort of financial security and the automatic respect his title had brought. His greatest difficulty came from the decision to give up his wife. Before departing London, he wanted to be sure he was well and truly gone from Kallista's heart, that he had no chance to reclaim her as his own. Although she had not rebuffed Hargreaves's attentions, it was, he told himself, possible he had seen nothing more than a single incident she had immediately regretted. But careful observation — from a safe distance — and gossip bought from household servants confirmed what he had seen in Berkeley Square. Kallista loved his best friend.

Reiner, who had used his time in London to meet with with his colleagues at the British Museum, learned through Alexander Murray, the Keeper of Greek and Roman Antiquities, that Ashton's wife had visited the museum frequently over the past several years, first on her own, and later with Colin Hargreaves. Everyone, Mr. Murray told him, was delighted the pretty young widow had found love again.

Even after learning this, Reiner prodded Aston to come forward, to tell his sister, at least, of his return, fearing his friend would regret having cut himself off from his family, but Ashton stood firm and refused. His nephew was now viscount, and if he no longer had Kallista's love, what point was there in slipping back into any part of his old life? Perhaps the dead were best left buried.

6

The heat of the day was upon us now, and the air in the drawing room cloyed and suffocated. I realize ancient statues cannot sweat, but I would have sworn I saw a glistening bead on the forehead of the fifth-century marble Dionysus that stood on a table beneath the large window. Margaret studied the man who claimed to be Philip, making no attempt to hide her stare. Colin appeared as calm as ever, but I knew he was churning beneath the surface. No one had spoken for some time, and although I suspected everyone was keen on having more whisky, we had missed luncheon, and spirits never combine well with empty stomachs.

I excused myself and went in search of Mrs. Katevatis, wanting to speak with her privately rather than in front of the group. I found her in the kitchen, making the spicy meat filling for the *kreatopitakia,* a pie of sorts encased in flaky pastry. She knew it to be my favorite.

She flung her arms around me and hugged me the way I imagined other people's mothers did when they found their children in dire need of comfort. I choked back a combination of tears and laughter, contemplating what my own mother's reaction to the current situation would be. *Horrified* would not begin to describe it. There could be no doubt she would blame me entirely, and somehow convince the rest of society that some deep flaw in my person had caused the scandal. Privately, she would despair, but even the thought of this brought me no comfort.

"I hope we did the right thing, letting him in the house," Mrs. Katevatis said, keeping me tight in her embrace. "His friend was in dire straits, I could see that at once, and it would not have been right to send them back into the storm."

"You had no choice," I said. "And he . . . did you know Lord Ashton well?"

"No, Lady Emily, I saw him on occasion but did not work in the house until you hired me. The maids recognized him immediately, and started weeping."

"They had no doubts about his identity?"

"None," she said. "Would you like to

speak with them?"

"No," I said. "What do I do now?" My voice was barely a whisper.

"Only you can decide that, my child." She kissed my forehead, and I wandered back to the others, who had moved into the music room, a space with smaller windows set high into the front wall and, hence, cooler — at least a bit — than the drawing room. Margaret was playing the piano while Colin and the newcomer sat across from each other, leaning close, deep in conversation. Jeremy brightened when he saw me.

"Capital, Em, you're back. Come with me. I want to see this island of yours." He linked his arm through mine and lowered his voice. "Let the two of them be. Hargreaves will get to the truth of the matter — it's the sort of thing he was made for." I motioned for Margaret to join us, but she refused with a quick shake of her head, and I knew she had every intention of eavesdropping as best she could. At the front door, Jeremy thrust a parasol at me. "I won't have your mother blaming me for the destruction of your complexion." He picked up his walking stick from the stand in the corridor, and we fled the house.

"Thank you," I said. "I didn't feel that I

should run off again, but I couldn't bear to stay."

"It's not like you, Em, leaving them to hash things out." We took the cliff path in the direction of Fira, the sun beating down on us. I welcomed its warmth; Philip's return had chilled me to the core.

"You told me I ought to," I said.

"Indeed, and you should, but it is out of character for you to resist intervening. Do you think they'll duel?"

"Duel? Colin? Don't be ridiculous." I squinted in the sun and opened my parasol.

"A duel, yes, that is just what we need. They're both decent shots, so I would have a reasonable chance of being the only man standing afterward. I could sweep you off your feet —"

"No, thank you. The last thing I need is a third husband." The very thought caused me to burst out laughing. I stopped walking. "Lord, this is . . . absurd. Is it not absurd?" The path narrowed and I stepped around a sharp rock jutting from it.

"Utterly and completely," Jeremy said. "Why don't we run off to Switzerland and live in sin? Hargreaves and Ashton can have each other."

"Colin has not done anything wrong."

"Has Ashton? If his story is true, he has

suffered losses so awful as to be nearly incomprehensible."

"Do you believe him?" I asked, moving out of the way of one of the island's many cats, which was charging toward us. We started walking again, passing more houses and a church as we drew closer to Fira.

"It would be impossible not to doubt him." He stopped and leaned against his walking stick. "The tale he tells is unlikely in the extreme. And, yet, here he is."

"Yes. Here he is."

"Do you believe him, Em?"

"I don't know what to believe. I had all but forgot the details of his face," I said, "but I recognized him as soon as he stepped into the doorway." I turned away from Jeremy and stared at the caldera, my eyes barely focusing. I felt tears smart and brushed them away with the back of my bare hand. In my haste, I had taken neither gloves nor handkerchief with me.

"You are certain?" Jeremy asked, turning me to face him.

"How can I be? I only knew him briefly before we were married and he died so soon after. He looks much older, but I suppose we all do after a decade."

"Quite. I can't claim to remember much about his appearance and I never knew him

121

particularly well, but while you were out of the room he reminded me of a time before you were engaged when the two of us argued over who would get to bring you a raspberry ice at Lady Elliott's ball."

"I never knew that." Our eyes met, and we started to walk again. "Jeremy, do tell me you were not considering courting me at the time."

"Heavens, no. Some dreadful girl had been clinging to me and I hailed Ashton as a means of escape. When he told me he was fetching raspberry ice for a lady, and that the lady was you, I knew battling him over it would send a strong message to the young person who would not let me be. I suppose it was a bit cruel."

"Not as cruel as letting her think you might fall in love with her would have been," I said. "You generally take a long view of things and act accordingly. Turn this way." We had reached the spot where the path diverged. One direction continued on to Fira, but I led us the other way, where a narrow trail turned to the west, leading across the rugged surface of Skaros, a rocky promontory jutting out from the island. Once the site of a medieval Venetian fortress, it stood all but abandoned now, save for the ruins of houses built in the eighteenth century and long since abandoned.

"So you don't think they will duel?" Jeremy asked.

"Of course not. What is there to fight over? I am legally bound to Colin. We have children."

"It is a crushing disappointment," he said. "I would have seconded Hargreaves, you know. But tell me, Em, can your marriage be valid if your first husband never died? I don't suppose there is an English solicitor anywhere on this island?"

"No, there is not, but I hardly think it matters. There is a valid death certificate that ensures the validity of my marriage," I said, having no confidence in my words. "Furthermore, the man claiming to be Philip stated clearly that he has no desire to disturb my domestic bliss. He only came here because his friend was in desperate need of medical attention."

"Did you examine the body?"

"No. Why would I?" I picked my way over a rocky section of path, grateful for my sturdy boots.

"Again, uncharacteristic, Em. Someone deposits a corpse in your house and you aren't inspecting every inch of it in hope of finding proof of foul play?"

"The situation could not be more straightforward," I said. "The doctor examined the poor man last night and he gave the cause of death as blunt trauma to the head."

"And you and I both know blunt trauma can only occur accidentally."

I frowned at his sarcasm. "Are you suggesting this man whacked his friend on the head and then risked both their lives going down that awful road in a storm simply to have an excuse to come to the house?"

"A house he owns if he's not dead." Jeremy poked at a rock with his walking stick. "You are correct, it doesn't make sense."

"None of it does."

"Can it really be Ashton?" Jeremy asked. "Is such a return possible, regardless of the explanation?"

"At present, I have more reason to accept him than not. I recognized him — his eyes. Who else could it be? Yet . . ." My voice trailed off. "How can it be he? I am utterly confounded." We had reached the midpoint of the path to the tip of Skaros. The heat had grown worse, and we had no water or other supplies with us. We were both breathing heavily from exertion, and perspiration soaked my shirtwaist. "Perhaps we should turn back. Your nose is starting to burn."

walk back passed quickly — more

quickly than I would have liked. I dreaded having to face my two spouses again. My mother might criticize my failure to faint when I saw Philip as proof of my lack of decency, but in my defense I should like to go on the record stating that most husbands, once dead, have the decency to remain so.

When we reached the villa, we spotted a young man in a khaki jacket and trousers, knee-high boots, and a pith helmet approaching the house.

"You must be Herr Reiner," I said, surmising as much from his clothing, which was appropriate for an archaeologist. "Your colleague told us to expect you."

"I am." He clicked his heels together and bowed neatly, his blue eyes flashing. "I presume you are Kallista — er, forgive me — Lady Emily? We did meet once before, years ago, at the site of the excavations at Ancient Thera. I would not expect you to remember."

"I am she," I said, "and I do recall our meeting. I understand you and my . . ." I could feel a stricken look cross my face. Jeremy, seeing my distress, interrupted and held his hand out to Herr Reiner.

"Jeremy Sheffield, Duke of Bainbridge," he said. "I understand you're a friend of the first husband."

"I apologize, Lady Emily, for the awkwardness of the situation," Herr Reiner said. "I am at a loss as to how one ought to proceed."

"It's rather warm, so a cool drink would be a good start," I said. "Do please come inside." This proved to be one of those rare moments where inane social conventions offer welcome solace. Everything, I suppose, has its purpose.

"Thank you, you are very kind." He hesitated. "I have some news for Ashton, but I worry he already has been overburdened."

"We heard about the death of your colleague, and I am most heartily sorry for your loss," I said. "Has something else happened?"

"Our expedition leader, Professor Hiller von Gaertringen, has already made the arrangements to accompany our friend's body to Athens, where his family will collect it. This morning, I went back to our camp — the local workers we had hired needed to be informed we would not be working today — and came upon the most dreadful sight. Ashton's tent has been destroyed and all his belongings smashed."

"The storm?" Jeremy asked.

"I don't think so, as nothing else in the

126

camp suffered a similar fate. It is as if someone did it deliberately."

"How terrible," I said. "Who would do such a thing?"

"I haven't the slightest idea," Herr Reiner said. "But he must be told."

"Inside," Jeremy said. "No point delaying the inevitable."

The others were still in the music room, where Margaret was playing a rousing rendition of "Say Au Revoir and not Goodbye," a song I found particularly inappropriate in the present circumstances. Colin pulled me aside at once. "Come upstairs," he said. "I want to speak with you privately."

The shutters in our bedroom remained closed all day against the heat of the sun, keeping the room deliciously cool. Colin pushed the door shut behind us and pulled me roughly to him, kissing me with the intensity of fire. I tangled my fingers in his curls, barely able to catch my breath. He raised me slightly off the ground, my toes leaving the tiled floor, and moved toward the bed, stopping when he reached it and setting me gently back on my feet.

"Apologies," he said, taking half a step back from me. "This is not the time." He closed his eyes and pressed his lips together. "I cannot lose you."

I took his face in my hands. "There is no question of that. It is only . . . what are we to do with him?" Suddenly I could not bear the oppressive darkness of the room. I went onto the balcony, slipping through the door so as not to let hot air into the house. Colin followed me, bringing with him the ewer of water and two glasses that had stood on a bedside table. I flopped onto a chair as he passed me a drink. He went to the edge, looked over, and then sat beside me, pulling his chair close.

"No one is below. We may speak freely, but should keep our voices down," he said. I nodded. "My emotions are a tumult, but I am more concerned for you. Are you all right?"

"As right as anyone could be in the circumstances," I said. "Do you think it really is Philip?"

"I was wholly incredulous at first, despite the physical similarities —"

"His nose looks different than I remember," I interrupted.

"Yes, but he explained it has been broken. That does alter one's appearance. I imagine the scar on his chin came at the same time. The time he says he spent in Africa and at archaeological sites would explain the lines on his face — he is a walking example of why your mother insists you carry a parasol in the sun — and of course we all change over the course of a decade."

"Yes, alas," I said. "And the scar on his leg? You recognized it?"

"I can't say so with precision. I saw the wound that caused it, and the scar looks like a good match. You, er, may have . . ." He cleared his throat. "You may have seen it more —"

"I was only vaguely aware of it." The words tumbled from my mouth and I scrambled to change the direction of our conversation. "Did you recognize him as your dearest friend? Not physically, I mean."

"When you left with Bainbridge, we picked up conversation as if we had spent no time apart," Colin said. "His manner and his way of thinking have not changed."

"What did the two of you speak about?"

"He is distressed at having come to us and wants everything to go on as if nothing has happened. He will return to the dig, and we to our lives."

"What about his family?" I asked. "Do they know he is alive?"

"No, and he is adamant that they not know."

"He is a viscount. He can't just walk away from his responsibilities."

"He did that years ago, and is confident the estate is in good hands with his nephew —"

"Who is only twelve years old," I said.

"And away at school, yes. The boy's father and Ashton's sister have matters well in hand. He has no desire to take back the title. He finds the life of an archaeologist suits him, and regrets only that he agreed to come to Santorini, as the decision has now caused you pain." A shadow crossed my husband's face.

"He had to know if he was working here eventually we would find out," I crossed my arms. "I visit Ancient Thera several times a year. It is only good fortune that has kept him from being exposed before now."

"Please do not judge him so harshly, Emily. If he is telling the truth, he is in an untenable situation. When he realized you were in love with me, it nearly killed him, and it took him years to move on from the blow," Colin said. "But now he has, and if he came here with the secret hope that he might, perhaps, be able to see you from afar once in a while, it is a small sin."

"Is he telling the truth?" I asked.

"The evidence points to it, for now at least. I cannot reconcile the breadth of his knowledge of our shared experiences any other way, but I cannot say with absolute certainty."

"You speak most calmly for someone who only a few minutes ago was acting as desperate as I feel," I said. A breeze kicked up from the sea, bringing welcome relief from the heat.

"Calm is my best armor," he said, his jaw firm. "I do not know the legal specifics of our situation. Whether our marriage —"

"Is valid." I bit my lip. "Jeremy and I were discussing the same thing."

"Is Bainbridge a solicitor now?"

"Don't be unkind. He is only trying to help."

"Forgive me." He stood and started to pace the length of the balcony, running his hand through his hair. "He has been a good friend to you, and for that I am grateful."

"Should we contact someone? I worry for the boys —"

"They are legitimate. There is no question of that." No one would dare disagree with Colin when he spoke in that tone.

"No?" I asked.

"The court would declare them so even if our marriage —" He stopped talking, tipped his head up to the sky, and blew out a long breath. "How can this be happening?"

"I tried to run, you know," I said. "I

131

couldn't bear to face it. Escape seemed the best option."

"If you hadn't come back when you did I would have set off for St. Petersburg in search of you."

"How did you know I was considering Russia?"

"You've always wanted to go. Whenever I'm sent there for my work, you beg to come along. Furthermore, I am well aware of your admiration for all things Fabergé."

"You know me so well." I tried to smile, but pain seared through me. How much longer would we be allowed these private moments if I were legally someone else's wife?

Colin sat back down, pulled me onto his lap, and kissed me again.

"You cannot do this in broad daylight," I said.

"Why not? On the privacy of our own balcony? With the door to our chamber locked behind us?"

"Is it still our own balcony?" I asked, burying my face in his neck. "I am most appreciative of this man's not wanting to cause us further distress, but can it be as simple as him returning to his camp and us remaining here? There is more going on here,

Colin, and I am afraid he may need our help."

"Whatever he may or may not need, he will not take me from you, my dear. That is the only certainty before us."

PHILIP
VIENNA, 1891

The excavation season — what a thrilling season! — in Turkey finished, Reiner had returned to Munich. Ashton, however, flush with earned income for the first time in his life and full of excitement after months spent unearthing treasures (even tiny ones), went to Vienna, where he had arranged to spend the winter working for a well-respected antiquities dealer. It had occurred to him that he perhaps ought not use his proper name, as eventually someone might draw a connection between Philip Ashton, archaeologist, and the Viscount Ashton, who had a reputation of sorts in the world of classical scholarship. "Philip," he decided, was innocuous and common enough to never draw attention on its own, but he adopted "Chapman" as his new surname, after his favorite translator of Homer's works. Mr. Chapman — how funny to be a "mister" after all these years! — had proved an asset to the team in Turkey, and looked forward to returning there in the spring. But for now, he had Vienna, a city he had always loved. It would be the perfect place to usher in the New Year.

No longer could he afford his favorite suite at the Hotel Imperial, so he rented rooms in a quiet part of town. He took to frequenting a café not far from his digs, and spent most evenings there, delighting in political and philosophical conversation with the other regulars. None of them knew him from his past life, but they all accepted him as one of their own after he gave a particularly passionate defense of Nietzsche's work. In the span of a few weeks, he had created another new world for himself, one in which no one judged him based on title or income. One quiet night early in the winter, an elegant lady, the picture of perfect sophistication, called out to him, her voice husky and rich.

"Can it be the Viscount Ashton?" She stared openly at him, her bright eyes dancing. "You must know just how shocked I am to see you. You look remarkably well for a dead man."

"Forgive me, I wasn't expecting —"

"You cannot claim surprise to learn I spend far too much time in this neighborhood," she said. "It is a favorite haunt of Hargreaves's, although he has always preferred Café Griensteidl to this place, despite the fact that his rooms are so nearby. I am certain you know that almost as well as I, but for rather different reasons. Sit with me, Ashton. I am a countess now — I have married since you last saw me — so we are both titled. Perhaps now we are equals you will call me Kristiana, despite the fact you never would before. I always wondered if that was because we did not know each other well enough or because you did not approve of my relationship with our mutual friend. Why are you in Vienna? He is already gone, you know."

"It is a long and convoluted story. I was in Africa longer than anyone knew," he said, sitting across from her and motioning for the waiter to bring him a coffee.

"I would imagine so, as everyone believes you are dead."

"I am surprised the news traveled all this way."

"It caused quite a sensation at the time. Hargreaves was devastated." Her tone suggested to Philip that she and his friend had fallen out since then.

"Do you still see him?" he asked. He prayed she would not notice the hope in his voice; it was beneath him. He ought not wish such a thing on Kallista.

"Only when my work necessitates it," she said. The waiter returned with fresh coffee for them both. She stirred hers despite putting neither sugar nor cream in it. "*Mein schatz* has, shall we say, moved on."

"To my wife."

"Yes." The countess licked the spoon before returning it to her saucer. "Wicked man. They are to be married, you know."

This hit Philip like the blow of a hammer on an anvil. "Married?"

"Don't look so crushed." She folded the newspaper she had been reading and set it to the side. "It wounded me as well, and I wasn't supposed to be dead. Which returns me to a subject about which I am most curious. Why did you disappear? I never suspected you had the constitution to follow Hargreaves's path of employment, yet —"

"She cannot marry him." His chest clenched, first with panic and then with growing anger.

The countess leaned away and draped her arm over the back of her chair. The posture ought to have looked strained, but instead her insouciance lent an air of permanent and sophisticated elegance to her every gesture. "Why shouldn't she? You haven't gone back to her. Are you forbidden to let her know you are alive?"

"Forbidden? No, of course not. I intended to let her know, but then I saw Hargreaves kiss her. Can you imagine how that felt? She did not mourn me."

The countess laughed. "I know we were never close, but I had not taken you to be so sentimental. Whatever did you expect her to do? Mimic your tedious queen and keep to her widow's weeds forever?"

"Of course not," he said. "I only —" He closed his eyes. "One would like to think it not quite so easy to get on with one's life after such a tragedy."

"I understand her mourning to have been rather unconventional, if you must know, but I assure you she did grieve." She shook her head and shrugged. "You must not want her back. If you did, you would have made your presence known at once, regardless of what you had seen. One would expect someone in your situation to have been catalyzed to intervene by the incident. The fact you did not tells me you are not sure you still want her."

"You could not be more wrong, Countess. I adore her."

"I insist you call me Kristiana," she said, leaning forward and placing her hand on top of his on the table. "I cannot tolerate formality from the dead. So you adore her. Did you follow her to Vienna? She has been here with him, you know."

"I did not know that," he said. "My work brought me here, not my wife."

"Your work?" Her lips curled into a wry smile. "How curious. Do tell me — what is your profession?"

"I am employed in an antiquities shop during the winter. For the rest of the year I pursue archaeology."

"An odd cover, but I know better than to ask questions," she said. "I presume you are no longer using the name Ashton."

"No. I have become Philip Chapman," he said.

Her eyebrows raised. "Suffice it to say I am aghast to learn you, Hargreaves, and I are in the same business. I always pegged you as an overeager dilettante."

He did not correct her error. "I am aghast as well. I would never have thought so refined a lady would engage in that line of work. He never told me, but you have given yourself away."

"Surely you suspected." She fluttered her eyelashes like an ingénue. "I always thought that was why you disapproved of me."

"I do not disapprove of you," he said. "So

they were both here, in Vienna?"

"They did not leave together, but neither is in the city now. You only just missed them."

"I would not have wanted to see the spectacle," Philip said, frowning.

"You would not have enjoyed it any more than I did," she said. "He loves her, more than he loved me, and from what I know, more than you loved her."

"You cannot know that."

"They are happy together," she said. "It revolts me, if you must know, but it would be unwise to try to separate them. We are both aware of how painful it is to lose love. Do you want her to know that feeling so well as we do?"

"He never did deserve you," Philip said.

"You do yourself no credit, *schatz.*"

"Don't call me what you called him. Terms of endearment ought not be transferable."

"Why not?" she asked, eyeing him closely. "You are more handsome than I remember. Perhaps the time in the wilds of Africa suited you."

"Where is your husband?"

"Berlin. You should come home with me."

"I cannot do that, Countess. I love her too much, and you are seeking to fill a hole in your heart that I will never fit."

She laughed. "You Englishmen do so like to be right, and here you are, succeeding at it extremely well. It is surprisingly good to speak with you. There are very few people who understand the delicacy of my situation when it comes to Hargreaves. You are the only of his friends he ever deigned to allow me to meet."

They sat for nearly an hour, dissecting their wounded hearts with the candor that develops easily between near-strangers who know they are unlikely to see each other again. Anyone watching would have thought them conspirators, the way they leaned together, speaking in hushed tones, but it was pain, not a mutual cause, that brought them together.

"I wish you would come home with me," Kristiana said. They were the only two left in the café, and Philip suspected the waiter would be pleased to see them go.

"You know I must not do that," he said. "I thank you, not only for the invitation, but also for your sage advice. I cannot bring myself to hurt her. If she loves Hargreaves, I shall not stand in the way of her happiness."

"I don't see that you have a choice — if

she is still married to you, she cannot marry him."

"Which is why, my dear lady, I am now Philip Chapman, who works in a very fine antiquities shop near St. Stephen's. You should call in, but be sure to use my new name. I shall only be in Vienna a few more months, then I'm off to Turkey in seek of more ancient relics."

"Ah, yes, archaeology." Her eyebrows lifted. "Fascinating. I should very much like us to meet again, but it is unlikely to occur. My own work has grown increasingly dangerous of late, and I fear this may be my final mission. I love Austria more than my own life, and will do anything to stop those who would attack her."

"Surely your work does not threaten your personal safety?"

She laughed and leaned forward over the table, her eyes flashing. "You play naïve quite well. I would not have thought you had it in you. There is no need for it with me. We may be embroiled in the espionage game, but I assure you we are playing for the same side."

"I will not allow you to distract me from my question. Is your life at risk?"

"There are abstract ways in which it always has been, but my current assignment has placed me more directly in the line of fire."

"Then it is too dangerous to attempt," he said.

"No, it is the most important of my career," she said. "I could not turn it down. Something you should understand well, as you appear to be engaged in a similar sort of subterfuge. Professional hazard, isn't it? I shall come out of it unscathed and then I shall stop. There comes a time when danger starts to lose its appeal."

"It felt different when you and Hargreaves were working together, didn't it?"

"More than you can imagine," she said. She rose to her feet and pulled around her the fur wrap she had draped across an empty chair. She held her hand out for him to kiss. "I already regret that I shall not see you again. When at last you do confront our friend, please tell him how disappointed I am to find him adopting such a bourgeois life. I expected better from him. And in your own work, I wish you good luck, Herr Chapman. I hope you never become as jaded as I."

7

Philip — I knew not what else to call him — looked dreadful when Colin and I returned to him and the others in the music room. His complexion had taken on a gray hue, and his eyes, sunken and dull, all but disappeared into his face. Herr Reiner had shared his news about the destruction of the tent, and while the gentlemen discussed it, Margaret, with what I am convinced was a deliberate desire to provoke, sat at the piano playing Mahler's *Lieder eines fahrenden Gesellen* and singing the composer's mournful lyrics bemoaning the loss of love. In the midst of this performance, Professor Hiller von Gaertringen called to collect Herr Bohn's body. Colin shook the archaeologist's hand and complimented him.

"I have read several of your excavation reports," Colin said. "Your work is most impressive. I do hope you will be able to further explore more of Santorini, and perhaps dig under the ash at Akrotiri." The eruption in the seventeenth century B.C. that had savaged the island buried the town of Akrotiri. Hiller von Gaertringen had ordered some of his men to do a preliminary dig there, and they had uncovered at least one house, but I imagine he could not spare the resources to excavate two sites simultaneously with the attention each deserved.

"Thank you," he said with a little bow. "I hope to as well, perhaps when I am through at Thera, but there is much to be done elsewhere, too, and I am already called to other sites. We shall see. I apologize again for the disturbance and thank you for taking in my men when they were in such dire need of assistance."

"Think nothing of it," Colin said. "I am only sorry more could not be done for Mr. Bohn. Please accept my condolences."

The German nodded brusquely, but I could see the emotion in his face and red-rimmed eyes. "I should take him now." He excused himself, gave Philip and Herr Reiner encouraging little slaps on the shoulders, and the three of them left to tend to their friend's body.

"I am aghast," Margaret said, abandoning the piano and flopping onto a settee. "How awful that poor Philip is left with a demolished tent after dealing with the death of his colleague."

"You have adopted the use of his Christian name? You must be feeling a tad more sympathy than earlier, although I would not have guessed that based on your choice of music," I said. "What caused the change?"

"He doesn't seem to want anything. I spoke most frankly with him while you and your charming husband disappeared. He plans to return to camp today, and they will go back to work tomorrow."

"So you now believe him to be Philip?" I asked.

She shrugged and nodded toward Colin. "You and Adonis seem to, so who am I to argue? I'm the only one who has never before met him."

I did not respond, still uncertain as to how I felt. "Can his returning to the site so soon be a good idea? He has just lost a friend."

"Getting back to work will help," Colin said. "Wallowing will not, and we must take action as well. I shall go to Fira and wire our solicitor about the legal aspects of the situation. Knowledge is preferable to speculation. I want to know precisely where we stand." I heard him go back upstairs after he left us, presumably to bid the archaeologists farewell and to see if they required any assistance with Herr Bohn's body. Soon they had all left the house.

"Greece, Em, is nothing like you promised," Jeremy said, rising from his seat and crossing to the small window. He opened the shutters. "I cannot fault the view, though. Margaret tells me this island may have inspired the legend of Atlantis."

"She is correct," I said. "Santorini is shaped like a crescent, but if you were to draw curved lines from its tips to the volcano and the islets near it, you get a sense of its appearance before the eruption."

Margaret joined him at the window, squinting. "It would have been circular."

"Yes. Plato wrote that the island sank into the sea," I said. "Imagine what might be in the depths of that water." I looked over Margaret's shoulder and gazed at the sapphire blue sea.

"You cannot claim the trip has been anything but diverting," Margaret said, turning to Jeremy.

He tilted his head back and forth, as if giving the matter serious consideration. "I have not thought about Amity for at least forty-five minutes."

"Progress," I said.

"And I look forward to the conclusion of the Greek tragedy currently unfolding before us."

"I am delighted to provide you with such amusement," I said.

Philip stepped into the room, leaving me no opportunity to scold Jeremy. "Apologies if I startled you," he said. "Herr Bohn is in good hands for his journey, so I wanted to pop back and invite you all to the dig. Perhaps a picnic and a tour, the day after next?"

"I thought you would never ask," Margaret said. I shot her a quizzical look that she pointedly ignored. "Thank you, Lord Ashton, I accept on behalf of all of us."

"Hargreaves already agreed," he said. "Kallista . . ." His lips caressed the word, making me feel distinctly uncomfortable. "Would it be too much to ask to speak with you privately? Outside, if we might?" I nodded and he stepped aside to let me leave the room ahead of him. He touched my arm softly to stop me as I turned toward the front door. "The roof terrace, if you don't object. I have long dreamed of standing there with you."

"Whatever you prefer," I said, mounting the stairs, my heart pounding. The sun would not set for another several hours, but already it hung low enough in the sky to have changed the appearance of the light caressing the island, its strong rays piercing the handful of clouds that dotted the sky above the volcano.

"You approve of the view?" he asked. I had taken a position an awkward five or six feet away from him at the low wall that served as a railing around the perimeter of the roof.

"No one could object to it."

"I know I shall never be able to adequately apologize to you, Kallista." He stepped closer to me, and I felt my body freeze. "Please, do not cringe. I have not brought you here to make any inappropriate advances or to implore you to return to me as my wife. I realize far too much time has passed to ask that of you. Waiting so long to come forward was an error in judgment on my part, but I swear I did it only because I could see that you truly love Hargreaves."

"Sir, I do not know what to say to you."

"Are we not allowed to reminisce at all?" he asked. "Do you care nothing for the time we had together, brief though it was?"

"Of course not," I said. "I grieved for you." I bit my lip.

"But not at first."

I met his eyes. "How did you know?"

"A reasonable guess, isn't it? I took you on a shorter than ordinary wedding trip and

149

then rushed off on safari almost the moment we returned to England. That can hardly have endeared me to you."

"It did not trouble me at the time. I understood how important the hunt was to you." I would have been ashamed to admit to him that I had not known him well enough to have missed him when he left me. Quite the contrary, I had found myself relieved to have the house to myself.

"Yet you deplore hunting," he said.

I looked down, scrutinizing the bright rug I had placed over the rough pumice surface of the roof. "Yes."

"But you never told me."

"I did not think my opinion on the matter particularly important."

"What did make you finally grieve for me?" He moved closer, and now stood only a few feet from me.

"Your journal," I said. "I fell in love with the man I found on its pages, and then regretted so very much I had not known you better when you were alive. I mean — when —"

"Don't," he said, and took my hand and gently raised it to his lips. "I shall always love you, Kallista. I am told you have a fondness for port, and I cannot help but

150

wonder if that stems back to our wedding night."

"You remember that?" I asked, looking into his cornflower blue eyes. "I did not expect one kiss to —"

"I could never forget."

"You had given me sherry before we retired and" — I blushed fiercely and looked down again — "told me I tasted of it when you kissed me. I asked you what your lips tasted like —"

"And I told you port." Our eyes met, and for a single wild moment I thought he might kiss me, and although nearly every sense revolted, a tiny space hidden deep in my heart half hoped he would. I shook sense back into myself and stepped away.

"Philip —" His name, after all these years, still sounded foreign on my lips.

"I told you, Kallista, I am not here to make inappropriate advances. You are Hargreaves's wife now." He fumbled in his pocket and pulled out a small parcel. "I have been carrying this with me for ages. It is something I bought for you years ago in Paris, with the hope you might accept it as a token of the new life I had thought we could start on my return. Instead, I give it to you now with the hope you consider it an offer of friendship. I do not expect you to immediately feel you can confide in me, but over time, we may come to be as easy with one another as you and Bainbridge are."

I took the package from him and unwrapped it, finding inside an exquisitely carved ivory brooch. "It is lovely," I said. "Thank you."

"It is my pleasure entirely."

I touched the smooth surface of the single rose's petals. "It reminds me of the one you gave me on our wedding day."

"I am glad you have not forgot," he said, and gently put his hand on my arm, only for an instant. "Thank you for indulging me with this little chat. I do so aspire to earning your friendship." He kissed my hand again, disappeared down the stairs, and then left the house. I remained on the roof, watching as he walked toward Fira. Only when I could no longer see him on the cliff path did I turn my attention to the magnificent view that stretched in front of me — the view curated, if you will, by Philip, when he chose the spot on which he built this house. Tears pricked in my eyes.

I did not hear Margaret approaching until she spoke. "You really must have something to eat. I've asked Mrs. Katevatis to bring dinner to us up here. It is diabolically early for it, of course, but given that we missed luncheon and never had even a bite of something with tea this afternoon, I thought nourishment in order."

"Thank you," I said, not turning around to look at her.

"Are you crying?" she asked. A choked sob was my only response. She embraced me. "I take it you truly believe him now?"

"Yes," I said, unable to stop my tears.

"This is a dreadful business, Emily, but you must look upon it as even more exciting than the most scandalous novel you have ever read. Can you imagine what Mary Elizabeth Braddon could do with such a plot?"

I laughed, despite myself. "She would probably have someone push me down a well."

"I am glad to hear you laugh. Regardless of what Colin learns from the solicitor, nothing can wrench the two of you apart. Even if you must divorce Philip and then marry Colin again, is that so very bad?"

"The scandal —"

"When have you given so much as a fig about scandal?" she asked. "Only think what it would do to your mother! I am of a mind to advise you to insist on divorce and remarriage even if it is not strictly necessary, just to aggravate her."

I laughed again, this time more heartily. "She would be well and truly put out, probably forever."

"And, hence, stop interfering. She might even abandon her much-vaunted efforts to impose upon you her views of child-rearing."

"Let us not get carried away, Margaret," I said. "She would never abandon that. They are, after all —"

"The only male heirs your father has," she finished for me. "Poor Henry. I can't pictures him as an earl."

"He is only a little over three. Give him time."

"It is good to see you smile." She dabbed at my face with her handkerchief. "Now, before Jeremy comes up and disturbs us you must tell me everything. What did Philip say?"

"We spoke of our wedding night."

"No!" I thought her eyes might pop out of her head. "In detail?"

"Nothing like *that,* of course. Well, not precisely, at least. He remembered a kiss."

"A kiss that you, too, remember?" she asked. I nodded. "Well, then, I suppose I must outright reject any doubts about him being whom he claims."

"I am afraid so," I said. "No one else

154

could have known the details of what occurred between us."

"Will you tell Colin?"

"I tell Colin everything."

"You might, my dear, want to amend that policy ever so slightly, if only in this single case. No one could object to keeping private moments shared with your first husband from your second."

"I agree in principle, but it is rather more complicated when one is confronted with both spouses simultaneously."

"Do what you like, but if you do not heed my advice, I shall be standing here, ready to remind you of my words when it all goes badly wrong."

"You are kindness itself, Margaret," I said. "Whatever would I do without you?"

PHILIP
MAGNESIA ON THE MAEANDER
TURKEY, 1892

Philip felt surprise at finding his work selling antiquities so fulfilling, although it did on occasion pain him to no longer be able to afford for himself the sort of prize pieces he had acquired as the Viscount Ashton with no regard for their cost. He had thought, when he first began the work, he would like to open a gallery of his own, but as winter slipped into spring and he traveled back to Asia Minor, where he and his friend Reiner were excavating with Carl Humann at the newly discovered Magnesia on the Maeander, he realized his passion lay in archaeology.

Kallista had married Hargreaves. He had read the announcement in *The Times*. He could no longer pretend she would ever again be his, and had, instead, to find something else on which to focus. Excavation proved a worthy successor, stimulating him physically and mentally, and bringing him endless satisfaction.

The dig filled him with exhilaration like nothing before. No thrill could compare to brushing away centuries of dirt to expose a perfectly carved statue, fixing together the fragments of a beautifully painted vase so it looked all but new, or restoring to their original glory the columns of a temple to Zeus. Collecting became almost an after-thought to him now, and he decided not to return to the shop in Vienna when the season ended. He would focus solely on this excavation, on its treasures and on the ancient people whose sandaled feet trod upon the pavement he helped to uncover. Scholarship brought more satisfaction than commerce.

He buckled his pith helmet under his chin and waved to Professor Humann as he set off in the direction of the Temple of Arte-mis. Every step he took on Turkish soil — land once called Ionia, part of the Greek empire, and the place that held the ancient city of Troy, a site more important to Philip than any other in the world — brought him closer to the heroes of his childhood.

Even as a small boy, he had felt a deep connection to classical mythology, but noth-ing had affected him more profoundly than reading *The Iliad.* If only he had discovered his archaeological fervor before Heinrich Schliemann, the German archaeologist who shared his obsession with Homer's stories, had died, he might have had the good fortune to excavate with him at Troy. He had heard rumors that one of Schliemann's team, Wilhelm Dörpfeld, might mount an expedition of his own, and if those plans came to fruition, Philip was determined to be part of the crew. He might have lost Kallista, but he could accept the city of Homer's epic as worthy consolation.

8

Some (initially, myself included) might have objected to our planned picnic with the archaeologists so soon after the tragic death of their colleague, but we Britons do not allow ourselves to become mired in despair, and evidently the Germans felt much the same. I woke up early on the morning of our outing to Ancient Thera and slipped onto the balcony off our bedroom while Colin still slumbered, his thick curls unruly and the bedsheet pulled down nearly to his waist, exposing the well-developed muscles of his bare chest. The scene looked almost ethereal through the mosquito netting hanging over the bed. Adonis himself would have wept to see such physical perfection. Had my husband not so thoroughly exhausted himself the previous night after we had left our friends huddled downstairs over a backgammon board, I would have been tempted to wake him, but as things stood, I felt he had earned his rest.

Mrs. Katevatis, knowing my habit of rising early, and far before Colin, had, along with a bowl of fruit, left outside our door for me a small pot of mountain tea, brewed from the Sideritis flower, a beverage the Greeks viewed as treatment for nearly any ill. I found it refreshing and always took a cup before breakfast when on Santorini. Helios and his chariot had already begun their daily ride across the sky behind me, and the rosy streaks of sunrise had started to permeate the western view, dyeing the water of the caldera a dark violet splashed with indigo. I had hardly finished my first cup of tea when Colin padded onto the balcony, the sheet bunched around his waist.

"If you are trying to present me with a distraction certain to keep me from Ancient Thera, I will tell you immediately you have succeeded," I said. "You should not show yourself outside in such a state."

"No one can see me but you," he said, looking skeptically at my teacup.

"Would you like some?" I asked.

"Mountain tea? I shall hold out and hope for something more drinkable."

"Do you mean to torment me, coming out here like that?"

"Not at all," he said. He split open a

160

pomegranate from the bowl on the table, scooped out some seeds with his fingers, and fed them to me, their tart sweetness mingling with the salty tang of his skin. "I am only trying to ensure you remember, when archaeological fervor strikes you later today, that there are other things, equally diverting, to be done at home."

"Only equally diverting?"

"That, my dear, remains to be seen," he said. "I am fully aware of how much you adore ruins." He went inside and turned his attention to his morning ablutions, while I was left to resent having to eat the rest of the pomegranate seeds without his titillating assistance. I could hear him humming the overture to *Don Giovanni* in the bathroom. Eventually silence and a whiff of shaving lotion told me he had finished, leaving the room free for my use. I finished my last cup of tea, took a final look over the caldera, and went inside.

Colin, moving faster than he ordinarily did in the morning, was already dressed, although his damp curls, his rolled-up shirtsleeves, and the jacket carelessly tossed over his shoulder suggested he had not taken much care with his appearance. To my mind, he looked even more handsome than usual. He kissed me as I passed him on my way to the bathroom and went downstairs in search of good, English tea.

Meg, my lady's maid, seldom traveled to Greece with me anymore unless I felt she required a holiday of her own. I rarely dressed in a conventional manner on Santorini, preferring instead to spend my days in cool cotton caftans or breezy tea gowns when inside and well-tailored suits that did not require a corset when exploring the island. As none of these items required assistance beyond that which my husband could supply, and as I was capable of braiding my long hair and pinning it on top of my head, I had not needed Meg to come with me. I laced my ankle-high boots and adjusted my skirt — adapted from those currently favored for bicycling — before buttoning my slim jacket. Pith helmet in hand, I collected the others and we set off for Thera.

We kept horses on the island, preferring them to the ubiquitous donkeys for everything other than the trek up from the port, and I had named them after the immortal steeds who pulled Helios' chariot across the sky each day: Aethon, Aeos, Phlegon, and Pyrois. Adelphos had them ready for us behind the house, and I mounted Pyrois, brushing his soft coat with my hand before pulling on my gloves and urging him to the trail that would lead us to towering Mesa Vouno on the other side of the island.

I have already described the steep road leading up to the site of the ancient city. As our noble beasts picked their way along the arduous path, I thought of all those who had made the trip before us, and considered with awe the sheer arrogance it must have taken to decide to build a city at such a height. No enemy army ever conquered it — its natural defenses were too great — and it remained populated and undisturbed through the days of the Roman Empire into the eighth century.

"Roman engineering," Margaret said, admiring the road. "Always a marvel."

"This far predates the Romans," I said. "Or else how could Theras have built the city?"

"I do not doubt he fashioned some sort of a road, but it is the Romans who engineered it to the precise state we find it today."

"They were remarkable copyists, the Romans," I said, ignoring her comment. "Yet who could blame them for wanting to steal every bit of Greek culture? Not every civilization can achieve what the Greeks did on its own."

"Are you planning to argue all day, or only

at select intervals?" Jeremy asked. "Hargreaves, back me on this matter. I propose no more than three fifteen-minute intervals every twenty-four hours during which you lovely ladies can duel over your respective historical passions. The rest of the time, I implore you to leave us in peace."

"You cannot claim the Greeks had the engineering skills of the Romans." Margaret paused neither to draw breath nor to respond to Jeremy. "Only consider the aqueducts —"

A cry interrupted what I am certain would have proved a lengthy and detailed lecture. "Ho!" Philip and Herr Reiner stood near the top of the road, waving and shouting to welcome us to their camp. Whatever damage had been inflicted during the storm and its aftermath had now been remedied, and the scene was one of precise organization. Three small tents stood in a neat row, evenly spaced in front of a large fire pit. Two larger tents on the other side of the plateau, Herr Reiner explained, housed their tools and the artifacts they uncovered.

"We have beer or water for you if you require immediate refreshment," Herr Reiner said, a broad smile on his face. His features, even and strong, were not precisely handsome, but imbued him with the appearance of reliability. We assured him we needed nothing; our canteens had kept us hydrated en route.

"I am pleased, as I am quite desperate to show you the ruins," Philip said. "Shall we explore?" He ushered us, ladies first, up the path to the top of Mesa Vouno.

"This pass where we have placed our camp, between Mesa Vouno and Profitis Ilias, the neighboring hill, is called Sellada," Fritz said. "Ahead of us, there" — he pointed — "we have found what appears to be a sanctuary. I suggest we continue to the city itself rather than start below. I know you have been here before, Lady Emily, but I am certain you will agree we have accomplished quite a bit since the time of your last visit."

The path snaked up the hillside, passing an early Christian church — built far too recently to be of interest to me — before flattening out and continuing in a straight line along the edge of the high plateau. From here, the awe-inspiring view stretched endlessly across the sea to other islands far in the distance. Directly below us was the black beach at Kamari, one of the two Ancient Theran harbors, the second, at Perissa, visible to our south.

"On a clear day, one can see all the way

to Crete," Philip said. "It takes little imagination to understand the strategic value of the site. One could keep an eye on an enormous swath of the Aegean from here."

Wildflowers lined both sides of the narrow path. The bursts of color springing from the dark, volcanic soil would soon fall victim to the burning heat of summer, but for now they were like the splashes of paint on an artist's palette. Colin squeezed my hand and grinned. "You are in your element here, standing guard over the ancient seas." He spoke quietly, so as not to be overheard, his lips close to my ear.

"If only you could throw me over your shoulder and take me to your walled city," I replied.

"I would never have manners as bad as Paris," he said, "and you, my dear, should aspire to a fate superior to Helen's."

In a few more yards the city emerged before us. I gasped. Although I had seen it before, so much more rubble had been cleared since my last visit that the place had entirely changed. The dirt path turned into pavement, some of it rough cobbles, some of it rectangles of smooth marble. To our right, as we continued walking south, buildings rose — some only a foot or so high, others intact enough to give a decent impression of what Thera had looked like fifteen hundred years ago. The city spanned the entire length of the plateau, a distance I estimated to be more than three thousand feet. As we continued on, past a gnarled pine tree whose scent filled the air with every breezy gust of air, the land to the east of the path widened and we began to see ruins on both sides.

Those to the west stretched much further than those to the east, where the mountain's steep slope limited the area useful for construction. To the west, stone stairs formed streets running perpendicular to the main road on which we stood. Unable to resist, I rushed up the first set of them, stopping only when debris the archaeologists had not yet cleared made them impassable. The remains of the buildings here were taller, and the width of the stepped street grew even more narrow the further up the hill it went.

"Come down here at once, Emily!" Margaret called from below. I followed her order, and gathered with the rest of our party in the center of the remains of the Basilike Stoa, a long building across from the Agora featuring a line of tall columns.

"Many of these columns are Hellenistic," Philip said, "although the Romans had their share of additions and renovations. We suspect the building lost its roof to an earthquake during the Imperial period. Further along, over to the east, you will see we have started to excavate a theatre built into the mountainside. We have found one or two private homes in its vicinity, but are focusing now on the city's civic buildings. The domestic ones we will save for another season."

A team of local men toiled in the theatre, and we watched for a while as they carefully and methodically moved dirt, rock, and bricks. Each object would be cataloged and labeled, and then set aside until the spot where it belonged could be discovered. It was not nearly so well preserved or so large as the theatre at Epidaurus, but already the semicircle of stones designating the stage was visible, along with the remains of the wall standing behind it, a structure of moderate height that would not block the view of the sea. What a spectacular backdrop for a play! One could clearly see the space that had been dug out of the mountainside in front of the stage to house the audience, but little remained of the long, stone benches on which they would have sat, row above row.

"Can we help?" I asked, pushing my

smoke-colored spectacles up on the bridge of my nose.

"Not now," Philip said. "Today is for picnicking and exploration, but going forward, we would welcome your assistance."

"Follow me," Fritz said. "We have everything ready for you."

"Jeremy!" I scowled, seeing he had taken out his pocketknife. "You are forbidden from leaving graffiti at this site."

"Archaeologists do object to that sort of thing, old chap," Philip said, slapping him congenially on the back.

Fritz led us to the far end of the city, all the way to the south, where he and Philip had erected a canopy, stretching from the remains of a tall, thick wall to nearly the edge of the cliff. Beneath it, they had placed chairs and a folding table, spread with a white cloth and set with the coarse, bright local pottery found in every village. Pomegranates, oranges, grapes, and figs filled a large bowl in the center of the table, and oval platters displayed pâté, a chunk of fresh Greek cheese, and a neatly sliced loaf of bread. Another, smaller bowl held black and green olives, and its twin nearly overflowed with the sweet, tiny, round tomatoes famously grown on the island.

"The pâté, I am afraid, comes from a tin,

but I assure you it is the best we have," Philip said. Fritz opened a bottle of wine and filled glasses for us all. We toasted to the excavations and to the island, then applied ourselves to the charming feast the archaeologists had provided. Once thoroughly sated, I stepped out from the canopy and into the sun, putting my pith helmet back on my head and holding it in place as I took in the view of the city. While I studied the top of the ridge, where the last row of ruins stood, I saw a flash of movement. A man with dark hair and dusty clothes climbed over a wall far in the distance.

"Who is that?" I asked. Fritz, who stood nearest to me, turned and followed my gaze.

"I do not recognize him," he said, and shouted out a greeting, asking the individual to identify himself. No response came, but the stranger started to run. At once, Colin set off after him, followed by Fritz.

Philip, his face pale, did not move. "How did he find me here?"

PHILIP
ATHENS, 1892

As Philip's second season with Carl Humann at Magnesia wound to a close, he considered his options. Reiner had already signed on to return the following year, but Philip had grown increasingly more dedicated to finding his way onto the staff of Wilhelm Dörpfeld, who, after spending years at Troy working under Schliemann, had taken over the excavations two years after the death of his mentor. Philip had read everything Dörpfeld had published and studied all of the excavation reports pertaining to Troy. Like him, Dörpfeld had a great desire to locate the sites mentioned in Homer's epic poems, which made Philip consider him a kindred spirit. Now the time had come to win a position on the crew working at Troy.

To start, he would winter in Athens, where Dörpfeld held the position of secretary of the German Archaeological Institute. He would beg an introduction, strike up a collegial — and professional — friendship with the man, and, when the time came, ask to join his work in Ilium.

His plan came to fruition more easily than he could have hoped, prodded along by an unexpected source. Jane Harrison, a middle-aged Englishwoman with a passion for all things Hellenic and a close associate of Dörpfeld's, took up his cause, and before more than a few months had passed, Philip was spending his time analyzing fragments of pottery and other objects Dörpfeld had collected with Schliemann in Troy. As soon as the weather allowed, they would go to the site, and Philip, who had visited there only once and had spent all of his time trying to determine where Achilles' tent might have stood, would now be able to contribute to the growing body of evidence about a place the world had once thought existed only in mythology.

Miss Harrison, whom he once might have dismissed as an eccentric spinster, proved herself knowledgeable and efficient. Dörpfeld had invited her to join them at Troy, and while this initially shocked Philip, he came to appreciate her even before they had left Athens. She had, apparently, lectured frequently in England, and proved wildly popular. She was working on a project about Ancient Greek religion, and had a grasp on classics superior to that of many of her male peers.

Watching her work, Philip could not help but think of his Kallista. He had loved her so, but had chosen her as a wife without even the slightest thought as to whether she might appreciate his intellectual endeavors. He had learned — through gossip and observation during his brief time with Reiner in London — that she had started to study Greek and apparently had an aptitude for it. Did Hargreaves cherish this part of her?

Hargreaves's work, which Philip knew often required lengthy periods away from England, would give her the freedom to pursue her studies, but would she, as Philip now began to suspect she might, long for a spouse who shared her passions? He tried to push the thought from his head, but on occasion allowed himself the indulgence of imagining she might welcome his return, if it came at a time when she found herself, perhaps, less enamored of Hargreaves than before. The glow of infatuation could not last forever, particularly if his friend — former friend — found her intellectual pursuits less than desirable. Philip pictured standing with her on the field at Troy, rosy-fingered dawn lighting her face as they praised the mighty Achilles before he set off to continue his excavations.

In his fantasy, he always had charge of the excavations.

He could build her an expedition house near the site. Gertrude Bell might have contented herself to live in tents while mapping Persia, but he wanted better for Kallista. She might decide to tutor girls from nearby villages, teaching them to read so they might better appreciate their ancient heritage. When he came home, dusty and hot from the dig, she would have his bath ready for him, and . . . well, some things were best not considered.

Instead, he focused on preparing for his departure to Troy. His time with Humann had given him good training in the basics of archaeology, and he felt confident he had gleaned everything possible from Schliemann's excavation reports. He familiarized himself with the system Dörpfeld had developed for analyzing the strata of a site. Schliemann and Dörpfeld had not agreed on everything, and Philip learned Schliemann had proved much sloppier in technique than Dörpfeld, who had been forced to intervene when Schliemann was poised to destroy the crumbled remains of a marble wall he did not recognize to be Greek. Dörpfeld showed him they were not, as Schliemann believed, Roman mortar.

Once he felt confident in both his knowledge and his technique, Philip learned how to reliably use a camera. Then, there was nothing left to do except pack his supplies, reread *The Iliad,* and wait for his departure.

9

Colin and Fritz raced along the ridge in pursuit of the fleeing man. I had run out from under the canopy to watch them. Philip followed, but hung back. I called to him, without looking away from the chase. "Who is that man?"

He shook his head. "I don't recognize him in particular, but he must have been sent by —" He stopped.

"Who?" I turned and stood in front of him.

"I worked at Troy for two seasons —"

"Troy?" I could not help interrupting, and must confess that all thoughts of the man Colin and Fritz were chasing after vanished from my mind as I spoke the word. "I adore Troy."

"You do?" he asked. "Have you been?"

"No," I said, turning to him. "Colin and I had planned to go as part of our wedding trip, but . . . Oh, Philip, I am sorry." His face had reddened at my words, and I instantly regretted them.

"It is of no consequence."

"Did they catch him?" Margaret asked, coming up beside us and jolting my focus back to the chase. I started up the cobbled path — Colin and Fritz had disappeared from view, over the far side of the hill — and could hear them shouting. Philip and Margaret followed close behind. By the time we reached the top, Colin and Fritz were standing silent and grim.

"Where is he?" I asked.

Colin nodded down the hill, where a crumpled body lay amid a mass of stones. "He wouldn't stop, and then he tripped and fell."

Fritz looked ill. "I never thought he would — all we wanted was to ask him what he was doing here."

"This is my fault," Philip said. "If I had never come here —"

"That is quite enough from all of you," I said, gathering my skirts and starting to carefully pick my way down the steep slope. "Is anyone going to come with me to see if he's still alive?"

He was still alive, although so far as I could tell, just barely. His breath was shallow, his leg was bent at an unnatural angle, and there was a gash on the side of his head, bleeding copiously.

"We shall have to move him," I said, "but not before we do something with his leg. He needs a doctor. Philip, go to Oia. Take Pyrois — he's my fastest horse. Find the doctor and bring him to the house. Fritz, Jeremy, and Margaret, go back to camp and collect anything we might be able to use as a stretcher. If you have got a medical kit, bring that as well."

"*Ja,*" Fritz said, slipping into his native tongue. "*Ich werde ihn bringen.*" The three of them headed toward the camp, Fritz keeping a firm hold on Margaret's arm as they made their way back up the hill.

Once they were gone, I turned to Colin. "We need something that can serve as a splint. Will you see what you can find?" He nodded. I removed my petticoat and began ripping it into long strips before turning my attention back to our patient. My stomach turned when I contemplated the sharp angle of the bone in his lower leg. Within minutes, Colin returned, brandishing Jeremy's walking stick, now broken into two pieces, and the tablecloth.

"Better than nothing," he said, crouching next to me. "It would be best if we could get the bone realigned. I have done it before. It will be unpleasant, but not impossible. I may be able to manage on my own —"

"I will help you," I said. "Tell me what to do.

Using his pocketknife, Colin cut the leg of the man's trousers off mid-thigh. He then held the leg, just below the knee, and directed me to grip above the man's ankle with both of my hands. I buried my teeth in my bottom lip, dreading what would come next. Colin pulled, while I held firm, and somehow he managed to straighten the limb. The sound of the bone slipping back into place sickened me. I turned away, just for a moment, to compose myself.

"Would you cut the tablecloth in half, please?" I asked Colin. He did so in a swift motion.

"Let me do the rest," he said.

"No. We need to keep him from moving. You are far stronger than I, and therefore in a better position to hold him still should he regain consciousness." My nausea and dizziness having passed, I took a deep breath and threaded strips of cloth under his leg at even intervals. He was not a tall man, so the two halves of the walking stick reached from his ankle to above the knee. I then wrapped my makeshift splints in the two halves of the tablecloth to pad them, placed one on either side of the leg, and secured them by knotting the strips of petticoat, tightening them until I was content that his leg was as stable as possible. Through all of this, the man did not so much as move a muscle.

"He must be in a great deal of pain," I said.

"It is a blessing he is not conscious," Colin said, "but astonishing that our moving the bone did not wake him."

I could tell from his tone he did not expect the man to live. "He does not look Greek," I said.

"Turkish, if I had to guess," Colin said. The man had a long, drooping mustache and his clothes and his build suggested he was of sturdy peasant stock.

Fritz, Jeremy, and Margaret returned, carrying with them a cot, a blanket, four canteens of water, and a medical kit. The slope was too steep for the cot, so they left it on the hilltop. I rummaged through the supplies until I found iodine. "Be sure he stays still," I said to Colin, and poured some of the disinfecting liquid over the injury on his head before covering it with gauze. The man did not move through any of this.

With great care, the gentlemen lifted him, Fritz supporting his head and shoulders,

Jeremy lifting his uninjured leg, and Colin, doing all he could not to disturb the splint, cradling the man's broken limb. Slowly, they made their way back up the hill and placed him gently on the cot. Transporting him was much simpler now. It took only two of them to carry the cot, which meant they could take turns on the way down to the camp.

Margaret and I went on horseback to the nearest village, where we found a farmer with a donkey cart who agreed to carry the injured man the rest of the way home. We lined the cart with blankets before transferring him to it and then slowly made our way down the terrifyingly steep road. The farmer drove with Fritz, whose Greek was the best of all of us, while I sat in the back with my patient. There was little I could do, but I did not want to take the chance he might wake up during the trip and find himself scared and alone. Colin, Jeremy, and Margaret rode the horses, slowing their pace to the barest walk so as not to pull ahead of the donkeys.

Philip and the doctor, who must have ridden at a shocking speed, were waiting at the villa when we arrived, and before long the man was settled into a vacant servant's bedroom in the back of the house, where Colin and I watched the physician conduct his examination. He complimented us on the care we had given him in the field.

"I shall stitch the wound on his head and replace the splint, but beyond that there is little I can do for him."

"Will he wake up?" I asked.

"He is in a deep coma, Lady Emily. I do not know if he will ever emerge." He left us with some morphine to administer if he did awaken, and promised he would come back the following day to check on his progress. After he took his leave, Colin and I joined the others in the drawing room, where they were sitting in silence, a half-drunk pitcher of lemonade on the table.

"What a terrible accident," Margaret said. "I have no desire to make anyone feel worse than I know we all do, but I wish we had not chased after him."

"What was he doing or planning to do that he ran away when confronted?" Jeremy asked.

"There is more to it than we know," I said, looking at Philip. "Is that not right?"

"There may be," Philip said. "I only wish I knew more."

"You said —"

He interrupted me. "Yes, I know what I said." He cleared his throat. "I have been plagued over the past few years by a gentleman who is convinced I have something that belongs to him. His view is entirely in error, but nothing I say makes even the slightest impact. He has sent his henchmen to rough me up on more than one occasion — hence the current appearance of my nose and the scar on my chin — and I believe this man to be one of them."

"What does he think you have?" Colin asked.

"I am certain you all recall the story of the Battle of Marathon," Philip said. "After winning his spectacular victory against the Persians, the Greek general, Miltiades, took the helmet he had worn in the fight to the Temple of Zeus at Olympia. It has since been discovered by archaeologists and identified as such by the carving along the base: 'Miltiades dedicated to Zeus.' "

"I have seen the piece in the museum at Olympia," I said.

"You have gone to Olympia?" Philip asked, surprise in his voice.

"I wanted to see the Praxiteles Hermes and the Infant Dionysus," I replied. "I am a fervent fan of the sculptor's."

"I have — had — a fine copy of his bust of Apollo in the house in Berkeley Square," he said. "Is it still there?"

Not knowing how much he knew about

the events following his so-called death, I decided now was not the moment to reveal to him that, for a time, the original bust had resided at Berkeley Square, and that its discovery had led me, briefly, to think Philip was a thief of antiquities. "So far as I know it is. Please, though — Olympia."

"Yes, quite," he said. "Or actually, we must now move to Troy. While digging there, in a location likely to have been part of the Greek encampment outside the city walls, I found a strip of metal — bronze — not far from the remains of a temple. It appears to be the bottom of a helmet, and carved on it —"

"Is it Hector's?" I leapt to my feet, unable to help myself, so excited was I at the prospect of something — anything — of the valiant man's having survived more than a thousand years.

"No, Kallista, it was not. It belonged to the superior warrior, Achilles."

This ridiculous description of Achilles raised my ire, but I did not correct Philip. That could wait until later. "How do you know it belonged to Achilles?"

"As was Miltiades' helmet, this, too was engraved: ΑΧΙΛΛΕΥΣ ΑΝΕΘΕΚΕΝ ΤΟΙ ΔΙ. Akhilleus dedicated to Zeus."

"How is it I have never heard of such a

thing?" I asked. "Surely such a discovery would have garnered considerable publicity."

"It would have, yes, if it had been made known," Philip said. "When I found it, I was far off from the rest of our group, working only with a single assistant, a native man who, until that moment, had proven competent enough. As I bent over the bronze, brushing the dirt from it, he struck me on the head with a rock. When I came to, both he and metal strip were gone."

"How can you be certain it was he who struck you?" Colin asked.

"I cannot, I suppose, but there was no one else in the vicinity," Philip said. "I staggered back to the main area of our dig and told my colleagues what had happened. No one believed me — no one expects to find firm evidence of the existence of Achilles — and they convinced me I had fallen victim to nothing more than petty theft. My watch, my compass, and the small amount of money I had with me were all gone."

"But the bronze —" I said.

"I was quickly convinced it had been nothing more than a figment of my imagination — a product of the head injury I suffered when I had been robbed. Everyone assumed the man, desperate for anything he

185

could sell, targeted me because I had chosen to work further afield than the rest of our team. I was content with the explanation until the following morning, when, upon exiting my tent, I nearly tripped over the body of the so-called thief. He had been strangled.

"The general consensus," he continued, "was that someone from his village had executed him, as theft from the Europeans, who are generally giving the natives good pay for honest work, is not tolerated in some quarters. I, however, read the situation differently. The way his corpse had been placed in front of my tent felt to me like a warning. I am certain I did discover a piece of Achilles' helmet, and that this man stole it, probably to give to someone who had offered him an exorbitant price for anything that could be sold on the antiquities market. My reaction to the piece could not have been more enthusiastic, and I explained in detail how rare and significant it was. Perhaps he decided to keep it for himself, to sell, rather than give it to his employer, if I may call him that, and said employer, dissatisfied, had him killed."

"If that were the case, why deposit him in your camp?" Colin asked.

"Perhaps the employer was never able to

locate the bronze and is convinced I still have it. All I can say with certainty is that someone has been hounding me ever since."

"Did you tell Herr Dörpfeld this?" I asked.

"I did, but he was not persuaded of the veracity of my story, particularly as further excavation where I had found the bronze yielded nothing of note. That, combined with the blow I had taken to my head and the fact no one heard even a whisper about the piece on the black market, led everyone to dismiss my theory out of hand."

"So why do you cling to it?" Margaret asked.

"Because twice more while I was at Troy, men came looking for me and asked what I had done with the Achilles bronze. When I had no acceptable answer for them, they threatened me. When my work at the site had finished, and I had moved on to Ephesus, their methods became more violent. I still bear the scars of their delicate attentions." He winced as he said the words.

"Have you gone to the authorities?" Colin asked.

"I have, both in Turkey and in Greece, but there is nothing to be done. There is no evidence to prove my story, and I have not the slightest clue as to the identity of the man sending others to do his dirty work for him."

"This is the first time you have had any contact with them here on Santorini?" Margaret asked.

"It is," he said. He had risen from his seat and now leaned against the wall next to a Monet painting of the seaside at Étretat. "Enough time had passed without an incident that I started to feel safe again. I came to Thera with Hiller von Gaertringen two years ago, and until today had all but forgot about Achilles and his bronze."

I watched him carefully as he spoke. His story, though outlandish, was credible enough, except for one point. Philip, Viscount Ashton, had written monographs praising Achilles and comparing him to Alexander the Great. He was a man who adored the Greek warrior in a way I, as a passionate admirer of Hector, could never understand. Having read every word he had ever written about his hero, no part of me believed Philip would ever have abandoned hope of seeing the Achilles bronze once again.

PHILIP
TROY, 1893

The death of their worker had left the archaeologists less jovial than usual, but this did not stop them from teasing Philip over breakfast the next morning. Being fully aware of the incredible nature of his story, he could hardly blame them. Who among them had not dreamed of finding something — anything — that might have belonged to one of the great heroes of the Trojan War? Dörpfeld told him to push the incident out of his mind, and sent for a doctor to tend to Philip's injury. His head still throbbed, but no one could make him believe he had imagined holding the bronze piece with Achilles' name etched into it. This was no hallucination brought on by concussion.

Three days later, his head no longer ached, but it took another fortnight before his colleagues stopped teasing him, calling him over to where they were digging only to laugh when he got there and say, look, this is not a shard of pottery, this is Achilles' sword, or a piece of his armor. Eventually, they tired of the game, and that was the end of the incident so far as they were all concerned.

No one claimed the dead man's body, but one of the men from the village, although unwilling to take responsibility for the execution, admitted someone might have killed him to punish his crime. He agreed to see to his burial, shrugging, saying someone would have to do it, and it might as well be him. The man had no friends. He had moved to the area only recently and had not made much of an impression on his new neighbors.

Philip, still convinced there were darker forces at work, went to the village and combed the man's filthy hut for anything indicative of a larger purpose for the theft, but he found nothing, and would have been prepared to forget about the matter altogether had two large, well-armed men not stopped him halfway back to the archaeologists' camp.

"I am Hakan and have been sent, along with my colleague, Batur, to tell you Demir knows you have what is his," the taller of the two said. Deep lines cut across his forehead, his face tanned the color of old leather by the sun. "It would be best if you returned it at once."

"First off, I don't have the slightest idea who this Demir chap is," Philip said, squinting in the bright sunlight. The men had positioned him at a disadvantage by forcing him to stand directly in its light. "Second, I can assure you I have nothing belonging to him or anyone else."

Batur, broad and built like an ox, pointed his rifle at Philip. "We will always be able to find you, so it would be best if you gave it back without requiring more persuasion."

"You are welcome to search me if you like," Philip said. "You'll find nothing."

"This is just a warning, my friend," Hakan said. "Demir is a man of business and does not like violence. He did not expect you to be carrying something so valuable with you. I will come next week to collect it. Be ready."

The following week, Philip made a point of sticking close to his colleagues and never worked away from the group. On Thursday, Hakan entered the site, demanding to speak to him. Dörpfeld at his side, Philip again explained that he did not know Demir and had nothing belonging to the man. Hakan uttered no response, only nodded and walked away across the plain, eventually disappearing from sight.

"These natives," one of the other archaeologists said as they sat around the fire that night. "Difficult to tell what they are ever thinking. I do hope this Demir doesn't have a daughter you've trifled with, Chapman."

"I would never do such a thing," Philip said. "All I can think is that the bronze —"

"There is no bronze, Chapman. Just some deceitful Turk who's trying to shake you down for money. Pay him off and forget about it."

10

After listening to Philip's astonishing tale — the second he had told us in the span of only a few days — the time had come to retire to our rooms to freshen up. Jeremy offered to lend Fritz a spare suit so he could change out of his working clothes, but Philip, looking rather sullen, refused Colin's offer to do the same.

"I must return to the dig," he said. "I want to make sure our men are all right."

"They will all have gone home, Chapman — er, Ashton, I ought to say." Fritz looked uncomfortable. "Apologies. Old habits and all that."

"Chapman?" I asked.

"It is the name I adopted so as not to draw attention to myself," Philip said. "I picked it in honor of the translator of Homer."

"Of course," I said. "His was the first I read and will always be my sentimental favorite. *Achilles' baneful wrath resound, O*

Goddess!"

"Your knowledge is impressive, Kallista," he said, his eyes meeting mine. "I had no idea you would take so readily to the Hellenic world. I only wish —"

"Upstairs," Margaret said, interrupting. "You too, Lord Ashton. You will accept Colin's offer of a fresh suit, as I can no longer tolerate the state of what you are currently wearing. *Filthy* does not begin to describe it, and you smell of horse."

He could hardly refuse after that. I waited downstairs for a few minutes, in order to give him and Colin time to find him something suitable to wear. I did not want to be present while they did so. There was something off-putting about one's first husband having to be dressed by one's second. Jeremy and Fritz had gone up as well, but Margaret stayed behind with me.

"Lord Ashton is a bit of a conundrum, is he not?" she asked. "Was he always so enigmatic?"

"Not to my knowledge," I said, "but I cannot claim to have been well acquainted with him."

"This odd incident with Achilles and the bronze and a mysterious Turk who has been chasing him across the Mediterranean — do you give it any credit?"

"There is a healthy market for stolen antiquities, and I have read any number of accounts of local workers pilfering things from archaeological digs. One hears about it in Egypt with great frequency. When people live in abject poverty, they will do nearly anything to supplement their inadequate incomes."

"To have found something, at Troy, with Achilles' name on it . . ." Margaret's voice dropped almost to a whisper and she had a far-off look in her eyes.

"It would be an extraordinary coup," I said, "but I wonder at the validity of the story. I am leaning toward agreeing with Herr Dörpfeld — Philip's head injury may have led him to believe he had found something of Achilles' when, in fact, it may have been something else altogether, if there was anything at all."

"You think it was simple theft?"

"If the dead man kept the bronze, this Demir would have found it on him, or in his home, and would not have needed to come after Philip. If the dead man had already sold the bronze, which would be unlikely in so short a time and in such an isolated location, I would expect there to have been something amongst his belongings to suggest an influx of money."

"If Philip found nothing, why is Demir still harassing him?" Margaret asked.

"Perhaps Philip owes him money and invented a fantastical story rather than admit he is in debt. How much can an archaeologist reasonably be expected to earn in a season? He was accustomed to living in luxury, but now has access to none of his former funds — he left his personal fortune entirely to me, and his nephew has the rest of the estate."

"He might very well find it difficult to adapt to a limited income," Margaret agreed.

"I shall have a quiet word with him after dinner and see if he would accept any help from me. It is his money, after all. He ought to have it back."

I heard the sound of doors closing and water running upstairs. The gentlemen must have sorted out their clothing situation, leaving Margaret and me free to do the same. Colin had just got out of the bath when I entered our room.

"What do you make of all this?" he called to me.

"Margaret and I are considering the possibility that Philip owes this Demir money —"

"Money is not a problem for him," Colin

said. "I had a frank discussion with him on the subject. He has managed to save quite a bit. He worked in Vienna for a while, as an antiquities dealer, and uses his connections in that world to sell pieces he has acquired with his income. He's done rather well."

"Is it all legal?"

He was rubbing his hair with a thick towel as he came into the bedroom. "Absolutely. He has been extremely careful about that. I would expect nothing else of him."

"I know we both believe he is who is claims," I said. "What convinced you he is telling the truth?"

"At first, I was too shocked to give the matter much useful thought," Colin said, "and then I focused on the implausibility of his situation. Having spent more time with him, I am inclined to say, yes, he is Philip Ashton. He recalls our shared history with admirable detail — some of our exploits at Cambridge with too much detail. Yet it is not the memories, but something in the way he speaks, the manner in which he expresses his opinions and tells a story, that strikes me. The scar on his leg is an extremely strong piece of physical evidence to add to the fact that he does look like an older Ashton, one somewhat the worse for wear. In the end, my view on the matter is influenced most by something you, my dear, are ordinarily better acquainted with than I. After much considered analysis of the evidence, and accepting I have no way to actually prove the matter, I *feel* he is the friend I've known since my school days. What about you? What made you believe him?"

"You knew him better than I," I said, my voice quiet as I slipped past him and turned the faucets to fill the deep tub.

"I do not like the recrimination in your voice. You are too hard on yourself."

"Do you not feel awful as well?" I asked. I threw my arms in the air and fought back tears. "This is ghastly. Have you had any reply from the solicitor?"

"Not yet," he said, "but Ashton is adamant he does not want anyone else to know he is still alive. So far as he is concerned, he is Philip Chapman, archaeologist; he wants no part of his old life."

"Can we leave it at that? What if he changes his mind in the future and comes forward and says we knew all this time he was alive? Would that not be worse for the boys?"

"I cannot believe he would do such a thing. It would go entirely contrary to his character. We shall know more when the solicitor replies. Until then, do your best not to let it trouble you. As for the rest, tell me what you really think. Has he said anything that you take as proof he is who he claims?"

I thought about our conversation on the roof, what Philip said about that kiss on our wedding night. "Yes," I said. "There are things no one else could know unless Philip was extremely indiscreet and discussed them with you. And if he had done so, I am confident you would not have shared them with anyone else."

"What did he say?" Colin stopped buttoning his shirt and looked at me quizzically.

"Nothing. It was nothing, just an insignificant detail from our wedding day."

"Something from the ceremony, or later?"

I knew precisely what he was getting at, and had no intention of discussing the matter further. "As I said, it was nothing of any consequence except that no one else could have known of it."

Colin drew a long breath and held it before loudly blowing it out. "I would prefer to remain ignorant on the subject." He returned to the bedroom, shutting the door to the bath behind him. Ordinarily, he would have left it open, so that we might converse with greater ease, and so he would know the instant I rose from the tub. He always liked to be on hand with a towel, a habit that often inspired him in certain amorous directions and led to our coming down shockingly late to dinner. I felt a strange pressure deep in my chest, and tears welled in my eyes.

When I emerged from the bathroom, he had already gone downstairs, without so much as a word. I slipped into what I knew to be his favorite of my tea gowns, fashioned from filmy cream-colored silk and trimmed with delicate lace at the cuffs, hem, and high neckline. Around my waist I looped a wide sash of the same silk, its edges detailed with a Greek key pattern embroidered in blue and gold. I pinned my hair in a loose bun on top of my head, not bothering to tame the escaping tendrils, as I felt they gave me a bit of a Gibson Girl style.

I took stock of myself in the mirror. An elegant gown and a fashionable pompadour could not hide the strain on my face.

I was not looking forward to the evening.

Dinner proved a more raucous affair than I had anticipated. The gentlemen consumed a great quantity of ouzo, given to them by Aristo Papadokos, the village woodworker who had become a close friend of ours —

an excuse, I suspected, to see Mrs. Kateva-tis, upon whom I was convinced he had romantic designs. We dined on the roof terrace, and by the time the last bit of baklava had disappeared, the sun had long since set, its light replaced by a silvery slip of moon. Colin, Philip, and Margaret were around the table arguing about something to do with Latin while Jeremy and I sat with Fritz on chairs pulled close to the railing, looking out over the dark expanse of caldera. Jeremy passed cigars to all of us, and Fritz balked when I accepted one.

"You do not approve?" I asked.

"Quite the contrary — I rejoice," he said. "I am surprised only because Ashton described you in ways so different from what I see having met you."

"How so?"

"I had the impression you were like a fragile flower. I could not have been more wrong."

"A fragile flower?" I crinkled my nose. Had I appeared as such all those years ago, when I married Philip? Granted, my education and my passions had not yet fully developed, but I did not believe myself to ever have behaved like a delicate debutante.

"Ashton probably wouldn't have liked her one bit if he had known her better," Jeremy said. "She is difficult. Impetuous, although I will admit if pressed on this that at least she may be improving with age."

I glared at him. "I changed a great deal after my husband's death, if I may still call it that. It would be useless to speculate how things might have turned out had circumstances been different."

"I am of the opinion that you turned out most heartily well," Fritz said.

"Thank you," I said. "Were you there the day he found the Achilles bronze?"

"No, I was working at Magnesia on the Maeander that season."

"What do you make of the story?" Jeremy asked.

"It is not easy to find sense in it, but I do believe his basic narrative. What we cannot be certain of is the bronze itself. No one had a chance to study it, so we can estimate neither its age nor its origin. Ashton, of course, wants it to have come from Achilles' helmet, but it just as easily could have been brought to the site by someone else much later."

"Alexander the Great visited Troy," I said.

"Yes, it was practically a place of pilgrimage to the ancients," Fritz said. "I exaggerate some, but no Greek man would have traveled through that part of Turkey without going there. The stories surrounding it were highly significant to their culture."

"What was his condition when you found him in Africa?" I asked. "Was he very ill?"

"Not when I first saw him. He was lean to the point of gaunt, but healthy. Sunburned. From his stories it was clear life with the Masai suited him in a way."

"Why did he leave them?" I asked.

"To come back to you."

I bit back the words I was about to speak. Jeremy, seeing the change in my expression, patted my arm. "There, there, darling. I am certain he would have come sooner had the hunting been not quite so good."

"Thank you, Jeremy," I said. "You are a source of true comfort."

"I am confident he had no real idea how much time had passed," Fritz said. "When we told him, he appeared genuinely horrified."

"I believe you," I said, flicking ash off my cigar before extinguishing it. I looked over at Colin, but he was too caught up in conversation to notice. If Philip had not tarried so long in Africa, Colin and I might never have married, a thought too awful to contemplate. For the first time since I had started traveling to Santorini, the villa began to feel more like a cage than a peaceful retreat. "Would you excuse me?" Smiling took an effort, but I did not want Jeremy or Fritz to follow me. Consolation offered no appeal, especially when my husband did not so much as look up when I started down the stairs.

I went first to the drawing room, where candlelight illuminated the Impressionist paintings on the wall. How I loved them — the way they captured light, and the way their colors so well suited the island. I paused before the portrait Renoir had painted of me, long before I had met him, using a photograph Philip had given him. I could hardly bear to look at it now, knowing the original image had been taken on the day of my first wedding. I removed it from the wall and called for Mrs. Katevatis.

"Could you please stash this somewhere?" I asked. "I don't want to display it anymore."

"But of course, Lady Emily, although I must say —"

A loud bang interrupted her. We looked at each other and rushed toward the back of the house, the direction from which the sound had come. Adelphos was already in the courtyard, making his way to the barn, from whence I could hear the distress of the horses. I ran after him, terrified they had come to harm, but was relieved to find them only startled.

"It was a gunshot, Lady Kallista," Adelphos said. I started to run again, this time to the room in which the injured man reposed. He was still unconscious, and so far as I could tell nothing had changed in his condition. By the time I returned to the courtyard, Colin and the others had arrived. My husband held me by the shoulders and looked me over.

"You are not hurt?" His dark eyes burned with intensity.

"No, I am unharmed. What happened?"

Mr. Papadokos, entering through the gate near the barn, laughed as he saw our frenzied state. "No need for alarm," he said. "The shot was fired in the air to celebrate an engagement in the village. You English are too skittish. It is —" he paused, then shrugged "— it is embarrassing."

I could not agree. The shot may have proved harmless, but in the shadowy courtyard, outside a house that held one man I had long thought to be dead and another who may have been sent on an evil errand, nothing felt secure. Uncertainty permeated the spring night, and I could not rest easy.

PHILIP
CONSTANTINOPLE, 1893

When the season ended at Troy, Philip debated his options, finding he welcomed the break from his colleagues and from the site. The Achilles bronze had caused him more than enough trouble and aggravation. He needed to make as much profit as possible from the objects he had acquired over the past months, some his share of the dig, others purchased from locals, and decided to try his luck in Constantinople. He thrilled when he entered the Grand Bazaar, the cacophony of foreign tongues and scent of exotic spices assaulting his senses. Today, he was no tourist looking for trinkets and souvenirs. He was a merchant, ready to ply his trade, and he had an appointment with a man who ran a respected shop, a man who had come highly recommended by both buyers and sellers.

"I assure you it is genuine," Philip said, eager to curry the shop owner's favor. "I am allowed a few pieces from the dig, ones not quite museum-worthy, but nonetheless beautiful and important. They would be valued by any collector. This pot is from Troy, and the painting on it tells me it is Mycenaean, from the Helladic period. See how it almost looks Minoan? They favored designs of this sort, floral patterns and sea creatures. Look at the detail on the nautilus on the front."

The robed man sitting across from him grunted. "It is not from the Trojan War and could not have belonged to Agamemnon."

"You're quite right," Philip said. "It is too early for it to have belonged to Agamemnon, although some might not agree with my precise dates for the piece. Regardless, it is a magnificent vessel." He watched as the dealer fingered it, examining it with a magnifying glass.

"It is genuine?"

"I have all the paperwork concerning the provenance. Herr Dörpfeld himself signed off on it. I could not have removed it from the site without his permission."

The dealer grunted again and called for a boy to bring them both tea. "I will buy the vase and the two spear points, but next time find me something better. Something gold."

"Would that it were so easy," Philip said,

taking the small pouch of money the man handed to him.

"You will count it here, Mr. Chapman, so I see that you know I am honest. I pay fairly."

Philip did as instructed, and once finished shook the dealer's hand and ducked out the low door of his shop and back into the teeming bazaar, ignoring the myriad merchants imploring him to come inspect their wares. He had no need for another carpet or brass lights or leather slippers. He wondered if coming to Constantinople had been a mistake. The man had paid him well enough, but would his goods have commanded a higher price in Athens? He did not think it likely. In London, perhaps, Paris, or Berlin. Next year he could venture west.

Or so he told himself, but even as he did, he knew he could never go. Not after the Countess von Lange had recognized him in Vienna. He could not risk being spotted again and had waited too long to see Kallista, who was now married to Hargreaves. His hesitation to confront her — and his disloyal best friend — had cost him her love, and he held little hope of getting it back. Better that he stay in the east and forget everything about his old life.

It certainly proved cheaper to live in the east. He had a small house in Athens now, something he would never have been able to afford in England on his meager wages. While he did not miss managing Ashton Hall and the rest of his estate, he had to acknowledge the unassailable fact that money made everything easier. He had become a good salesman and had earned a tidy sum buying and selling antiquities, but he would never be able to approach the luxurious level of his former lifestyle.

Surprisingly, this did not trouble him. He loved his work, from the alternating extremes of thrill and drudgery while excavating to the nervous excitement that came from negotiating a sale. His best results with the latter had come not from the paltry items he was allowed to take from the dig, but from pieces he spotted in villages, things the locals did not value and would give him for a pittance. He would never take advantage of them, but what they considered to be a fortune was an insignificant amount to him, even in his reduced circumstances. Reselling the piece in Athens or Constantinople or even Cairo to a dealer whose clients were wealthy Europeans — that was where the real money was made.

If he opened a gallery of his own he would

make still more, for he knew the dealers turned an outrageous profit after paying him, but he feared it would be too risky. He did not want to interact directly with Western clients. His world would come crashing down if anyone recognized him, and he could not face having to reinvent himself again.

What he truly desired was to go back to Santorini, the one place on earth that made his soul sing. He wondered if Kallista ever used the villa, or if it sat, neglected. She might have sold it. Much as he wanted to return to the island, he feared he might be too easily identified there. Few foreign visitors came to the Cyclades, and those who did were more likely to visit Delos or Naxos than Santorini, so he had stood out, and many of the locals, especially in Fira and Imerovigli, had known him on sight. In a few years, perhaps, enough time would have passed for them to have forgot him. He would be patient for as long as necessary. Santorini was worth the wait.

11

Mr. Papadokos continued to laugh as we all stood in the courtyard near the barn, and before long the gentlemen had joined him. I blame the ouzo. They all thought it was a good joke, my having been stricken with terror at the sound of one innocuous gunshot. Margaret and I stood apart from the others, our arms crossed, looking disapprovingly at their antics, which now included Mr. Papadokos teaching them Greek folk dances. Colin had the advantage, as this was not his first ouzo-fueled evening with the woodworker. It was only a question of time before more men from the village appeared and the strains of violin music accompanied their shouts and stamping feet.

"They are like children," Margaret said.

"I could not agree more," Jeremy said, coming up behind us. "It is mortifying to observe. I myself insist upon much higher standards of behavior."

I boxed his arm and grinned. "You are a model of good breeding."

"Why are you unwilling to take part in the fun?" he asked.

"I understand this particular incident was harmless, but we have in the house a man suffering from grievous injuries who Philip claims was sent to threaten him. Are we to believe his nemesis will stop now? Should we not be taking measures to secure his safety, not to mention ours?"

"Personally, I could not be less concerned. If someone wants to shoot me, I do wish he would get on with it. Tedious business, waiting around." He took a cigar from his jacket pocket and rolled it between the fingers of his right hand. "This trip, may I remind you, is meant to provide consolation for my wounded and insulted heart. Instead, it is making me start to think I would have been better off subjecting myself to the matrons of London and their desperate attempts to marry me to their daughters."

"You know that is not true," I said.

"I may be teasing, just a little," he said. "However, Em, I do think it is unfair of you to subject me to not only one, but two, of your husbands. It's bloody awkward. And just when I had finally started to get used to Hargreaves."

"Only imagine what it must be like for Colin," Margaret said. "He may be all stiff upper lip and what have you, but I have never seen him so troubled."

"Impossible to see anything beneath that implacable countenance," Jeremy said.

"Don't be unkind," I said. "You are quite right on one count, though, Jeremy. We are here to amuse you, and I refuse to let anything stand in our way. Philip can defend himself without us for one day at least. Tomorrow we will cross the caldera and visit the volcano. Perhaps we will even indulge ourselves with a dip in the hot springs. I trust you have a swimming costume?"

Before he could answer, Philip swooped toward us and looped his arm through Jeremy's. "Come along, Bainbridge, that's quite enough fraternizing with the ladies. If anyone understands heartbreak like you do, it is I. Join me and together we will forget all of our sorrows."

Margaret and I stayed for only a little while longer. When we bade the gentlemen good night — they showed no signs of abandoning their dancing in the courtyard, and, as I predicted, several more village men had joined them — Colin pulled me aside, to the shadows of a dusty alcove of the barn, and kissed me with such passion I nearly lost my balance.

"Why don't you come upstairs with me?" I murmured, barely pulling my lips from his.

"Can't, not now." He stepped back, then leaned forward and kissed me again, quickly this time. "You ought to sleep. I will be late."

I admit to being somewhat vexed by this, but made sure to give him no indication of my feelings as I went inside. Margaret confessed to being exhausted, so we parted outside our bedchambers, but Morpheus eluded me. I read for a while, first *The Iliad,* but found that Homer's poetry soothed me not at all, and so discarded it in favor of Mary Elizabeth Braddon's *Sons of Fire,* but its setting — Africa — put me off, and I decided to abandon literature as a source of consolation. I blew out the lamp, tucked the mosquito netting around the bed, and did my best to sleep.

As anyone who has struggled with insomnia knows, trying to force sleep is at best a hopeless business. Slumber is unimpressed by suitors. I lay on my left side, then flipped to the right, then stayed flat on my back. I sat up when a sound from outside caught my attention. The strains of music still wafted through the open shutters from the courtyard behind the house, but I also heard voices coming from the front, muffled, and the banging of furniture, accompanied by shushing noises and deep, masculine laughter.

I slid out of bed, getting tangled momentarily in the mosquito netting, and went to the balcony, the smooth tile of the floor cool against my bare feet. The rail was not iron, but solid plaster, in the Cycladic style, and quite deep, at least a foot — more wall than rail, really, so I could skulk behind it and peek over the top just enough to see Colin and Philip adjusting chairs on the terrace below. The red tips of their cigars glowed in the darkness as they sat.

"I never thought we would do this again," Colin said, his long legs stretched in front of him. He had removed his jacket and his collar, and the top buttons of his shirt were open. A glow of yellow from the drawing room windows shed just enough light on the scene for me to watch them. "I have missed you, missed our talks."

"And I you, old boy," Philip said. "Glad I could at least leave you a wife as compensation for the loss of our friendship."

"Don't —"

Philip laughed, low and steady. "I do not mean to disparage you. We always had so much in common it cannot come as a surprise that we should both love the same woman. Although you must admit that prior to Kallista's winning your affection, your attention strayed in a very different direction. Older and catastrophically sophisticated, if I recall."

"Don't remind me," my husband said.

"I saw Kristiana in Vienna some years back," Philip said. "You left her devastated."

"Kristiana never let anyone devastate her." He paused. "She is dead now, at any rate."

"Dead? Are you quite sure?"

Something — perhaps the ironic tone of his friend's voice — made Colin laugh. "I realize that your question is most prescient given your . . . may I say, resurrection? You and I never discussed it — for obvious reasons — but Kristiana was an agent for the Austrian government and died trying to stop an unprincipled Englishman's attempt to catalyze a war between Britain and Germany."

"In that line of work it would not be unheard of for her to have staged her death, would it?"

"No, but in this case, I know exactly what happened. Unfortunately, she is dead. It still pains me greatly to say it."

I sank down, my back hard against the plaster wall at the edge of the balcony. He had loved Kristiana, long ago, and had admitted as much to me before we were married. I, too, regretted her demise — she had been killed defending the Austrian state, and it was unfair of me to begrudge Colin remembering her with fondness all these years later. Emotions frequently refuse to bend into nice, rational packets.

"I'm sorry, old boy," Philip said. "It had to be a blow."

"Thank you."

After that, they sat in silence for so long I started to grow bored. Margaret and I would never have tolerated such a lag in conversation. I had just about decided to return to bed when Philip spoke again.

"You love her, don't you?"

"Emily?" Colin asked. "More than anything. I did not think someone could ever be so dear to me."

"Yes, you can imagine my shock at having found you so well and thoroughly domesticated."

"She is not like other wives."

"I wish I had —" Philip sighed. "There is no use wishing."

Colin did not reply. The scent of their cigars filled the air. I wanted to peek over the edge again, and try to read the expression on my husband's face, but I dared not.

The risk of exposure was too great. I did not want to be caught eavesdropping. That said, I must admit, as I always attempt to be absolutely candid, I should have felt mortified at listening to what the men below thought was a private conversation. Yet I found I could not pull myself away.

"You have children?" Philip asked.

"Three boys."

"One is your ward?" Colin must have nodded, for Philip continued as if his question had been answered. "It was good of you to take him in. And your oldest will inherit when Earl Bromley dies?"

"Yes," Colin said. "The irony is not lost on me."

"She adores you," Philip said. "She never once looked at me the way she does you."

"She did not have the time to —"

"Please, do not try to comfort me. I am happy for you, but if I am to be honest, I must own I am happier for her. No man could be a better husband and partner; she is lucky to have you. Seeing her again has been like a dream, despite the obvious difficulties of the situation, but I am well aware my presence here is troubling to her."

"You had to know it would be," Colin said.

"I did. I shouldn't have come to the villa. If Bohn hadn't been so terribly injured in his fall —"

"You did what was necessary."

"I shall return to the dig and keep my distance from you all."

"I hate to lose you again, Ashton. Your friendship has been the most important of my life." I had never heard a tone quite like this in my husband's voice. It very nearly cracked.

"I do not think, old boy, there is any way for you to have both me and her. It would cause her nothing but pain, and I have already been the instrument of too much of that."

"I shall come see you at the dig, before we leave the island, and perhaps . . ."

"That is more than I deserve, but I will not refuse the offer."

They returned to their companionable silence, and I slunk back inside, consumed with guilt. I did not want to keep Colin from his friend, and determined I would do my best to show them both we could peacefully coexist. I recalled Philip telling me he hoped we could someday be as easy with each other as Jeremy and I were, and I saw no reason such a goal could not be achieved. That decided, Morpheus came to me at last. I did not stir, even when Colin came to bed, and could only tell he had been there when

I woke in the morning and saw his clothes strewn about the room.

A glance at my watch told me I had indulged in a rather extravagant lie-in, so I hurried to dress. By the time I went downstairs, breakfast had long since been cleared away, but Mrs. Katevatis appeared out of nowhere with a dish of yogurt drizzled with honey and walnuts for me.

"I knew how exhausted you must be when Nico brought your tea down, cold and untouched. Are you feeling well?"

"Yes," I said. "Only tired, but much better now. Thoroughly refreshed, in fact." I heard Margaret on the terrace in front of the house and, taking my yogurt with me, I joined her there. The chairs Colin and Philip had occupied the previous evening remained pushed close together, and I felt a slight pang looking at them. "Where is everyone?"

"Colin and Jeremy are arranging for a boat to take us to the volcano," Margaret said. "Philip and Fritz are gone."

"Gone?"

"They left at the crack of dawn, without saying goodbye to anyone but Mrs. Katevatis, who said they were eager to get back to their work."

"I am sorry to hear that," I said. "I had

hoped they would join us today."

"I do not think Professor Hiller von Gaertringen would look kindly on them treating his dig as a holiday adventure."

"Quite right," I said. "Will they come back to dine with us?"

"They will not be back," Colin said, opening the gate that led to the cliff path and ushering Jeremy onto the terrace in front of him.

"We should at least invite them —"

"No, Emily," Colin said. "We must let them to their work."

Jeremy made a display of studying his boots while Margaret feigned interest in a bird squawking in a nearby tree. I bit my lip so hard I drew blood.

"He did not even say goodbye." Tears stung my eyes and I blinked them away.

Colin stood in front of me, awkwardly shifting his weight from one foot to the other. "It would have been too painful, my dear," he said, his voice barely audible. "You must let him go, whatever the toll it exacts. There is no other way forward."

PHILIP
TROY, 1894

Sacred Ilios, built upon the plain . . .

Philip would never tire of the view of what, to him, was nothing short of a holy place. Hills erupted from the landscape in the far-off distance, but it was the plains in the valley of Scamander that fired his imagination. Dörpfeld felt confident that the level on which they were currently focused — Troy VI — housed the city of Homer's epic, and Philip could not have agreed with more fervent enthusiasm. The experience of being there, of touching the walls beneath which Achilles had fought, nearly overwhelmed the Englishman. On rest days, he would hike the distance between the ruins and the sea and try to imagine how it had looked, all those centuries ago, with camps teeming with tens of thousands of Greek soldiers filling the now-empty space. Occasionally, he would dig on his own, no longer afraid menacing individ-

uals would jump him should he find anything of import.

His confidence proved unwise. Two weeks
before the end of the season, he received a
visitor in his tent, long after everyone in the
camp had succumbed to slumber. Hakan,
tall and lanky in the robes of a nomad, a
turban wrapped around his head, crouched
over him, brandishing a long knife and holding it close to Philip's throat.

"I know what you have," he said. "And I
will not rest until I have retrieved it for
Demir."

12

When I awoke that morning, I realized I might not be able to convince Philip of my sincere desire to be his friend, not now that he had exiled himself to the archaeologists' camp at Ancient Thera, but I could, somehow, persuade Colin we could come to terms with the inherent discomfort of the situation. I would do anything necessary to ensure he did not lose the dearest companion of his youth, the man who understood him in ways that even I might not have.

Because I had arisen so late, we did not have time to stroll along the cliff path on our way to the boat that was waiting for us. Instead, Adelphos brought donkeys to transport us, as well as our enormous picnic lunch. I suspected Jeremy of adding several bottles of champagne to whatever Mrs. Katevatis had packed. The day was fine, the molten orb of the sun blazing down on us as the beasts of burden plodded along, following the curve of the island.

Once we reached Fira and began our descent, the air changed, as it always did, the breeze that cooled us at the villa seemingly stopped by the tall rocks of the cliff. Whenever I commented on this, Colin pointed out the flaws in my theory: If the cliffs were stopping the breeze, the effects would be felt on the opposite side to where we were, and, if anything, we would be blown back against them. I refused to listen to him. In my mind, some ancient force misdirected the wind here, allowing it to be felt again only when one had stepped onto a boat and relinquished his or her fate to the sea.

I admit, once again, to succumbing to the lure of the dramatic. Greece has that effect on me, and I will never, while walking its hallowed ground or sailing the seas on which Odysseus traveled, believe the Olympians do not still rule Hellas.

The captain of our little boat was Kyros Katsaros, a local fisherman who had long ago become a friend, and who happily abandoned his ordinary work whenever we wished to be ferried either to the volcano or to one of the other small islands in its environs. We always paid him at a rate superior to what he could have earned otherwise, and his wife, a beautiful young woman who I liked to imagine was descended from sea nymphs, encouraged him to do all he could to persuade us to hire him with ever-greater frequency. Kyros helped Margaret and me over a narrow plank and onto the deck. Jeremy followed, but Colin leapt straight from the pier onto the boat, and before long our journey was under way.

We skimmed through increasingly deep water — even at the port, the depth was too great to allow a ship to drop anchor — as the boat moved toward Nea Kameni, one of the small islands in the caldera. Born from volcanic eruption, its black basalt surface harbors little life. Only a few flowers sprout from its soil, and the loose, rocky path leading from the northern shore to the volcano's crater crosses a bleak landscape that brings to mind a line written by the first Baron Lytton in his novel *Pelham:* "A mysterious and unearthly communion of the soul with the beings of another world."

Jeremy stretched out on the deck of the small boat, placing his hat over his face to avoid sunburn. Colin, an enthusiastic sailor, pulled ropes and assisted Kyros as he guided us to our destination. Once there, the fisherman carried ashore the large baskets containing our supplies and told us he would have everything set up in a cove on the red-hued shoreline by the time we returned from the volcano.

The smell of sulfur hung heavy in the air as we started up the path, and I had no trouble imagining the terror the ancient inhabitants of the island must have felt when ash and pumice rained from the sky onto their homes. There is something arrogant about hiking up the side of a volcano, as if one is taunting Hephaestus, daring his anger to materialize in spewing lava and fire. The last eruption on Santorini had occurred fewer than thirty years ago, and although there were no signs of another brewing, I felt a bit daring whenever we traveled to this side of the caldera.

"As if Hargreaves would risk losing you to an ill-timed flow of lava," Jeremy said, when I expressed this sentiment to him. "I assure you, there is nothing brave in our actions today. The air is dreadful, though, isn't it?"

"Wait until you get to the hot springs," Margaret said. "The smell is even stronger."

"Remind me again why we came?" Jeremy asked. Margaret took him by the hand and dropped her head onto his shoulder.

"My dear boy, *you* came for distraction," she said. "*We* came to make sure you don't fling yourself into the volcano."

"Couldn't one be distracted in a casino instead?"

"That did not turn out well last time," Colin said. I looked at him with surprise that he would so callously refer to the events Jeremy had suffered in the south of France, but his comment elicited from Jeremy a hearty guffaw that made me doubt entirely the possibility of ever fully understanding the thinking of gentlemen.

We continued up the gentle slope until we stood at the edge of the volcano's crater, looking down at a large expanse of rock, mainly dark, but interspersed with random profusions of rust-colored stones.

"And thou, fiery world, / That sapp'st the vitals of this terrible mount / Upon whose charr'd and quaking crust I stand — / Thou, too, brimmest with life!" I recited.

"Another of your dreadful ancient poets?" Jeremy asked.

"Not at all. Matthew Arnold, writing in our own century about the philosopher Empedocles, who died when he flung himself into the crater at Mount Etna. Some claim the volcano spit back out one of his sandals, but I am not convinced."

"An inspiring story, Em." He looked perfectly bored; I knew it to be an expression he cultivated with great care. I reached down, picked up a piece of pumice, and tossed it at him. He caught it effortlessly with one hand.

"Astonishing how light it is, isn't it?" I asked.

"Quite. And I had feared you were flinging rocks at me in an attempt to cause injury," he said with a grin, and then pointed over my shoulder. "Look back to Fira. What a view!"

"Worth the smell of sulfur?" I asked.

"I withhold judgment until I have had a little sea bathing."

We skirted the circumference of the crater, and then, finished with the volcano, started back down to shore, where our picnic awaited us.

"I don't think I shall swim today," I said. "The water is too cold for me."

"You promised me hot springs, Em, and now you tell me they are cold?"

"There are sections that are quite warm," Margaret said, "but the surrounding water is cold enough to put off us ladies. Furthermore, we will be much freer to watch and comment on your athletic prowess if you are out of earshot."

Colin and Jeremy disappeared behind a large rock, where, presumably, they would change into their swimming costumes before diving into the clear water. Margaret and I removed our boots and stockings and, bunching up our skirts, waded in the shallows while the gentlemen bobbed up and down in deeper water.

An unfamiliar voice called out from beyond the beach. I turned, but saw no one and moved through the water away from the hot springs, following the sound around a jumble of tall rocks that protected a small inlet. There, on the shore, stood two gentlemen (I use the term loosely), out of view of anyone not in the water, arguing animatedly. I slipped closer to the shore until I reached the rocks, which were large enough to conceal me, and I could now recognize the men's language as Turkish.

Having very little of the language at my command, I could not understand much of what they said, but distinctly made out the name *Chapman,* as its inherent Englishness stood out from the foreign tongue. I saw Margaret approaching me, and with a finger to my lips, I shushed her, and pressed up against one of the rocks. With effort, I could peek just beyond its surface to catch a glimpse of the men. One, tall and lean, his face nut brown from the sun and heavily lined, appeared to be taking out a great deal of anger on the other, a broad and muscular man, with no hat protecting his bald head. A knife hanging from his belt glimmered in the sun.

The tall one said *Chapman* again, and I watched Margaret's eyes widen. I had pulled my head back down so as not to be spotted, and we made ourselves as small as possible behind the rock. My heartbeat quickened when I heard the crunch of their feet on the pebbles of the beach, but they did not enter the water or approach us. When their footsteps faded, Margaret and I quietly returned to our own side of the beach, where Kyros had our picnic waiting.

I hailed my husband, who swam like a fish and would have stayed in the water until sunset if allowed. Jeremy, floating on his back, languidly made his way toward the shore, reaching it long before Colin, who, though swimming at a far faster pace, took what could generously be described as an indirect path to us. Once they had toweled themselves off and changed back into their clothes, spreading their striped swimming costumes on rocks in the sun to speed their drying, they joined us on the blanket Kyros had spread on the pebble-covered beach.

We all sat on overstuffed, soft pillows and immediately tore into the spectacular dishes

Mrs. Katevatis had packed for us: tyropita and spanakopita, their fillings — cheese in the former and spinach in the latter — almost bursting from the flaky pastry encasing them. There were also plump dolmades (grape leaves full of rice and spiced meat), salty feta cheese, and tomatoes, along with bread she had baked early in the morning and a bottle of crisp white wine made on Santorini.

"How can you say with any confidence they were speaking of Ashton with menace?" Colin asked, as I recounted for him what Margaret and I had observed. "I know you do not understand much Turkish."

"It was apparent in both their tone and their gestures," I said.

"You cannot possibly claim to know simply from tone and gestures they were directing malice toward Ashton. Or if he even was the topic of their conversation."

"You must admit it is too much to believe it to be a coincidence that they spoke his nom de guerre," Margaret said. "I would perhaps be skeptical, too, if I had not heard it myself —"

"You wouldn't believe me?" I asked, raising my eyebrows.

"You do have a flair for the dramatic, my dear," Margaret said. "It is one of your finest qualities."

Frustrated, I shook my head. "Regardless of what you think, I am confident they were talking about Philip. Am I to believe there is someone else called Chapman on Santorini at present?"

"Perhaps they were discussing Homer," Jeremy said. "I have seen you engaged in violent arguments on the subject, particularly when it comes to translators." He popped a dolma into his mouth.

"We ought to warn Philip," I said.

"Warn him of what?" Colin asked. "The fact that two men of indeterminate origin had a conversation of indeterminate topic that may or may not have included a reference to the false name he has been using?"

"Yes, exactly," I said. "He told us Demir is a Turk, and now, whatever their origin, two men speaking Demir's language are here, near where Philip is working. I would be concerned even if they had not said his name. Do you want him to suffer the same fate as the unconscious man back at the villa?"

"I hardly think it is wise to condemn an entire nation of Turkish speakers on the basis of one story of dubious credibility," Colin said.

"I thought Philip was your dearest friend,"

I said. "Now you speak as if you don't trust him and are content to let him, too, be injured."

My husband's eyes darkened slightly. "The man in our villa was injured because he chose to run away from us rather than identify himself. We have no evidence — none — that his presence on the island is connected to Ashton in any way at all."

"All of our nerves are strained at present," Margaret said. "Why don't you have some more wine?"

"My nerves are quite fine, thank you," I said. I threw down my napkin and stormed away from them.

"Em!" Jeremy called out as he followed me along the beach. I walked faster until he pulled on my arm, stopping me. "What is going on here? Why are you arguing with Hargreaves? I realize I ought to be encouraging you, and probably would if I thought divorce would ever become socially acceptable, but as the chances of you leaving him are slim, I must say you are . . . overreacting to the present situation."

"Overreacting?" My hand ached to slap him.

"Ashton is a grown man, capable of taking care of himself. What you and Margaret saw on the beach is at best a sketchy indication that two gentlemen may or may not be referring to him in conversation." I was looking away from him, down at the rocky beach. He bent over and forced me to meet his eyes as he continued. "How do you think it makes your absurdly handsome husband feel when you make such a display of worrying about Ashton?"

"I was not making a display."

"Call it whatever you like," Jeremy said. "Just try to be a little less insistent about us all having to be thinking about Ashton constantly."

I did not think his words were entirely fair, and I was still convinced the men on the beach had been talking about Philip. Furthermore, Colin knew better than most I would be concerned about any person in Philip's situation. This was not about Philip because he was Philip; it was about common concern for someone who might be in grave danger.

"Someone ought to tell Philip. That is all I have endeavored to say. I fail to see the controversy."

"I know you, Em, and I know right now in that pretty head of yours, you are fuming because you are thoroughly convinced you would feel the same about anyone you thought to be in a precarious situation. I also know this to be true, and it is a credit to your character that you do not stand by quietly when you can prevent something awful from happening."

"So you agree we should warn him?"

"No, Em, I don't share your opinion that he is in imminent danger he can't ward off on his own. Your judgment is clouded by something — guilt being the obvious culprit. It looks to me as if you are desperate to save him from being harmed again, perhaps because you had no way of helping him when he was in Africa. Furthermore, there's the little matter of your having married his best friend."

I felt the skin on my neck prickle, and I sighed. "There may be some truth to what you say."

"Heaven save us all." He rolled his eyes. "You are making me miserable, Em, for if I have started speaking the truth, then I am further away than ever from my goal of being the most useless man in England."

"Have you considered the possibility that you could be useless while in England and useful when abroad without irrevocably harming your reputation?"

"Inconceivable," he said. "Have you forgot how quickly gossip spreads? Particularly when one is an incredibly wealthy and —

dare I say? — more than moderately handsome bachelor duke? What do I have in the
end other than my bad reputation? I shall
protect it at any cost."

Philip
Constantinople, 1894

Much though Philip had been loath to leave
Troy at the end of the season, the visit paid
him by the knife-brandishing Hakan had
softened the blow. He had not mentioned it
to any of his colleagues. It would only
remind them of the story at which they had
scoffed after he had lost the Achilles bronze,
and he had no desire to say anything that
might make them think less of him, not
when they had begun to accept him as their
professional equal rather than as a mere
dilettante-dealer turned archaeologist.

Dörpfeld did not plan to return to Troy
the following season, and rather than following him to a new site, Philip had agreed
to join Fritz Reiner, who would be working
with Carl Humann at Ephesus, the magnificent Greco-Roman city in western Turkey.
Humann was delighted at the prospect of
having Philip back, having seen much
promise in his work in Magnesia on the

Maeander, and Philip was eager to see his friend Reiner again.

So Ephesus it would be, but first he would spend another winter in Constantinople. It would not take long to sell the antiquities he had acquired over the season, but this time he intended to go about it more slowly, because along with money, he wanted — needed — information. Who was this Demir who'd sent Hakan with a knife to his tent in Troy? Someone interested in ancient artifacts in general, or someone who wanted the Achilles bronze in particular? The former sort of chap was not likely to incite violence.

It could not be argued the bronze was anything less than a spectacular find, although one did wish that more of the helmet were intact. Even in its mutilated state, something uncovered at Troy featuring Achilles' name so prominently would draw a handsome price, but most members of the public would be more impressed with gold jewelry, like that Schliemann had found at Troy. He'd had his wife photographed wearing it, and claimed it had belonged to Helen; all the newspapers had published the story. Jewelry was the sort of thing — splashy, its value obvious — along with monumental statues and beautifully carved friezes, that tended to command the highest prices on the antiquities market.

Whoever wanted the Achilles bronze was bound to be as obsessed with Homer's hero as Philip. And obsession, he knew, could prove dangerous.

As he made his rounds from dealer to dealer, Philip made discreet inquiries, insinuating he had heard rumors of something of Achilles' having been stolen from the dig at Troy. He had worked there, he explained, and was cognizant of the fact that nothing of the sort had officially been found, but, he explained, he knew that locals often pocketed objects when they could.

No one he questioned admitted to having heard of any such thing. One dealer, however, suggested that he, an honest man — he repeated the phrase three times to convey its truth — would not be approached by anyone in possession of something looted from an archaeological site. He was aware, naturally, of others less scrupulous than he, and if Mr. Chapman wished to be introduced to that sort of dealer . . .

"I am told a man called Demir . . ." Philip paused, partly for effect and partly because he did not know how to finish the sentence.

The dealer straightened in his chair.

"Demir? You know him?"

Philip tried to modulate his voice and regulate his breathing, which was becoming rapid. "By reputation, only, I am afraid."

The man nodded. "It is he who would have information about the sort of piece you are seeking. I, you must understand, have great respect for Demir, but in my own humble shop, I do not deal with such objects. I am an honest man — as Demir is, too; I would never offend him. I, however, do not have the connections he does."

"Can you put me in touch with him?" Philip asked.

After a lengthy back-and-forth that primarily involved the dealer's proclaiming his honesty and Philip's praising him for his scruples before offering a rather large bribe, the man agreed to set up a meeting.

The following evening, just after eight o'clock, Philip found himself on the Asian side of the city, in a seedy alley, ripe with the scent of sewage and rotting vegetables. More Gypsies than Turks resided in the neighborhood, and the dealer had told him in no uncertain terms to take precautions against attack. He had armed himself accordingly, and kept a hand on the revolver in his pocket as he waited. When the eerie strains of the night's final call to prayer came from the nearest mosque, its sound bouncing and echoing off the quarter's decrepit buildings, Philip began to look around more earnestly. Before the muezzin had finished, a boy of no more then ten approached him, holding out a small bronze statue of the god Hermes, the sign for which he had been told to watch.

The child led him through a maze of back alleys and narrow streets until they reached a rickety wooden building, designed to mimic those favored by Ottoman officials, but of much lower quality in both material and construction. Philip pulled open the door, at which point the boy pressed the statue into his hand and disappeared into the darkness. Philip stepped inside, unsure how to proceed.

A broad, muscular man who did not speak met him at the door and glanced at the statue Philip showed him before leading him into a small room lit by a single oil lamp hanging from a chain. Its scattered glow, colored by the mosaic of its glass globe, provided scant illumination, but allowed him to just make out the features of his guide. His black eyes and hooked nose were foreboding enough, but were made all the more imposing by a long scar that crossed the entire length of his face, from forehead to neck. A second man, seated at a rough table, leaned away from the light, keeping his face in the shadows.

"Please sit," the man said, his voice refined. "I am Demir and you are Philip Chapman, enterprising archaeologist and seller of antiquities. You are looking for something that belonged to the great Achilles?" His command of English was impressive, and he spoke in a manner that suggested he had been educated in Britain rather than in Turkey.

"I am," Philip said, lowering himself onto a stool. "A specific piece. A bronze."

"Yes, I am familiar with the details." He raised his eyebrow in a manner that made Philip uneasy. "There is, however, no such item. If there were, I would know about it. What makes you think it exists?"

"Rumors. I worked in Troy, at the excavations, and our workers sometimes did not share all their finds with us."

"Your employer Dörpfeld did not offer them bonuses for significant objects?"

"He did."

"And does he not pay fairly?"

"He does, but you and I are both aware of other sources that pay better."

"Indeed, and I am that source, at least in Constantinople. No one pays better than

I. Which means, unfortunately for you, the cost of acquiring such a piece would be not insignificant."

"But you have nothing matching the description?" Philip asked.

"Indeed not, though I, too, have heard stories." Demir looked at him with an unnerving stare. "If we are to work together, I demand absolute honesty from you. I see you smile, as you make the mistake of believing that because I deal on the black market, I am no better than a thief."

"Not at all, I assure you."

Demir waved his hand dismissively. "I am not interested in your assurances. I would like to know more about the rumors I have heard concerning a certain English archaeologist who claimed such an object was stolen from him." His eyes darkened in a terrifying manner.

Philip swallowed hard. "Yes. That was me."

"You think I do not already know this? You are not as intelligent as I expected. I do not appreciate your game. Do you come here to accuse me of stealing from you?"

"No, I —"

"You are an amusing man, so I will not kill you. Not now, at any rate. But never again come to me under false pretenses."

"I have not done so now." Philip felt

13

The sea had grown rough by the time we started our return trip from the volcano, and this, combined with heat, sunburn, and displeasure at what I had seen on the beach, left me in a foul mood. Back at the villa, I went straight to my bath, eager to wash the film of volcanic dust from my body. I scrubbed my hair clean, then ducked down to rinse out the suds. That accomplished, I leaned my head against the porcelain and slid until the water reached my neck. I lingered for some time, mulling what Jeremy had said to me. How had I managed to make such a bungle of everything?

Colin had not yet come up to our room, and although his mood had showed no signs of distress or discomfort during the rest of our visit to Nea Kameni, I could not help but worry I had hurt him. When my fingers began to prune, I climbed out of the tub and pulled on a comfortable, bright caftan.

increasingly confident. Demir knew his story, and this encouraged him. "You have sent men to harass me over this piece — a piece that was stolen from me."

"You misunderstand my associates, Mr. Chapman. They made inquiries as to the location of the piece and have informed me you insist you do not have it."

"I don't have it," Philip said, "and I cannot understand why you are bent on believing otherwise."

"I find most men incapable of telling the truth the first time they're given the opportunity. Asking a question repeatedly, with encouragement as necessary, is the only way to an honest answer. Why did you come to me on the pretense of looking for the bronze, when your true purpose was to beg me to call off my men? I do not appreciate lies and subterfuge."

Though he felt sweat beading on his face, Philip nearly laughed at the irony of Demir's statement. "I do want you to call them off, but it is your persistence regarding the object that tells me you are the only person capable of tracking it down. I want the bronze back. I do not know who has it, but I am happy to pay for the piece — whatever price you demand. Will you tell me the moment you learn where it is?"

"You are very determined," Demir said. "It is a quality I admire. Furthermore, I find you wholly untrustworthy, a quality I often find useful in acquaintances. I shall contact you periodically to inform you if I have any information for you."

"I shall be at Ephesus once I leave Constantinople."

"I knew that already." He smirked, as did his henchman, lurking in the background. "I will always know where you are."

"And you are certain — quite certain — no one has the Achilles bronze?" Philip asked.

The man shrugged. "You are the only one who has ever claimed to possess it."

"The man working with me that day was killed. Surely that supports my story. It certainly horrified me."

"Yes, yes, this tribal justice is sometimes most unsettling to you Westerners. I would think nothing of it."

"I am convinced he took the bronze from me, and I want it back. At any cost."

Demir narrowed his eyes. "Yes, I do not doubt you will pay almost anything to retrieve it. I will be in touch, Englishman." He rose from his seat and left the room, the burly man accompanying him, but not before he first extinguished the oil lamp, leaving Philip to feel his way out in the dark, terrified he had set something in motion he did not quite understand.

I could hear Jeremy and Margaret on the terrace below, but saw no sign of my husband. I decided to wait for him and sat on the balcony, reading Sophocles' *Antigone* until I heard his familiar step in the corridor outside our room. Tossing the book aside, I raced to the door and flung my arms around him as soon as he opened it.

"This is unexpected," he said, kissing me, but only quickly. "I would take matters into hand in an entirely different way were I not so filthy."

"Where have you been?" I asked. "You were in a better condition when we arrived home."

"I received a response from our solicitor. He says the matter is most complicated and he would prefer to discuss it in person when we return to England."

"That is disappointing," I said. "I had hoped for a clear and immediate resolution. But surely reading a telegram did not leave you covered with dust."

"No. I rode to the excavation and told Ashton what you saw and heard. I may not agree there is anything to it, but I could not in good conscience ignore your intuition when it has on so many other occasions proven to be correct."

"Thank you," I said. "You do know I

would have felt the same concern for anyone, not just Philip, don't you?"

"I know it well, my dear." He peeled off his jacket and started to unfasten the buttons of his shirt. "Ashton was grateful. He is rather skittish. I pressed him as to the cause, but he assured me I ought not concern myself. He does not have the bronze, and eventually whoever is looking for it will have no choice but to accept that."

"His tent and his possessions were mangled by someone in the midst of a dreadful storm," I said. "That does not suggest an individual who is likely to give up his quarry."

"I agree with you, but Ashton now believes Reiner misread the scene, and that the destruction was likely due to the storm itself." He kicked off his boots and headed for the bathroom, flinging his shirt to the ground on the way.

I scowled. "How can he believe that when no one else's tent suffered even the slightest damage?"

"He is aware of that and credits it to the same bad luck that has haunted him since his ill-fated safari in Africa."

"Is there anything else we ought to do?" I asked.

"No," he said, disappearing into the bathroom.

"Then that settles the matter," I said with a shrug.

He popped his head back into the bedroom. "Settles the matter?"

"You know I have always respected your opinion. If you do not consider further action necessary, I agree."

"If I did not know you better —" he started.

"No one could know me better." I put my hands on his chest, the hard muscles still warm from the exertion of riding. "And I would have it no other way."

"Leave me to my bath, wicked woman," he said, a familiar glint in his eye. "I shall see to you when I am finished."

We passed the following fortnight in a state of calm respite. Colin borrowed Kyros's boat and took us on a cruise around the island. We walked into Fira and visited the small museum in town, whose collection grew with each new season of Professor Hiller von Gaertringen's excavations. It now included some very pretty pots as well as numerous older objects, including the stark but charming Cycladic figures from island civilizations predating that of Pericles'

Athens by several millennia. Each afternoon, we chose a different vantage point from which to view the sunset, sometimes hiking all the way out to the top of Skaros, sometimes taking the horses to Oia, on the northernmost tip of the island, and sometimes staying at the villa, watching from the comfort of the cushioned benches of our terrace, while munching on fresh fruit and drinking cool wine.

Our patient, whom the doctor from Oia was now visiting only every third day, had showed no signs of improvement, but we took the fact that his condition had not further declined to be encouraging. Beyond his presence in the house, the events surrounding Philip's arrival were no longer a topic of our conversation. Margaret decided Jeremy ought to marry one of the beautiful local girls and spent a great deal of time searching for a suitable candidate for him, much to his chagrin. I could almost have believed Philip's return to have been nothing more than a dream, were it not for the increased vigor of Colin's marital attentions to me. Although his efforts were much appreciated, I could not help but wonder if he was trying to erase any memories I might have of similar, shall we say, activities. If so, he need not have bothered, but I was not about to tell him that, given the spectacular results of his endeavors.

"The time has come for us to consider our next destination," I said one morning when the two of us were taking breakfast on our balcony instead of on the terrace with our friends. "We are all thoroughly relaxed from our stay here, and it would be best if we left before Margaret starts marriage negotiations with any of our neighbors."

"We could go to Rhodes," Colin said. "Bainbridge might like the crusaders' palace there."

"I was thinking we should go to Olympia. It is not a simple journey, but the excavations there —"

"Perhaps it would be best to ask Bainbridge. He is, after all, the one meant to benefit from the trip."

I had no choice but to agree, and was heartened when Jeremy warmed to my suggestion of Olympia.

"I quite fancy a run around the stadium there," he said. "You know how put out I was at not being given a medal when they brought the Olympics to Athens in '96." His younger brother had competed in the marathon, and Jeremy, who had climbed down from the stands to run the last leg of the race next to him, felt his own exertion more worthy of recognition than Jack's.

"Capital!" Margaret said. "We shall stage a race, but only if you agree to dress in proper ancient attire."

"You shall not catch me there, Margaret," Jeremy said. "I know they were, er, unclothed while competing. Emily told me when we were at Delphi."

"I am beginning to believe this trip is having a deleterious effect on you," she said. "What fun am I to have if you don't remain your willfully ignorant self?"

Colin made arrangements for the boat that had brought us from Athens to collect us. It would arrive in five days and, instead of returning us to the capital, take us on a leisurely cruise around the Peloponnese, docking at Katakolon, a short distance from Olympia. As our departure approached, I oversaw our packing, and had nearly finished with my final trunk when a commotion outside the house brought me to my balcony.

Below, Philip and Fritz, in a hideous state of disarray, perspiration causing dust to stick to every exposed inch of their skin, had arrived on donkeys that looked only slightly less disheveled than their riders.

"Heavens!" I cried, and they looked up, Fritz waving an exhausted greeting. "What has happened? You two look a fright."

Philip, clutching at his arm, slid from his donkey and collapsed on the ground with a dull thud. I ran back inside and downstairs, calling for Colin, and rushed to the front of the house, where I knelt next to the fallen man. His arm was bleeding — the result, I deduced from the rent in the sleeve of his jacket, of a bullet.

"I never intended that you would see me in such a state, but Reiner insisted we come," he said, meeting my eyes and giving me a weak smile before his lids shut and he slipped from consciousness. My husband, only a few steps behind me, appeared almost the next instant, with Jeremy and Margaret fast on his heels. Colin carried his injured friend into the house, back to the Etruscan room where he had stayed before, and placed him on the bed.

"We need iodine to clean the wound," he said as he removed his friend's jacket and ripped the sleeve of his shirt to expose the injury.

"I shall fetch the doctor," Jeremy said. "I know the way to Oia."

"I will go with you," Fritz replied, but I stopped him.

"No, you stay," I said. "Tell us what happened." With a quick nod, Jeremy was off and Margaret had gone downstairs to get iodine from Mrs. Katevatis, who kept in her kitchen every supply for which one could ever find a use.

"Wir haben ohne Unterbrechung durchgearbeitet —"

"English, please, Fritz," I said.

"Ich bitte um Verzeinung. We had been working without interruption for these past weeks, everything going extremely well. The professor is due to return tomorrow or the next day, and we wanted to have as much of the stoa cleared as we could before his return. We found an exquisite Roman decoration that —" He stopped himself. *"Es tut mir sehr leid.* I forget myself. The details are not important. Today Chapman — Ashton — went down to the site of the theatre to check our workers' progress there, but before he reached it, someone started shooting at us."

"At all of you, or only him?" Colin asked.

"It is difficult to say, Hargreaves. It happened so suddenly. No one was hit but him. His wound —"

"Is superficial," Colin said. "I have seen much worse. The bullet did little damage and exited cleanly. He passed out due more to exertion and stress than blood loss, and should recover fully in a very short time. I have stopped the bleeding. The doctor will be able to determine how many stitches he needs to close the wound. I myself would say he requires approximately five or six."

I studied my husband's face and wondered when, exactly, he had seen much worse and how he knew so much about treating bullet wounds. I was aware the work he undertook on the Continent on orders of the palace was often dangerous, but I had not ever considered the matter in detail, fearing that doing so would cause me too much agony while I was awaiting his return.

I snapped myself back to attention. "Your workers?" I asked. "How are they?"

"Unharmed, but frightened. We will have trouble persuading them to return to the site tomorrow."

"You cannot think of starting back up so soon," I said. "No one should return there until we figure out who did this."

Margaret appeared with iodine and smelling salts, which Mrs. Katevatis believed had the power to arouse anyone from any state, a tenet she clung to despite the fact they had done nothing for the other injured man currently under our care. They did, to her delight, bring Philip around at once.

"What a mess I am," he said. "Deepest apologizes for once again disrupting you in this manner. You must think my aim is to turn the villa into a hospital."

"Think nothing of it," I said. "Did you see who did this to you?"

"I did not. Was anyone else hurt?"

"No," Fritz said. "The men are safe."

"Safe at home, I imagine," Philip said.

"Yes, I saw no point in making them stay today, but will speak to them about coming tomorrow."

"I will go with you," Philip said. "My pain is trivial. My usefulness may be limited somewhat, but I will at least be able to assist."

"You cannot even consider it," I said. "You are staying here. There will be no further discussion of the subject."

PHILIP
ATHENS, 1894

Philip had meant to spend the entire winter in Constantinople, but after completing, more or less to his satisfaction, the selling of the artifacts in his possession, he decided instead to go to Athens. His conversation with Demir had initially frightened him, but as the weeks went by, he began to feel emboldened, and started to reach out to his contacts in the antiquities market in the Greek capital. By the time he arrived in the city, he had arranged meetings with three dealers who'd promised knowledge of objects not officially for sale.

Of these men, none had heard the story of the Achilles bronze, but each perked up when Philip told the tale. He judged the second dealer, a man called Simonides Floros, the most likely to be able to help him, and went so far as to give him a payment — not exorbitant, but larger than Philip would have liked — as a retainer of sorts. In return, Mr. Floros would have his contacts begin to make inquiries about the piece.

That done, Philip felt a rush of relief. Soon he would have positive confirmation about what the sellers of illegal antiquities knew or didn't know about the bronze. Either Mr. Floros or Demir — or both — would ferret out whatever there was to discover. Then he would at last know whether Demir was hunting him because he had somehow learned the truth — that Philip still had the object in his possession.

He fingered the stiff spot in the bottom of his jacket where he had carefully sewn a small pocket behind the lining, only as large as necessary to contain the thin strip of bronze. Every inch of his body burned whenever he felt it. He should never have taken it and, having done so, should never have lied about the other man stealing it. But what else could he have done? The man had tried to steal it, and Philip still did not quite understand how he had managed to keep it from him.

The sun had been low in the sky. He and Erkan, a Turk, had worked later than their colleagues. Dörpfeld had agreed to let him dig a series of test trenches in this area, partly because he wanted to be as thorough as possible with his excavations and partly because, Philip suspected, he admired Philip's devotion to Homer's great works. They frequently discussed the poetry in camp, after the day's work was done, and although Dörpfeld's primary focus was on the city of Troy, he agreed that going further afield, into the area of the Greek's encampment, could unearth a trove of information. Archaeologists know rubbish heaps can reveal all kinds of fascinating details about the lives of ancient peoples.

No one else had worked so late that evening, and Philip and Erkan were too far away to be easily seen from camp. The moment Philip had felt the hardness of metal in the dirt, excitement had filled him. He cleared the area, first with his hands and then with a brush, revealing a glint of bronze. His initial disappointment at the size of the piece — clearly it was nothing more than the fragment of something, nice, but not spectacular — faded the instant he saw the great hero's name scratched into the surface. He touched it, reverently, and as he read the inscription — ΑΧΙΛΛΕΥΣ ΑΝΕΘΕΚΕΝ ΤΟΙ ΔΙ. Akhilleus dedicated to Zeus — his hand started to shake. He knew of the discovery of Miltiades' helmet at Olympia, with words on its base following the same formula. Could this be a piece of Achilles' helmet? The very one he had worn when fighting the Trojans? Perhaps — almost certainly, as what other helmet would he dedicate to Zeus? — the one that had protected him the day he killed Hector?

Erkan, ten feet away, was not paying the slightest attention to Philip. He did the coarser work, digging the initial trench and moving dirt as necessary. He showed no interest in archaeology beyond the money it brought him, and revealed no aptitude for the finer techniques of the work. Philip watched, wondering if the man had seen the bronze, and started to breathe rapidly as the realization of what he was about to do began to sink into his soul.

He could not bear to be parted with this piece. He knew it belonged in a museum, he knew scholars should be allowed to study it, and he knew to keep it for himself would be akin to an act of blasphemy. But he could not — would not — stop himself, and as he took it in his hand, his back to Erkan, he felt as if he were watching the scene from above, as if some other person were committing the crime. The bronze felt heavy in the breast pocket of his coat. He buttoned the pocket closed, his heart racing, and crouched in the dirt, trying to catch his breath.

He never managed to quite compose himself. Truthfully, not ever again after that, no matter how many years passed. For all the pleasure he got from having that small bit of bronze he believed Achilles had once owned — worn, even — the crushing blow of knowing he had become a thief to get it tormented him.

But that guilt paled next to the constant fear and paranoia with which he now lived. Fear of exposure, of course, of losing the respect of his new colleagues, of tarnishing his name. But did the latter truly matter? He had invented Philip Chapman and could adopt another identity if necessary. At least he told himself he could. But he loved this new life of his, and could not fathom having to leave it behind. Death would be preferable.

And death might be precisely what he would face, for when he called out to Erkan that the time had come to stop work, the man stepped toward him, a menacing look on his face.

"What did you take?" he asked. "I saw you put it in your pocket. I saw the gleaming metal."

"Don't be ridiculous," Philip said. "No metal freshly removed from the ground after thousands of years would be gleaming, un-

263

less it were gold, and I can assure you had we discovered such a thing, you would have heard my cries of delight long before you noticed any gleaming."

"I saw what you did."

"You are mistaken." He took a firm tone. "I keep my compass in one pocket, and my watch in another." He pulled the watch out, as if to prove his point. "You must have seen me returning it after I had checked the time."

"I saw what you did."

No matter how Philip replied, Erkan kept repeating that same sentence, each time closing the gap between them. Little by little, the man came closer, looking fiercer with each step. When Erkan pulled back his arm, his hand balled into a fist, Philip struck first, a clean hit to the jaw.

They had struggled — fought — and somehow Philip came out victorious. He had never felt anything like the rush of watching the man slink away from him. It was superior to anything a man could experience even on the plains of Africa during a successful hunt. He had saved himself — his reputation, his livelihood — and he had saved the remnant of bronze. Nothing would make him part with it now.

He had been fortunate, though, that his

opponent had run away too soon to see Philip collapse, unconscious. Erkan's blows had taken a toll, and Philip hardly remembered growing unsteady on his feet before falling. If Erkan had seen, the bronze would well and truly be gone, in the hands of someone who cared not for its historical significance but only for its monetary value. Philip would protect it and keep it safe. No one could appreciate it more than he. No one had more right to possess it. It would be his forever.

14

Dr. Liakos and Jeremy arrived from Oia in a cloud of dust. The doctor, whom I had almost begun to consider a friend, given how frequently was he at the house, confirmed Colin's diagnosis of Philip's injury, and closed the wound with a row of neat stitches before checking on his other patient. I followed him to the small room in which the stranger reposed.

"Is there any hope he will wake up?" I asked.

"It is impossible to say, Lady Emily. In cases like this, I cannot predict. He is not yet dead, which is favorable, and his leg is healing nicely. But his brain . . . Only time will tell if his injuries were too great."

"If he does regain consciousness, will he be able to speak?" I asked.

"Again, he may or may not. I would not venture to guess."

"I wonder if anyone on Santorini might

recognize him? I hate to think of his family worrying, not knowing what has happened."

"As I told you when I first saw him, he is a stranger to me, and I have not heard of anyone having gone missing," Dr. Liakos said, returning his instruments to his leather satchel. "The island is small, and if someone were lost I would likely hear about it."

"Of course," I said. "Families would contact you to see if the person in question had been injured and was in your care."

"Yes. Most likely he is a visitor."

"Yet his clothes did not suggest him to be a man of means traveling for pleasure."

The doctor shrugged. "He might have come looking for work and went to the excavation in search of employment."

"If that were the case, he wouldn't have run away when we called to him." I sighed. "I shall take up no more of your time with idle speculation. Thank you again for coming all this way."

"It is no trouble, Lady Emily. I shall return tomorrow to look in on Mr. Chapman. I do not expect any complications, but we must keep an eye out for infection."

After he had gone, I went into the kitchen, where Mrs. Katevatis was looking over the shoulder of the maid as she washed the breakfast dishes.

"There is still something there," Mrs. Katevatis said, pointing to a spot on a pan. "You must get every last bit, you know, if you ever want to stop doing dishes and start cooking." The maid nodded and scrubbed harder.

"Do not be too rough on her," I said.

"You are lucky she does not speak English," Mrs. Katevatis said, "or I would have to throw you out of my kitchen. I will not have you making her think I will accept any lowering of my standards."

"You may rely on my uncompromising support of your standards," I said. "Come sit with me in the courtyard. I would like to have a word about our injured man."

"Which injured man?" she asked.

"Not Lord Ashton."

"Who now wants us to call him Mr. Chapman," she said. "Remarkably foolish, if you ask me. I will brew us tea and meet you in the courtyard."

A quarter of an hour later, we were seated at the wooden table behind the house. The air felt considerably warmer here than in the front, where the breeze from the sea offered respite. Our mountain tea, though hot, was thoroughly refreshing, and like its black counterpart somehow managed to have a cooling effect despite its temperature. I am told that in India, even during the hottest days of summer, a nice cup of tea is more beneficial than cold water, although I admit to a certain skepticism on the point.

"I would like to try to ascertain the identity of the injured man," I said. "Dr. Liakos does not believe him to be local. Do you agree?"

Mrs. Katevatis nodded. "I have never seen him before, and no one in the village has heard anyone is missing. His clothes look Turkish to me." She wrinkled her nose and made a noise as if she were spitting. She would never forgive the Turks for the four hundred years they subjugated the Greeks to their rule before her nation won its independence in the early part of our century, and held every individual Turk personally responsible for the affront.

"Do foreigners often come to Santorini looking for employment?" I asked.

"What do you think? We have barely enough work for those of us who live here. This is not Athens. We are a small island."

"There are some foreigners who come here, though," I said. "Those who work on the ships that stop in Oia."

"The captains of those ships live in Oia, but even so there are not many foreigners. He could, I suppose, be a sailor."

"I would like to ask Adelphos to help me identify him. Would you object?"

"No, my son is always a good help. You are wise to make use of him."

"Could you send him to me in half an hour? There is one task I must complete before speaking with him."

When Adelphos and I rendezvoused in the courtyard, the young man listened to my words with a serious look on his face, nodding his head in understanding, but remaining silent until I had finished proposing my plan: He would question as many as people as possible to determine whether any of them remembered the man arriving on Santorini. If we were lucky, one of them may even have ferried him from another island.

"I will do as you ask. It is no problem," he said, after sitting, contemplative, for a moment. "It is a sound idea. Someone must have seen him. The only trouble is how will they know if they recognize him?"

"You can describe his clothing, but also, I have this for you." I had made a sketch of the man's face. Adelphos looked surprised when I handed it to him.

"You did this? I had no idea you are such a talented artist. You should be with the archaeologists. Mr. Reiner tells me they are always looking for someone who can draw."

"You're very kind, Adelphos. It is a reasonable facsimile, but I assure you I lack the hand of a true artist. Furthermore, the archaeologists have cameras, which give a much more exacting image of the original."

"I do not agree. A photograph cannot show us the soul of a man. I see a menace in his face, even with his eyes closed, that his features alone do not communicate. Yet you have managed to show just this in your drawing. It will be a great help on my quest."

Adelphos pulled himself up very tall and threw his shoulders back as he spoke this last sentence. It might have been his use of the word *quest,* but I could not help seeing him as a modern incarnation of the ancient hero, ready to take up the mantle from his ancestors. Jason and Heracles would have recognized the noble look on his face as he took on the task, and even though he would face neither harpies nor Stymphalian birds (although he might argue he too well understood the trouble of the Augean stables), I did not doubt he would handle any challenges with the single-minded determination required to succeed.

That settled, I went in search of my husband, but Margaret intercepted me before I found him.

"Do you not find all this awfully contrived?" she asked. "Philip turns up only days before we are set to leave the island? His injury is not life-threatening, but inconvenient enough for him to require a certain length of time recovering, and that, of course, is better done in a comfortable villa than in a tent. Given the manner in which he received said injury, he had to know we would never allow him to go back to his excavations right away."

"What are you saying, Margaret?" I asked. "Do you suspect him of having orchestrated being shot?"

"Yes, yes I do," she said. "I do not trust him."

"I agree the timing is an odd coincidence, but that alone does not mean we should condemn him." I chewed on my lower lip. "Yet . . ."

"All his protestations about not wanting to disrupt your happy household ring false to me. The man is still in love with you."

"He wants nothing from me."

"So he claims at the moment."

"I cannot entirely agree with you, but it hardly matters now. I am determined to speak with the other men who were at the dig this morning. One of them must have seen something, and whoever shot Philip is likely still on the island. I shall have a quiet word with Fritz to learn where their workers live. And then, perhaps, you and I could go for a ride. I know you would like to further explore the island."

Margaret delighted at the suggestion. "I am passionate about island exploration. I am of the mind that we ought to leave the gentlemen behind. Do you agree?"

"We don't want a large party, but Colin could be a useful addition, so long as he does not insist on taking matters into his own hands and excluding us altogether; but I can manage that. Our questions might be more willingly answered if they are asked by two ladies, concerned only for the safety of the rest of the crew."

"So you propose to tell Colin everything *and* let him come with us?" she asked, tossing her head back and throwing her hands in the air. "It is as if I hardly know you."

"I will initially allow him to believe we intended to go on our own," I said, "but will of course let him be part of the scheme."

"Of course?"

"I cannot be anything but transparent with him when dealing with matters concerning Philip."

"I own a slight disappointment at hearing that, as I do adore a clandestine expedition, but must compliment you on your, shall we say, maturity."

"Maturity has nothing to do with it, I assure you," I said. "Aside from the obvious complications that could arise, we need the others to know where we are going. There is, after all, someone on the island with a gun he is happy to use for nefarious purposes, and although I find it difficult to believe he would point it at two ladies, one can never be too careful. Which is why I am happy to let Colin accompany us."

Colin all but howled when I told him my plan, but I overcame every objection he threw at me, primarily by inviting him to join us. He countered by saying he could go on his own, at which point I all but howled. This had the desired effect, and as soon as Margaret and I had changed into something suitable for a long ride, we headed for the stables.

"Nicely done, Emily," Colin said, as I slipped my boot into the stirrup and flung my leg over Pyrois' back. "You knew I would never agree to letting you and Margaret go alone, and you also knew you were more likely to convince me to accompany you than to convince me I shouldn't go alone."

"Thank you," I said. "You were easier to

manage than I had hoped, but, then, I do know you awfully well."

"I recognized your strategy at once and decided not to fight you," he said. "The manipulation was superfluous."

"Believe whatever you like, my dear," I said.

We rode straight to Kamari, the village nearest to the site of Ancient Thera, where Fritz had told me their workers lived, and had timed our arrival so as to not conflict with the traditional rest period in the afternoon following lunch. There was not much to Kamari beyond a collection of small, dusty houses and a handful of olive trees, under which sat, so far as we could tell, all the men of the village, on a collection of mismatched chairs they must have brought from their houses. They rose as we approached.

"Greetings," Colin said in Greek. "We are here to learn who disrupted the peace on your island today, and to make sure none of you was hurt."

"We are all unharmed," one of the men said.

"I am most heartily glad to hear it," I said, dismounting from my horse. Margaret, whose modern Greek was not so good, nodded, but could contribute little to the conversation, which left her free to observe in detail the reactions of everyone to whom we spoke. "The excavations are important, not only so the world may learn more about the glories of your ancient ancestors, but also because they bring good employment. We do not want to see your income disappear because of one bad apple, or, olive, if you will." My attempt at humor did not translate well into Greek, and two of the men assured me I would find nothing but the finest olives in Kamari.

"Will Mr. Chapman live?" another man asked.

"He is not seriously injured," I said, "and will recover fully." The men breathed a collective sigh of relief, many of them nodding vigorously at the news.

"Did any of you see the coward with the gun?" Colin asked.

"No. We were all working," the first man, who introduced himself as Milos, answered. It appeared he was the leader of the group.

"Were you all at the theatre?" I asked.

Most of them nodded, but one man, younger than the others, shook his head. "I am Vasilis. I had gone to the camp because Mr. Chapman needed another basket for sorting things. I did not see him fall from the shot, only heard it."

"That is very important, nonetheless," I said, "because you were on the only safe route down the mountain from the site. Did you see or hear anything else unusual?"

"No," he said.

"You were in the camp when you heard the shot, correct?" Colin asked.

"I was. I ran back to the site as quickly as I could. I forgot the basket."

"I am certain it was not missed," Colin said. "Did you pass anyone on your way?"

"No. If I had, and it was a stranger, I would have stopped him," Vasilis said. "I knew something was wrong."

"Think very carefully," I said. "As you were running, did you catch a glimpse of anything at all — a bit of cloth, perhaps, or just the hint of movement?"

"I did not."

"Did you hear anything?"

"Only my heart pounding from running." He grinned.

"Were any of you working down lower on the mountain, in the cemeteries?" Colin asked.

"No," Milos answered again. "Mr. Reiner told us to work on the theatre and stoa to prepare for the big boss's return, so no one was in the cemeteries."

"Was anyone taking a break — a rest — at

the time of the shot?" I asked.

"No. We had stopped only a little before then and were all back at work," he said.

So the shooter had been paying attention. He could have climbed Mesa Vouno at any time, most likely early in the morning, before Fritz and Philip had stirred from their tents, and hidden himself somewhere away from where the work was taking place. By waiting until after the men's break, he ran less risk of being seen when he took his position and aimed his weapon.

"What happened after the shot?" Colin asked. "Did anyone apprehend the perpetrator?"

"We tried," Milos said, "but there was no one to be found. He must be an unholy man to be able to vanish so completely."

"He had no gods on his side, that much is certain," Colin said. "How long did you remain at the site after Mr. Reiner had removed Mr. Chapman?"

"We all went down at the same time," Milos said. "Mr. Chapman did not want us to stay and place ourselves in danger."

"Have you watched the road since then?" I asked.

"No one, madam, has gone up or down. We have a man positioned at the lowest bend in the road. No one could come down from Mesa Vouno without passing him."

Colin and I looked at each other, thinking with one mind. Taking Milos and Vasilis with us, we rode to the bottom of Mesa Vouno, up the first straightaway, and around the first curve. There, a black puddle of thick blood next to his head, lay the villagers' lookout.

PHILIP
EPHESUS, 1895

Philip did not like to think he had become complacent over the previous year, but the fact he had not had a single visit from a nefarious person since having established ties with Demir in Constantinople and Mr. Floros in Athens had allowed him to breathe a long-held sigh of relief. He congratulated himself for making alliances with these two figures, despite knowing they operated on a side of the law he could not find acceptable, let alone admirable. But who was he to sit in judgment of them, now he had allowed his own morals to lapse?

As always, when he recalled his own sin, he felt for the bronze, still safely sewn into the lining of his jacket. He almost never allowed himself the luxury of taking it out and examining it, fearing he might be caught. But knowing he possessed it was enough. Its physical presence brought him contented pleasure.

Reiner delighted at their reunion, and the two friends sat up late next to their fire after their first day at Ephesus. John Turtle Wood, an Englishman and a railway engineer, had begun digging at the site several decades ago, and although he found the remains of the famous Temple of Artemis, the structure — if one could even call it that — was in diabolical shape. Mr. Wood could not persuade the people financing his work to continue to do so.

They ought, Philip believed, to have been more impressed at participating in the discovery of the remains of one of the Seven Wonders of the Ancient World no matter how little of it survived, but the longer he worked in the field, the more he came to see that the moneyed classes did not always have altruistic motives, despite their so-called superior blood. In a fortunate development for the intellectual edification of the human race, Herr Humann had come to Ephesus, along with Professor Otto Benndorf of the University of Vienna, with enough official backing and funds to embark on an excavation of enormous scope. Benndorf had even ordered a house to be built in Selçuk, the nearest town, to serve as headquarters for the project.

The dig was extraordinarily well organized, and before long Philip and Reiner each had charge of a separate section of the city as the team methodically made its way through the site, which included an enormous theatre and the impressive two-story façade of the Library of Celsus. The work exhilarated Philip, and the dread that had been his constant companion since that fateful moment at Troy began to dissipate. Sometimes days, and then, eventually, weeks would go by without him pausing from his work to search the horizon for someone who had come for him.

When not consumed with archaeological fervor, his thoughts would turn to Kallista, but he pushed them away, knowing he could not have her, not as things now stood. Fortunately, archaeology provided all the satisfaction he required and missing her became something he could tolerate.

His peace proved short-lived. Hakan appeared early one morning, dressed in the robes of a local peasant, the clothes hanging on his frame in a way that made it impossible to believe they were his but instead suggested they were a disguise meant to fool the locals but not an Englishman.

"Demir believes you might be in a unique position to offer him assistance," he began. "He has heard you paid a sum of money to a colleague of his in Athens to provide a service Demir has, up to this time, provided to you without payment. Does this arrangement strike you as fair?"

"I assure you, sir, I meant no slight by my actions. Mr. Floros insisted I pay him, and if Demir requires similar compensation, I do not object."

"Demir, unlike this Greek friend of yours, does not . . . what did you call it? . . . require compensation. He has entered into a business arrangement with you and wants something in return. Money he can get from anyone. You, Meester Chapman" — the man's accent made Philip's assumed name sound sinister even to himself — "could, for example, help Demir acquire the finest antiquities available from this site."

"Naturally, I would be happy to sell him everything I am allowed to take —"

"You misunderstand, I think. Demir does not care about *allowed.* He cares about the quality of the objects he acquires for his many clients."

"I would expect nothing else from a man of his discerning taste." Philip folded his arms, looking around and feeling divided between wishing someone would come and interrupt this increasingly uncomfortable conversation and praying that no one would hear a word the man was saying.

"So you will secure for him things he might not get otherwise, yes?" Hakan asked. "Things governments and firmans don't always allow to be taken out their country of origin?"

"I can only do what our firman allows," Philip said. "Violating it could lead to our permission to excavate being rescinded altogether."

"You are a smart man," he said. "Demir says you went to Cambridge. I am told they like racing boats there, do they not? Sculling, it is called? We have fine rivers here in Turkey. They might not be so forgiving as those you have in England. It is easy to drown here. You will find a way to do what Demir wants. There is no other option, you see, so we will all be happy and drinking tea together in Constantinople before long."

Hakan turned around and walked away without giving Philip time to reply. Philip was still watching his figure grow smaller in the distance when Reiner clapped a hand on his shoulder.

"Was he looking for work?" Reiner asked.

"Yes, but he liked neither the hours nor the pay," Philip said, shocked at how easily the lie came. "I doubt he will return."

15

I choked back bile as we stood around the fallen man, who Milos told us was called Alastor Kallas. He had been married only two years and his wife had given birth to a baby boy less than a month ago. Margaret had retreated behind some nearby scruffy plants to be sick. Colin crouched next to the body, examining it carefully.

"Did any of you hear another shot?" he asked.

"No," Milos said. "If we had, we would have come here without delay. If we had arrived more quickly . . ."

Colin turned Mr. Kallas gently onto his side so that he could better see the fatal wound. "I am afraid it would have made no difference. The back of his skull has been crushed — Emily, do please look away; you will not want to see this — and he must have died almost at once after receiving the blow."

I took my husband's instruction in the spirit in which he gave it. I had remained composed at enough scenes of grisly death to feel no further need to prove my mettle, but as I stood, my back to the others, I feared I would be sick. I closed my eyes for a moment and then opened them and stepped further away from the cloying metallic smell of blood, searching for clues on the road in front of me.

"Colin," I called. "I may have found the murder weapon." He and Milos were at my side at once. Vasilis, tears streaming down his face, remained next to his murdered friend. I pointed to a large rock on the ground, off the side of the road, nearly against the hill. The surface bore the evidence of its use. My stomach churned.

"Emily, you and Margaret must take Vasilis back to the village. Someone needs to speak to Kallas's wife —"

Vasilis interrupted. "I will not leave him."

"I will go with you, madam," Milos said. Margaret, the pallor of death coloring her face, walked back toward us, but stopped well before she reached the body and stood trembling in the middle of the road. Colin went to her, scooped her off her feet, and carried her to her horse, which she somehow managed, with his help, to mount. Milos took the reins attached to his donkey in one hand and held on to the bridle of her horse with the other, walking between the two animals so Margaret need not do anything more than remain upright. I followed behind, Pyrois skittish, as if he sensed something was wrong.

Back in the village, the men were still beneath the olive tree. Milos said nothing to them as a group, but pulled one of them aside, and spoke to him in low tones. The man's grizzled face crumpled at the news. Alastor Kallas was his son. As the others comforted him, Milos went in search not of Alastor's wife, but of her mother, whom he felt should tell the new widow what had happened. I offered to accompany him, but he refused my offer. Graciously and with thanks, he explained it would be easier for her to hear without a stranger present.

Margaret had slid off her horse and was now leaning against the side of a building away from the men. I went to her, passed her my canteen, and forced her to take a drink.

"The water is bound to be hot and awful, but it will do you good," I said.

"I did not think I would react this way," she said. "I am so very sorry, and thoroughly mortified."

"You ought not be," I said. "It was a hideous scene. No one should have to observe such a thing."

"You are stronger than I realized. How many times have you faced this? And yet you manage to go on and do whatever is necessary, regardless of a churning stomach."

"No more talk like that," I said. A high-pitched wail came from inside one of the houses, and we knew Milos and the girl's mother had given her the awful news. "We will need the police, but I don't know if there are any on the island. Dr. Liakos may be able to help us. Why don't you and I return to the house and send Jeremy or Fritz to fetch him?"

"We should wait for Colin," she said.

"He is perfectly capable of handling things here," I said. "Go back to your horse. I will be along presently, as soon as I have explained to Milos what we are doing. He will tell Colin."

Margaret remained silent the entire way back to the villa, and when we entered the house, she retired to her room without so much as acknowledging the gentlemen, all three of whom were on the roof terrace and had called down greetings to us. I followed her and knocked on her door, but she begged me to leave her be, so I sent Mrs. Katevatis up to her, on the pretense of drawing her bath, and stayed in the corridor outside her room until I could hear the two of them talking. Mrs. Katevatis had nearly mystical powers when it came to comforting others, and I was glad Margaret had seemed to succumb to them.

Knowing my friend to be in capable hands, I climbed the stairs to the roof, where the gentlemen leapt to their feet upon seeing me. Philip, his arm bandaged and in a sling, had regained his color. I told them to all sit back down, and scolded Philip for having got out of bed — he ought to have been resting — and then described for them the events of the day. Upon hearing of Mr. Kallas's death, Fritz choked back a sob and Philip turned a sickly shade of gray. Jeremy immediately expressed concern over the man's death, but then inquired after Margaret.

"She saw the body?" he asked.

"She did. You know the effect such a thing can have —"

"Indeed I do," he said. Some years earlier, Jeremy had accompanied me on a walk through Hyde Park, during which we stumbled upon a similarly grisly scene. It had

taken a great deal of whisky to get him —
and me — through the aftermath. "Should
I go to her?"

"She refused to let me in," I said. "Mrs.
Katevatis is with her now."

"We need to return to Kamari immediately," Philip said, rising. "We cannot let
our men think we have no concern for their
well-being."

"Sit back down at once," I said, ignoring
the shock on his face. "They do not need
anything from you right now, particularly as
your presence is what appears to have lured
this miscreant to the area. Would you have
him stalk you again, and perhaps miss and
hit one of the villagers instead? Do they
need another death in their community?"
The harshness of my words took me by
surprise.

"Hargreaves is with them," Jeremy said.
"He will have told them you have not
abandoned them, but are staying here for
the safety of everyone."

"I will go tomorrow," Fritz said. "Today it
is best that we leave them undisturbed to
mourn."

"An excellent idea," I said. "In the meantime, it would be helpful if you, Philip, told
us everything you can about what precisely
you think is going on." I looked directly into

290

his eyes and held his gaze.

"I have already told you everything I can," he said. "That is, everything I know. I am as much in the dark as the rest of you. This Demir believes I have something of his and he has become increasingly violent."

"Perhaps it is time to find something to give to him," I snapped. "Unless you are content to let his henchmen terrorize innocent people?"

"It is not fair of you to be angry with me," he said, his tone scolding. "You do not know everything —"

"You just said I know everything you do." I stopped myself from stamping my foot. "I am going to freshen up. You, Philip, should retire to your room at once to rest so your injuries heal more quickly."

"I am quite fine here, I assure you."

He answered me sharply, responding precisely as I'd thought he would. His rebuke told me he did not like his former wife — or, more likely, any lady — speaking to him with such candor and force, and I'd suspected he would refuse to follow what he viewed as an order from me. Pleased that I had managed him so neatly, I went back down the stairs, but paused at the bottom before going any further. Once the gentlemen had started talking again, and it became clear Philip was involved in the conversation, I felt confident he would not come down in the immediate future.

I crossed the corridor and headed directly for the Etruscan room, closing the door and locking it behind me. On the wall above the bed I had caused to be painted, by an extremely skilled artist, a fresco in the Etruscan style, depicting three musicians with their instruments against a background filled with trees, birds, and other decoration. A niche on the wall opposite the door contained a spectacular amphora from the sixth century B.C. that was still in possession of its pointed lid, covered with geometric patterns. Mermen frolicked along the top of one of the sides, dogs on the other, and below, the artist had painted a wide variety of waterfowl.

I looked around the room, not sure where to begin, feeling not even the slightest guilt at what I was about to do. Philip had brought nothing with him from the camp other than the clothes he was wearing and a small bag he had hung across his chest. I remembered seeing it after he had fallen from his donkey, and now I found it on a bedside table. Without any hesitation, I opened the buckle and looked inside.

The contents — a notebook, a pencil, a

penknife, a spyglass, a revolver, and a box of bullets — disappointed me. I opened the notebook, expecting to see the handwriting so familiar to me after having read his journals, but instead found only sketches of Ancient Thera. He was an excellent draftsman, the drawings clear, detailed, and accurate, but the pages contained nothing to indicate why he was being targeted. According to his story, the Achilles bronze fueled all of the current violence, but I found it hard to believe anyone would focus this many years on what seemed nothing more than a futile chase. Surely this Demir person would realize he would be better off spending his time harassing someone in possession of something he had a chance of actually acquiring.

I felt along the bottom and sides of the bag and realized I had missed one of the inside pockets. In it, I found a small statue, bronze, of the god Hermes. I thrilled at the discovery, until, upon closer inspection, it became clear the piece was a modern copy, and not a particularly good one. I returned it to the bag.

I would never be convinced the storm had mangled Philip's tent the night of Herr Bohn's death. The destruction was deliberate and with specific purpose. If Demir's lackeys had not found the bronze there or on Philip's person during one of their numerous attacks on him, why would Demir continue to waste resources pursuing it after all this time? No rational man would continue the pursuit, unless he had a solid reason to believe Philip did, indeed, have the object.

I searched the rest of the room, even under the mattress, but found nothing further. Undaunted, I went down through the kitchen and into the courtyard, where, as I has suspected, Philip's clothes, along with Fritz's, had already been washed, and were hanging on the line to dry. I glanced up at the roof, but saw no sign of the gentlemen watching me from above, and then checked the pockets in each pair of trousers and both jackets, as well as Fritz's shirt. Philip's, too damaged to merit repair, was nowhere to be found. Satisfied that the pockets were all empty, I went in search of the maid, who told me Mrs. Katevatis had burned Philip's shirt, its bloodstains having rendered it unusable even as a rag. The jacket, she said, could be saved.

Frustrated, I returned to the clothesline and felt through the pockets again, focusing on the myriad number of them in the jackets, before turning my attention to the seams of the garments. The trousers revealed nothing of import, but on the inside of one of the khaki jackets — the one I recognized to be Philip's — I spotted a small repair in the lining, beneath which lay something hard and inflexible, no more than six inches long. I ran to the kitchen and grabbed the first sharp object I saw, a paring knife, and used it to rip open the stitches. I could hear the blood pulsing through my veins as I reached inside with a single finger, and felt the cool touch of metal. Continuing with great care — I anticipated what I had found — I pulled open the lining so I could gently remove the object. I trembled as I touched it and placed it on my open palm, holding it up in the sunlight, the inscription confirming my suspicions:

ΑΧΙΛΛΕΥΣ ΑΝΕΘΕΚΕΝ ΤΟΙ ΔΙ.
Akhilleus dedicated to Zeus.

PHILIP
EPHESUS, 1895

This last visit from Hakan caused Philip ongoing distress. He could no longer sleep. Every sound in the camp, every voice in the distance startled him. Reiner commented he was not looking well and worried his friend would fall ill, but Philip assured him it was nothing a little rest would not cure, and he asked Humann to allow him some leave to recuperate, saying he would go into town, consult a physician, and stay for a few days. Obviously, he had no intention of doing any of this, but he needed an excuse to leave the site in search of something to satisfy Demir. He did not have enough time to go far, but he covered as much ground as he could on horseback, combing village after village and buying whatever antiquities he could find from the locals.

His spoils lacked the panache he believed would be necessary to impress Demir. He had two small but adequately decorated red figure pots, a badly damaged sculpture a foot and a half high that might have been Artemis, a handful of prehistoric spearheads, and a tiny but lovely bronze of Hephaestus. No one would believe any of them, except perhaps the last, worthy of stealing, but he hoped that, if presented in the right way, they might convince Demir that he was at least trying to do what the man wanted. After all, Philip could not guarantee the Turk he would ever uncover something spectacular enough to tempt the man's clients. Archaeology was not predictable. One might work for years without finding something the outside world would consider exciting, as John Turtle Wood had learned the hard way. Demir would have to content himself with whatever Philip presented him.

The difficulty, of course, would come if something truly extraordinary did turn up in the course of their excavations. Demir would get word of it, and Philip hated to think what might happen then. He might be able to pocket a few coins, or even a small statue, but the mere thought of doing so troubled him, and objects of that sort surely would not be enough to satisfy Demir anyway. Philip had already stolen once and had no intention of ever doing it again.

He continued to work, his dedication never wavering, but found himself plagued by feelings of paranoia and fear with ever-increasing frequency. Peace eluded him altogether. Even when he turned to *The Iliad,* in which he had always before been able to escape whatever was happening around him, he could not focus.

One morning, as he sat sorting an enormous heap of potsherds and considering his plight, excited shouts rang out over the site. Like everyone else, he stopped what he was doing and ran to see what had happened. Reiner was standing with Humann, who was wiping sweat from his brow.

"It is extraordinary," he said. "Where is Benndorf? He must see this." In the trench below, the first signs of a significant find emerged from the dirt. The curly-haired head of a life-sized bronze statue stared out at them. Reiner returned to his task, using a soft brush to clear the rest of the face.

"It must be a Roman copy," Philip said, jumping into the trench and assisting his friend, working to remove the harder chunks of earth away from the body of the sculpture — assuming, of course, more of it had survived than simply the head. His work was rewarded quickly, and he grew more and more excited as together the archaeologists revealed a figure that, although not intact, was in a condition remarkable for its age. The pieces would have to be carefully fitted together, but that would prove no problem, and, eventually, the sculpture would be restored to its former glory.

The mood at the dig turned celebratory, and the men returned to work fresh with inspiration, dedicating themselves to finding the next magnificent souvenir of this once-great city. Benndorf and Humann agreed with Philip's initial assessment of the piece and, after weeks of excavation and study, announced it had been copied from a Greek original and dated from the middle of the first century.

A month after they had come to this conclusion, Philip received a visit from Hakan.

"Why did you not secure the bronze sculpture for Demir before its restoration began?"

"Have you any concept of its size?" Philip asked. "I could never have moved it on my own, let alone stored it somewhere without anyone seeing."

"You could have taken just the head. That alone would be worth —"

"Look here, I will not destroy what I am meant to protect," Philip said. "Taking the head would have been tantamount to an act of violence against our cultural past. I shall not participate in any such thing."

"So I should tell Demir to expect very little from you, yes?"

"I am doing my best," Philip said. "I have some items for you. They are not of the caliber of the statue, but they are not worthless. I will meet you at sundown on the road to Selçuk and give them to you."

"There is a well three miles from the city. I will wait there."

Now came the most delicate part of Philip's plan. He had done nothing illegal — he had bought these objects in the open, from villagers, but he had to make it appear to Hakan that he had pilfered them from the dig. At the same time, he could not let any of his colleagues suspect he was stealing, so going overtly to meet the man was out of the question.

As sunset approached, and the day's work wound down, he told Reiner he was going to Selçuk, and was deliberately vague about the purpose of his trip, wanting to make sure Reiner would not offer to come with him. Reiner's guarded reaction to Philip's stumbling explanation told Philip his friend suspected him of seeking out the comfort of a willing local woman, a thing Philip would never do — he adored Kallista too much and would never betray her, even if she had not extended the same kindness to him — but he saw no way out other than letting Reiner believe the worst. Better he think Philip weak-willed than guilty of something far more sinister.

And, so, he stood alone at the well as sunset approached, his horse tied to a nearby tree, the antiquities packed carefully into parcels, ready to be handed over. No one came for more than two hours. Philip grew increasingly anxious as he waited, starting every time he heard the sound of hooves on the dark road. This was an intolerable way to live.

When Hakan did at last arrive, it was not via the road. He emerged from the darkness behind the well, as if he had made his way across the coastal plain without the benefit of so much as a lantern. Furthermore, he was not alone. Batur, his brawny compatriot, had accompanied him.

"You are late," Philip said, trying to sound more confident than he felt.

"You are disappointing," Hakan said. Philip reached for the bundles, but the man slapped his hand down. "I do not think you give Demir objects worthy of his attention, and I would teach you to do better next time." With that, he nodded, and Batur commenced a beating the likes of which Philip had never before experienced, leaving him on the ground, bleeding, his nose broken. He could hardly see out of his swollen eyes.

"I will take what you offer to Demir," Hakan said, watching as Batur used water from the well to rinse his bloodied hands. "And you will remember this, will you not? I think you will not disappoint us again."

16

I slipped the piece of bronze into a pocket of my khaki jacket, a near-perfect match to Philip's, and returned his to the clothesline. I considered repairing the seam that had held the piece and waiting to see how long it would take for Philip to notice it had gone missing, but decided, on balance, I did not wish to delay confronting him for quite that long.

I went into my room — I had not lied about my desire to freshen up — and drew a bath. While the tub filled, I held the bronze on my palm, hardly able to comprehend the historical significance of the words carved on it. I am no lover of Achilles, but even I felt moved at the sight of something that might very well have belonged to the mighty warrior. Part of me — a very small and juvenile part — wanted to smash it to bits, invoking the memory of Hector as I did so, but I resisted this unseemly urge; I would never destroy something of historical value. I wished I knew more about bronze in general, as I had no way at all of making an attempt to date the piece, but I was willing to accept Philip's reasons for believing it to have come from the time of the Trojan War. My eyes misted as I faced the possibility it might even be a shard from the helmet Achilles wore when he slayed noble Hector.

Not wanting to let it out of my sight, I took it with me into the bathroom, placing it on a chair before I stepped into the tub. Once scrubbed clean, I pulled on a simple tea gown, picked up the bronze, and went to Margaret's door. Mrs. Katevatis was no longer with her; my friend had regained her composure and all but drowned me with apologies.

"You must stop," I said. "I cannot stand one more act of contrition."

"I have always believed myself strong enough to face any adversity," she said. "Now I must revise my theory. I do not surrender, however, only now find it necessary to train myself to better react when facing horrors."

"You might, instead, try avoiding having to face horrors."

"You are my best friend, Emily, and horrors follow you wherever you go, so there's no hope of my avoiding them altogether. I am fortunate not to have been struck down myself before now. The least I can do is prepare myself."

"I am glad you are feeling better," I said, welcoming the return of her sarcastic spirit. "I have done something rather under-handed, but, in the circumstances, I cannot be faulted for it." She sat, dumbfounded, as I explained to her what I had found, and how, and she nearly grabbed the bronze out of my hand the moment I produced it.

"Do be careful," I said. "It is extremely old."

"It is extraordinary," she said, holding it close to her eyes to better examine it. "Can it really have come from Achilles' helmet?"

"It is possible," I said. "More important at the moment, however, is how we deal with its presence in the house."

"You have not yet confronted Philip?"

"It would be best to wait until Colin returns," I said. "We have no way of know-ing how Philip will react."

"Or Fritz," Margaret said. "He will be shattered to learn his friend is a thief."

"At least now we know why Demir has not given up trying to secure the piece. He must have known all along that Philip had it."

"He really ought not to have been carrying it around with him all this time," Margaret said. "It was downright reckless of him. He should have locked it up somewhere secure."

"Yes, but knowing Philip as I do, I do not think he could have borne being parted from it," I said. "He all but worships Achilles — he wrote a monograph lauding him and filled volumes of journals praising him. The fact he has carried the bronze safely with him for so long, assuming he kept it in a similar manner for all these years, proves a certain wisdom to his scheme. Despite repeated attempts, and even attacks, Philip never lost hold of it."

"Until now," Margaret said. "How fortunate Mrs. Katevatis insisted on washing his clothes. I wonder that he did not protest when she took them from him."

"It would have drawn attention to what he was trying to hide," I said. "Furthermore, he was in no condition to intervene."

We decided to wait for Colin in the courtyard, as he would return to the house on horseback, and, hence, go to the barn before coming inside. We could make him au courant with my discovery before any of the rest of the party knew of his arrival.

In the meantime, we visited the nameless

man still residing in the small servants' room at the back of the house. I hold firm the belief that those unconscious are not necessarily wholly unaware of what is happening around them, and therefore spoke to the man, explaining to him we had in our possession the piece his master had sent him to find. If he only could wake up, all of his troubles would be over.

Margaret rolled her eyes while I did this, and dragged me out of the room when I was done. "We have no idea who sent him — if anyone sent him — or why. It is entirely possible he has no connection to any of this business."

"I only meant to encourage him to try harder to recover from his injuries. The mind is powerful, Margaret, and if dangling a little information spurs it into action, he may awaken sooner than he would have otherwise."

"Unless you've terrified him into staying unconscious forever."

"Don't be absurd," I said. "If he did not come to Santorini on an ill-fated mission to harm Philip, he will not have the slightest idea of that which I spoke, and then, if we are lucky, curiosity to understand my meaning may inspire him to heal."

"I am warming to this idea, Emily," Margaret said. "Perhaps we should take turns sitting with him, telling him thrilling stories but stopping before we get to any sort of resolution. That should make him positively desperate to recover. I could start with something from Caesar's account of the Civil Wars. Do you suppose he knows any Latin?"

"Highly unlikely," I said, thanking Mrs. Katevatis as she deposited two glass cups brimming with fresh mint tea.

"You could try *The Iliad,* perhaps, but I suspect he may be Turkish, and if that is the case, he might not enjoy a story in which the Greeks come out victorious. Although *The Odyssey* —"

The clatter of hooves announced my husband's return, saving me from having to explain to Margaret that I was not prepared to read the entire *Odyssey* to the unconscious man. That said, I did appreciate the enthusiasm she brought to her idea, and I could not fault her for trying to come up with any scheme that might shed light on the mysterious events surrounding Philip.

We met Colin in the stables and pulled him into a storeroom next to that building, where, in complete privacy, we could show him the Achilles bronze. His tanned brow furrowed as he studied the piece. "It appears to be genuine," he said, "but I am no expert. I . . ." His voice trailed off, and I found myself surprised he had not reacted more strongly to what we had told him. I had narrated the story, but Margaret's frequent bursts of elaborately imagined embellishment had lent a whimsical air to the tale, something I thought he would have at least acknowledged with the wry raising of his eyebrow or a pointed look in her direction.

"Do we know positively the coat is Ashton's, not Reiner's?" he asked.

"Yes. The hole from the bullet is still very much in evidence."

Colin nodded, but did not speak.

"Do you think we ought to confront him immediately?" Margaret asked. "I am convinced it is the best way forward. He may run off when he realizes it is gone, so we must prepare ourselves for the possibility. Jeremy might —"

"Philip Ashton would never steal something." Colin's voice, preternaturally calm, commanded attention. "This cannot have been in his possession."

"Yet clearly it was," I said.

"I know Ashton better than any of the rest of you. He would not steal." My husband's countenance clouded and his eyes flashed.

309

"I appreciate your feelings on the subject," I said, "but there can be no question on the matter. Unless you are suggesting Reiner took it and hid it in his friend's coat?"

"Yes," Margaret said. "I could believe that. It would explain why Philip has always insisted he doesn't have anything belonging to this Demir or whatever his name is and why the man has continued to behave as if he knew Philip did have it."

"You misunderstand the point of my statement," Colin said. "If this bronze has been hidden by the man currently in my house, then that man is not Philip Ashton."

"Much though I admire your continued defense of your friend's character," I said, "are you now claiming you do not believe he is Philip?"

"Can you claim you are absolutely certain he is?" he asked.

"Yes, as certain as anyone could be," I said. "I told you, he knew things no one else could."

"Have you doubted him from the beginning, Colin?" Margaret asked.

"No," he said. "Well, initially, yes, of course. Anyone would be skeptical. Once my initial shock wore off, and I started to analyze the matter rationally, I had grave doubts."

"But you came to the conclusion he is Philip," I said. "You told me as much."

"That is correct. As he did with you, he shared memories of conversations and events from the past that I had discussed only with him. The scar on his leg helped to convince me. But regardless of anything else, I will never believe Philip Ashton to be a thief, no matter what the circumstances."

"You did not react so strongly to the idea when, a decade ago, I suspected him of having been involved with stealing from the British Museum," I said.

"No, and when the theory proved incorrect, I realized how unfairly I had treated his memory. I ought to have been his staunchest defender."

Margaret watched him closely and then looked at me. "If I may be so bold, I would like to suggest that neither of you is the best judge of any of this. You both knew him and shared private thoughts with him, but you also — forgive me — you both have struggled with feelings of betrayal after the two of you fell in love. Guilt may be clouding your judgment."

"If guilt were guiding me," Colin said, "I would be unlikely to question his claims. He has accepted our marriage with a dignity not many could muster and has asked nothing of us."

"Your last point is precisely why I cannot agree with your change of heart," I said. "If he is not Philip, why on earth is he here? What could he possibly gain by claiming a false identity?"

"Perhaps the scheme was born out of necessity," Margaret said. "He may have murdered a man in Constantinople and could only escape justice if he adopted a new name —"

"Do not get carried away," Colin said, studying the bronze again. "I see no point in further delay. Let us go to him."

PHILIP
EPHESUS, 1895

"You must stay completely still," Reiner said as he cleaned the gashes on his friend's face. "I do not want to get iodine in your eyes." Philip had only just managed to make it back to camp, his injuries causing him enormous pain, and he had turned to Reiner for help. Fortunately, although he was battered and bruised, nothing was broken other than his nose, and he felt confident he would be able to resume work after a good night's sleep.

"I should never have been on that road so late," Philip said. "It was as if I had sent an invitation to every brigand in the region."

"We have had no problems with local crime," Reiner said. "I would not have thought your actions unsafe."

"I caught someone on a bad night."

"Did he get anything of value from you?"

"A little money, but nothing else." Philip caught himself before claiming the man had stolen his watch, realizing its chain still hung from his pocket. "Apparently he missed seeing I have a watch."

"He attacked you so viciously." Reiner said, frowning. "It makes no sense. It is as if he were more concerned with causing injury than robbing you."

"I would have much preferred simply being robbed."

"It reminds me of that day in Troy when you were attacked."

"That was an entirely different matter," Philip said. "The object of that attack was clear — the man wanted antiquities to sell."

Reiner looked away. "You were so adamant you had found that bronze and that he stole it. And now this. It makes me wonder . . ."

"Wonder what?" Philip asked, unwilling to wait, preparing himself for the worst.

"I ought to have believed you," he said. "I am sorry to have been so skeptical. Maybe you did find something there — your Achilles bronze — and maybe it was stolen from you. And maybe this man tonight attacked you believing you still have it."

Philip had only an instant to choose his course of action. How much should he tell his friend? He could never admit to the theft, but had Reiner presented him with an opportunity to tweak his story in a way that might solve his problem with Demir? Thoughts flew through his brain, and he processed them as quickly as he could, realizing what he had to say. "I told the truth about finding the piece and stand by my original story. You are correct regarding what happened tonight. The man told me over and over that he wanted the bronze, and that I could expect more suffering in the future if I did not give it to him — all the while kicking me in the abdomen." He winced.

"The dead man in front of your tent. Who killed him?"

"I have never been able to puzzle that out," Philip said. "I suspect he was working for someone else, and that he did not give the bronze to whomever it was intended for."

"But if that person had him killed, would he not have taken the bronze at the same time?" Reiner asked.

"Not if it had first been sold to another party —"

"For a higher price," Reiner finished. "But finding no evidence of this left the original buyer with the belief you have had the piece all along. Let us return to Troy and try to find out what happened. No doubt he hid his earnings before he was killed. Someone in the village must know something."

"I fear far too much time has passed," Philip said.

"Is there nothing that can be done to convince these people you do not have what they seek?"

"I have tried everything, even going so far as to put the word out to black-market dealers. Nothing will convince them."

"What if we found the bronze?" Reiner asked. "Once we handed it over to these people, that would be the end of the matter."

"First, how would we ever find it?" Philip asked. "And second, how could we live with ourselves knowing we had put an object so important into the hands of villains, forever away from scholars?"

"We would of course involve the police, who would intervene at the final moment and retrieve the bronze while arresting these thugs."

"Thank you for believing me, Reiner." Philip nearly choked on the words. "It means a great deal to me. I wish there were some way to remove myself from this mess, but I fear there is none. I shall leave Ephesus at the end of this season and hope that wherever I go next, I am more difficult for them to find."

And so he made his decision. He could have agreed to Reiner's plan, without even having to confess to theft. It would not have been difficult to orchestrate a scheme for retrieving the bronze — a series of fictional late-night meetings in Constantinople, an exchange that involved some egregious (and also fictional) amount of money. Philip knew if the bronze were gone, it would be nearly impossible to find it again, but he doubted Reiner would suspect him. Who would not believe one could lure almost anything out of the hands of unscrupulous men by offering the right price?

Yet Philip did not choose this option, and as he sat in his friend's tent, he discovered an astonishing truth about himself: He cared more about the Achilles bronze than about his own well-being. He would prefer to keep hold of it and live with the anxiety and nerve-destroying worry that came from knowing Demir's men would eventually track him no matter where he ran; he would submit himself to violent treatment again and again rather than give up his prize.

There was only one other thing that mattered to him so much. Kallista.

He had been away from her for far too long.

17

The sunset had already started to color the sky as Colin, Margaret, and I climbed up to the roof terrace. I stood at the top of the steps, pausing to take in the beauty of the scene — the sparkling water of the caldera, the bright streaks of red and gold smudging the blue heavens — and considered that Hephaestus rather than Helios would likely govern the fiery conversation about to explode.

"I have been worried sick about the two of you." Jeremy was on his feet and at my side almost before I saw him move. "How are you holding up? I know, Em, you claim to be made of iron or steel or some sort of ridiculous metal, but —"

"Fear not," Margaret said. "We are both quite well. Sad, of course, but coming to terms with what happened."

"An awful thing," Fritz said, offering her a seat. "Poor Kallas. And his wife. We really must do something for her."

"Yes, quite," Colin said. "It is particularly distressing given it might so easily have been prevented."

"I am consumed with guilt," Philip said. "The villagers were trying to help me. They did not want the man who shot me to escape. If I had not been —"

"If you had not been so dishonest, they would never have been in danger," Colin said.

"Hargreaves!" Philip fairly flew to his feet and looked at Colin with disbelief. "What can you possibly mean by saying such a thing?"

"I shall make no attempt to prettify the situation," my husband said. "Explain this at once." He held the bronze out for all to see. Philip reached for it, but Colin pulled it away. "I shall not let you get your hands on it again."

Fritz, his jaw slack, rose to his feet. "Is it the Achilles bronze?"

"Indeed," Colin said. "Can I trust you, Reiner, to look at it without absconding with it?"

"Of course." Fritz's words sounded almost mechanical as he gently accepted the slim piece of metal from Colin's hand. "Akhilleus . . . *Das ist ja unglaublich* . . . to hold such a thing . . . to . . ." He shook his head slightly, as if trying to free himself from the awe inspired in him by the artifact. "How did you find this, Hargreaves?"

"I found it," I said. "Your dear friend has had it all this time."

"That is impossible," Fritz said.

"Ask Lord Ashton if you don't believe me," I said, glaring at Philip, who started at hearing me address him by his title.

"Ashton?" All the color drained from Fritz's face.

"It is far more complicated than they would have you believe," Philip began. "Yes, I am now in possession of the bronze, but —" He stopped, sank back into his chair, and buried his face in his hands. "No, I cannot lie anymore."

"You told us the truth about finding it at Troy," Fritz said. "Is the lie that you claimed it had been stolen from you?"

"I have carried this guilt for so long I do not know how I shall live without it," Philip said. His body seemed to shrink and his eyes looked dead. "What I told you in Troy was mostly true. I found it and the man working with me attacked me in an attempt to steal it. We fought, and to this day I do not know how I managed to thwart him. Perhaps Achilles himself fought with me —"

"I will stand for none of that," Colin said. "Proceed without embellishment."

"I defeated my opponent, somehow," Philip said, "but then succumbed almost at once to my own injuries. When I came to, I realized I still had the bronze, which I had slipped into my pocket for safekeeping."

"You put it in your pocket before the man attacked you?" I asked.

"Yes."

"So you had already decided to keep it for yourself," I said.

"No, not entirely, although I do admit to being tempted," Philip said. "After regaining consciousness and finding it still on my person, I —" He stopped and sighed. "I took it as a sign that I ought to keep it, that it was a talisman of sorts, that —"

"That your passion for Achilles mattered to you more than scholarship," I said. Margaret touched my arm and gripped my hand.

"I am afraid you are all too correct. A madness consumed me, and I decided never to part with the object. The next morning, when I nearly tripped over my attacker's body in front of my tent, I considered coming forward and saying I had recovered the bronze from his corpse, but could not bring myself to do so. I am ashamed of my weakness."

Colin made no sound while Philip spoke, his eyes dark and bold as he listened.

"Did you not think you might then be in danger?" Margaret asked. "Someone killed the man, and what better motivation for the act than securing the bronze?"

"You make a keen observation, and I confess I did as well, but it did not daunt me. I suspected the man had failed a cruel employer for whom he was supposed to get anything of value he could from the site."

"But why would the man have told said employer he ever saw the bloody thing? Do please pardon my language, ladies," Jeremy said. "Why not keep his mouth shut until something else of value turned up?"

"I can only imagine that my reaction to the find made the truly exceptional nature of the piece clear to him," Philip said. "And, although I can only speculate, I have spent a great deal of time over the past years considering what happened and have come to the conclusion that he had dangled the idea of the piece to someone else, someone he thought might pay better."

"Whatever happened then is irrelevant now," I said. "What we must contend with is a stolen artifact that must be returned to the proper authorities without delay. You, Philip, must do it yourself if you are to retain any shred of dignity."

"Yes," Fritz said. "We must correct this at once."

"And in doing so," I said, "you will remove the threat of danger you have faced for so long. As soon as your nefarious friends learn the object is safely in the hands of a museum, they will know there is no longer any point in pursuing you."

"I do not think you understand these people, Kallista," Philip said. "They will find me and destroy me. Prison would offer me no protection."

"Right." Jeremy sat down, crossed his legs, and folded his arms. "I must interject, as the lot of you have no ability to view this situation objectively. I can almost exclude you, Hargreaves, from my judgment, for you are free from the passion for antiquities that consumes the others, but your relationship to the accused, if I may call him that, precludes you from being able to separate your emotions from rationality."

Colin, leaning against the wall, his arms crossed over his chest, looked at Jeremy in astonishment before turning away from the group. The fact that he was not pacing, as was his habit when faced with a stressful situation, worried me.

"Jeremy —" I started.

He did not let me continue. "I find it inconceivable anyone cares so very much about one lousy little piece of bronze, no matter what one can read on it, no matter who found it where. Yes, to scholars of Ancient Greece, it has enormous significance. But on the black market, why on earth would any dealer — or whatever these fellows call themselves — become so obsessed with such a thing? Better he should hunt down the treasures of Egyptian pharaohs or something like the gold mask we saw in the museum in Athens. The one that bloke who fancies Troy found and said belonged to the chap who went after Helen? Can't remember his name."

"Agamemnon," I said.

"Precisely," Jeremy said. "I can see you are all horrified by my lack of specific knowledge on the topic, but let me assure you my level of disinterest is far closer to that of the average person than any of yours. Normal people do not sit around worrying about things that happened ten thousand years ago."

"More like three or four thousand, actually," Fritz said.

"Yes, yes, I have utter faith in your dates,

Herr Reiner." I could tell Jeremy was enjoying this. "The material point remains. Someone bent on earning a fortune selling pilfered antiquities would have given this up as a bad job years ago."

"If only you were right," Fritz said. "Sadly, the market for such things —"

"I do not speak of these things in general," Jeremy said. "I refer specifically to the bronze in question. You do still have it, Hargreaves? Can't have it slipping away now." Colin did not reply to this inane question. He remained standing, away from the table around which we were gathered, his back to us.

"I do appreciate the point," I said. "Why would someone pursue this so relentlessly?"

"No one would," Jeremy said.

"Yet clearly someone is doing just that," Margaret said. "Someone who has resorted to violence again and again."

"You are all falling straight back into his trap," Colin said, turning hard on his heel to face us again. His dark eyes blazed. "What evidence do we have for any of his claims? If he lied about stealing, he can just as easily have lied about what happened after."

"How dare you?" Philip's countenance flushed. "I have stood by and watched you

325

steal my wife, keeping out of your way because of the deep respect I have for her. I will not tolerate any further insults from you."

"I would be more than happy to discuss your shortcomings in greater detail, but believe it would be best if we did so outside, away from the ladies." Colin's voice was deadly calm.

"There is no need for any of that," Fritz said. "I can attest to the attack at Troy, as could the rest of the archaeological team. And I assisted him after he had been badly beaten in Ephesus."

"You saw the attack?" Colin asked.

"No, but I —"

"Then you do not know the identity of the perpetrator?" Colin continued.

"No, but —"

"So we are left to take on faith Mr. Chapman's version," Colin said, glaring at Philip when he opened his mouth to speak. The look silenced him. "For all we know, he hired someone to rough him up to lend credibility to his story."

"Why would I have done that?" Philip asked.

"I haven't the slightest interest in considering the question," Colin said. "Your credibility is shattered. It would be best for everyone if you took yourself off and returned to whatever life it is you actually ought to be living."

"What are you suggesting?" Philip stood, his hands balled into tight fists.

"I apologize if I did not make myself understood," Colin said. "I did not offer a suggestion. I meant to say, quite clearly and without question, that I do not believe anything you have told us from the moment you entered this house."

"Colin —" I started, but he silenced me with a raised hand.

"You have taken advantage of our goodwill and you have tormented my wife. I will stand for it no longer. Leave at once."

"That is quite enough." Now I stood. "He cannot leave, not when we know someone is trying to physically harm him. To allow him to do so would be inhumane."

"He is not Philip Ashton," Colin said, "and if he wants to stay under my roof for another night, he will confess his true identity." Philip blanched, and I thought I saw a hint of moisture in his eyes, eyes I had recognized the moment I saw them.

"First off, if we are to be technical regarding the subject, this is my house, and my roof, and I shall decide who stays here," I said. "Do not let your anger get the best of you."

"Is there some question of his identity?" Jeremy asked. "I thought he had proven to us all that he is who he claims?"

"I *claim* nothing," Philip said. "One does not need to *claim* to be the person one has been since birth. It is simple enough to establish one's identity, even after all these years, when one has the truth on one's side."

"Right now, the only thing we must discuss is what to do with the bronze," I said. "Colin, will you go to Fira and wire someone at the Archaeological Museum in Athens?"

"Nein," Fritz said. "Herr Dörpfeld would want the piece to go to Berlin or Vienna."

"That can all be figured out," I said. "For now, we need someone in a position of authority involved."

"The moment I send the telegram we must assume Chapman's enemy will be alerted to it," Colin said. "If he cares so much, he no doubt has more than one person operating on his behalf on the island. He may even have someone in this house."

"He most certainly does not," I said. "I trust all of our servants implicitly." I pulled my husband aside in order to speak to him privately. "I have never seen you so governed

328

by your emotions. You are the one I rely on to provide calm in a storm, yet you appear determined to make this tempest even worse."

"He has taken advantage —"

"What he has done matters not to me at present. We must secure the bronze and stop any further harm from coming to Philip or anyone else."

He squeezed my hand with such strength I feared he would crush it. "You are quite right," he said. "I have let my emotions run away with me. When I think of him speaking to you privately about intimacies —"

"Stop," I said. "There is no value in discussing this now." We rejoined the others and I laid out my plan. "A wise man does not act in haste, so I propose we wait until morning to send any telegrams. Philip, you and Fritz will remain here as long as necessary until —"

"Until you hand me over to the police," Philip said. "I cannot argue. I deserve far worse."

"No," Fritz said, a sudden strength in his voice. "I will not stand by and let you be arrested for a mistake made during a time when you were suffering so greatly. Your mind was not clear. You had lost everything — your name, your fortune, your wife —

and I am of the opinion that we must forgive your transgression. We will return the bronze to the proper authorities, and can determine the best way to do this, but whatever we decide it will not include making you pay any further for what you have done."

PHILIP
ATHENS, 1896

When the season at Ephesus ended and Philip started for Athens, for the first time in years — really, since he had left England after seeing Hargreaves kiss his wife — he allowed himself the luxury of thinking about Kallista again. His love for her had not dwindled a bit. If anything, his heart desired her more ardently. But he had chosen a different path, one that had proven challenging and satisfying. And now that he no longer worked in Ephesus, perhaps he would enjoy a little peace, at least until Demir's henchmen caught back up with him.

When he first told Reiner he meant to leave Ephesus, his friend tried to convince him to stay, an effort Philip appreciated, as he understood the significance of the site and both the pleasure and the satisfaction of undertaking his chosen work there. He would not be swayed, however, and confessed to Reiner he believed he had no choice but to go because of the ongoing threat from the man who had beaten him. Reiner declared that then he, too, would leave, and that together they would find another dig to join.

What Philip could not have imagined was that Reiner would come to him, only three weeks after they had departed Ephesus for Athens, where they both planned to spend the winter, with several enticing possibilities for the subsequent season. He'd contacted the leaders of expeditions in Paestum, with its three magnificent Doric temples in southwest Italy; in Leptis Magna, the sprawling site of a Roman city in northern Africa; and in Sicily's Valle dei Templi, a shockingly well-preserved area full of Greek temples, near the city of Agrigento. Reiner offered one last option, apologizing as he described it.

"It is a site not so spectacular as the others, but I am well acquainted with the man leading the dig, Friedrich Hiller von Gaertringen. We were students together at Tübingen, studying ancient history. He has obtained a firman to dig at a site that, while on a far smaller scale than Ephesus or Troy, will prove fascinating nonetheless: Ancient Thera, a city built by colonists from Sparta in the eighth century B.C., on the Aegean island of Santorini. I can assure you Hiller von Gaertringen would not choose to work somewhere without merits. He is one of the most competent archaeologists I have ever encountered. I thought I would mention the site, as it is more isolated and away from the ordinary path of tourists."

Philip could not have hidden his shock, his astonishment, his joy, at what he immediately viewed as a turn of good fortune. "Thera — this is more than I ever could have hoped, Reiner," he said, leaving his friend befuddled.

"I must stress that it is not a fair trade for Ephesus."

"Santorini is a place close to my heart," Philip said. "My villa was there — is there — only now it is hers. Kallista's. I would never dare disturb her or let her know of my presence, but the mere fact I may be on the island at the same time as her — that is more than I could ever have hoped for. I cannot thank you enough, dear man, for this opportunity. Just to be near her will be a gift. I shall never be able to repay you."

18

"Not turn him in to the authorities? You cannot ask that of us," Colin said when Fritz had made his extraordinary pronouncement imploring us to keep Philip from being held responsible for the theft. Jeremy laughed quietly, shaking his head, but Margaret, her eyes soft, looked as if she might be at least partly convinced by the idea.

"Indeed I can," Fritz said. "I understand how close you and Ashton were before, but I am the one who has stood by him since our party stumbled upon him in Africa, and I now know him better than you. I saw the physical effects of his illnesses and all those months living in the bush, and I saw that the only thing keeping him alive was the hope of being reunited with the woman he loves. Can you imagine the pain he felt when he realized she no longer mourned him? When he realized she had pushed aside her memories of him to make room for a new life with his best friend?"

I swallowed hard listening to this, and tugged at the lace on my cuffs, not knowing where to look.

"No one argues it was anything but a terrible blow," Jeremy said. "Most blokes would have wanted revenge. Pistols at dawn. Although he did know Hargreaves to be a good shot, so he might —"

"I would never have done any such thing," Philip said. "I chose not to interfere. I saw that the world and those in it whom I love had gone on without me, and although that caused me pain, I could not fault any of you. You believed me to be dead, and life is for the living. I rejoice that you found each other, and when it became clear to me how deeply you cared for one another, I made the conscious decision to step back."

"I told him it was foolish," Fritz said. "That he should go to his sister, and reclaim his title and position in the world, but he refused."

"I did not have the heart to rip my nephew's inheritance from him," Philip said. "I had lived for nearly two years without the trappings of my title — and I owe my very survival to you, Reiner, in those early days; without you I would not even have had the funds to buy a simple meal. But once I began to work, I found a new purpose in life. I —"

Colin interrupted, curling his well-formed lips. "Yes, we have already heard that part of your fantastical tale. If you have nothing further to add by way of providing evidence as to your identity, my verdict on the matter remains the same: You are a fraud and an impostor."

"I am happy to provide whatever proof you wish," Philip said. "Ask any question you like. Shall we revisit our days at Cambridge? Recall evenings spent at the Eagle over too many pints? Discuss the particulars of an ill-planned excursion to find the Colossus at Rhodes?"

"I am happy to go over the details of any of those."

"What about the time you climbed to the roof of the Wren Library at Trinity and Lundt spotted you? You convinced him not to report you by promising him a bottle of that whisky we used to take from your father. We had to go all the way to Anglemore Park to get it, because we could not find any in the house in Park Lane."

"It was from a small maker who would not let it be sold in England," Colin said.

"My father brought it from Scotland him-self."

"When we went to London in search of the whisky your mother forced us to go to that awful ball — I can't remember who hosted it —"

"Of course not, because you weren't there," Colin said. "You have proven to be in possession of a basic knowledge of my past. Hundreds of people knew about my father's whisky preferences, and it is not difficult to determine the name of the porter at Trinity College. I was embroiled in any number of scrapes during my student years, and a little judicious poking around the Oxford and Cambridge Club could give you the details of many of them."

"Shall we discuss Kristiana, then?" Philip asked. "In front of your wife?"

Colin pulled back his shoulders and straightened to his full height. "You need not try to dissuade me from my beliefs by threatening my wife, who already knows everything there is to be said about the countess."

"Everything?" Philip crossed his arms. "I doubt that."

"That is quite enough," I said. "I will hear no more."

"Then I am afraid, Kallista, you should

retire to your room, as I have a great deal more to say."

"Look here, chaps," Jeremy said. "There is no need to make the ladies uncomfortable —"

"Hargreaves has just told us she knows everything," Philip said.

"I do," I said. "He loved her, but that was before he met me, and he was hurt, deeply, when she was killed working for the safety of her country in a position similar to his own work for the crown."

"I was thinking of a specific night, Hargreaves, that first time in Vienna, when you took her back to your rooms and then, much later, at her request, went to the Hotel Sacher in search of a piece of their famous torte," Philip said. "It was nearly three o'clock in the morning and you had to persuade the night clerk to let you into the kitchen so you could get it. You took it home and fed it to her. Do you require more details? I shall continue if you insist, but it would only hurt Kallista."

My face grew hot. No one likes to hear stories of a spouse's previous loves, particularly in front of one's friends.

Colin narrowed his eyes. "I do not remember recounting that story to anyone."

"I would not expect you to," Philip said.

"You told me on the evening she rejected your proposal of marriage. We had consumed rather a great deal of whisky."

My heart thudded against my chest. I could not speak and did my best to appear more composed than I felt.

"Are we quite finished here?" Margaret asked. "I see no point in further discussing any of this. We should all go to bed or retire to read or write letters or something. It has been a dreadful day."

"I quite agree, Margaret," Jeremy said. "Em, will you walk me downstairs? I find myself suddenly fatigued."

"I appreciate what you both are trying to do, but assure you it is unnecessary. I am not so fragile that hearing this makes me want to run off to bed," I said, pulling myself up tall and finding my voice. "Colin, I may not have known every particular detail of your relationship with the countess, but I did know you proposed and that she refused you. Am I shocked you were upset after that and turned to your friend for whisky and gentlemanly consolation? Hardly. Am I surprised you once brought her torte in the middle of the night? It sounds like just the sort of thing you would do for someone you love." I swallowed hard.

"This ought not have been discussed in

such a setting," Colin said, looking at our friends.

"No, it ought not," I said. "And the subject shall not be mentioned in such a way again."

"We cannot stand by and pretend this theft did not happen," Colin said.

"Of course we can," Fritz said. "And if you insist on notifying the authorities, I will swear to them it was I who took the bronze."

"I will not let you do that," Philip said. "I —"

"It is a ridiculous, if noble, threat," I said, "but one that would collapse under even the slightest scrutiny. Colin, if Philip goes to jail, is it possible Demir could harm him there?"

"Yes," Colin said, glowering at Philip. I had never before seen him so agitated.

"Then we must find a way to prevent that," I said. "What if I make overtures to these shadowy figures of the black market? I could let it be known I have an object I have acquired by dubious means and have decided to sell. When word spreads that it is the very bronze Demir has been harassing Philip for —"

"He will still attack him, believing he sold it to you," Colin said. "I am afraid there is no easy way to avoid the consequences of this particular action. I shall go to Fira and telegram the museum in Athens to ask how they would like us to proceed." He kissed me before he went downstairs, but instead of a quick peck, he pulled me close to him, one arm around my waist, his other hand resting on my cheek, and he took his time about it. Although I admit to being rather too distracted to be certain, I thought I heard Margaret whoop. Much though I enjoyed the forceful nature of the kiss, I knew it to be the primal display of a man marking his territory and could not entirely approve of the action. Which is not to say I entirely disapproved of it, either.

When he had gone, Philip asked me to come with him to the back of the terrace, away from my friends, so that we might talk without them hearing. Once we were alone, he said, "I owe you my deepest apologies, Kallista. It was wrong of me to speak the way I did, but my name is all I have, even if the greater world does not know it. Hargreaves's change of heart and rejection stings, but that does not excuse my behaving in a most ungentlemanly manner. I hope you can forgive me."

"It is of no consequence," I said.

"You still believe me, don't you?" he

asked, his pale blue eyes radiating earnestness.

"I —"

He took my hand. "I remember so vividly the night I fell in love with you. It was in Lady Elliott's ballroom — a dreadful night, really, until I saw you. You were wearing a gown of the palest shell pink, all ruffles and flounces and lace, and your cheeks flushed the identical shade, not from a feeling of embarrassment or modesty, but from the heat of dancing. You sat out not a single tune, but I noticed how carefully you chose your partners. You spurned several extremely eligible gentlemen, clearly having no interest in title or fortune, and instead danced with younger sons and elderly fathers."

"I had not gone to the ball in search of a husband," I said, pulling my hand away. "I only wanted to dance."

"That may be, but your behavior suggested to me you required more from your life than a title and a comfortable allowance, and the moment I realized that, I started to hope you might consider me as the gentleman who could give you something better. I loved you wholly from that moment on."

I pressed my lips together. I hardly remembered the night of which he spoke. It had made almost no impression on me at the time, but his words echoed almost perfectly another description I had heard of the evening, from Colin, nearly ten years ago, when he had agreed to help organize for me the details of a trip to Paris. We were in the library at Berkeley Square, and I had commented that he and Philip must have spent many pleasant hours there. He assured me they had, and explained it was in the library that Philip had told him he had fallen in love with me. His words were kindly intended, meant to give a young widow consolation, but instead they stunned me. It was the first time I had heard anything that led me to believe Philip had genuinely cared for me. Until that moment, I had assumed he wanted nothing more than a standard society match.

"I am afraid I do not remember the evening so well as you," I said.

"You cannot have forgot the dress, though?" He smiled conspiratorially and raised an eyebrow.

"That I may remember," I said, feeling myself begin to blush.

"You were but a girl then," he said, "and the woman you have grown into is nothing short of amazing. When I imagine what we might have had — exploring the world together, our mutual love of Ancient Greece acting as our compass —"

"I only began to study Greece after reading your journal," I said. "Had you not disappeared in Africa, I might never have come to be so devoted to ancient history."

"You would have," he said, reaching his hand up as if he meant to touch my face but pulling it back before he could do so. "Your ardor for the subject always lurked within you and eventually would have come out. I know you have translated both *The Iliad* and *The Odyssey*. I should very much like to read your versions."

"We should not discuss these things."

"I know it is wrong, but I cannot stop. I do not want to." He stepped closer to me. "You are dear to me, and I shall always hold a special place in my heart for you."

I fidgeted, finding his proximity discomforting. As if he could read my thoughts, he retreated, just a bit, and spoke in a less intimate, clipped tone. "Again, I apologize for any pain I have caused." He took my hand again and pressed it to his lips. "You do believe me, don't you? You recognized me. I could see it in your eyes the moment I stepped out of the villa."

"Yes," I said. "I did recognize you." I

began to feel the way I had that first day we arrived on the island, when I stood on the terrace speaking to him in private: confused, and yet, somehow, calm and happy.

"I hope you know that whatever happens, I shall always be a friend to you, Kallista. Anything you need, I shall endeavor to provide, even if it is nothing more than the opportunity to discuss Homer with someone who shares your passion for it."

"Yes, but you prefer Achilles to Hector, a position I find intolerable."

He laughed. "Only because you are caught up in the notion that man's best is enough, when Achilles' semi-divinity enables him to —"

A loud clattering on the stairs interrupted him.

"Lady Kallista!" Adelphos called as he rushed over to me, grabbing both of my arms. "I have found the man you seek. I have him. He is in the barn. I tied him up there. You will come right away?"

PHILIP
SANTORINI, 1896

Before the start of his first season at Thera, as he wintered in Athens, Philip had considered again changing his name, as it might make it more difficult for Demir to find him. Reiner had suggested the scheme, assuring him that Hiller von Gaertringen would hire him on Reiner's recommendation, even if he could not, with this new name, claim any prior experience. Philip saw the wisdom of the idea, and very nearly agreed to it, but in the end decided he had already lost too much. He had worked hard to hammer out his new existence, and he was proud of the work he had done in Magnesia, Troy, and Ephesus. He would remain Philip Chapman.

He reached this conclusion only after giving full thought to the implications, not wanting to foolishly make it easy for Demir to continue harassing him. He kept his name, but that did not stop him from engaging in a certain amount of subterfuge specially designed to throw Demir off the track. He informed his archaeological colleagues he planned to spend the next season in northern Africa exploring Roman ruins before agreeing to join another excavation. He wanted to see Petra and Leptis Magna and, he had to admit — leaning close to gain their confidence — he felt a certain pull toward Egypt. He had never believed he would give even the barest consideration to abandoning the Greco-Roman world, but owned that a trip through the land of the pharaohs might prove a temptation too great to resist.

When the time came to depart for the season, he did not go directly from Piraeus to Santorini. Instead, he took a boat to Alexandria and played tourist in Egypt for a fortnight, waiting there until he felt certain no one was following him. He then sailed to Tripoli, where thence, at last, he boarded a ship that would call at a number of ports, one of them Oia on Santorini.

As a result, he was late getting to the dig, but he had told Herr Professor Hiller von Gaertringen to expect this — pleading vague family commitments — and his new employer had not objected. The site was small enough that the professor, along with

Reiner and Gerhard Bohn, would be able to manage adequately without him for a few weeks.

Once he arrived on Santorini, Philip wondered how he would ever bear leaving the island. He had taken fewer than twelve steps into the picturesque village of Oia, with its blue cupolas and curving white arches, before he came to what he realized should have been an obvious conclusion: No place on earth could compare to Santorini, with its bright skies and arid landscape. He loved the hot, dry summers, with their infrequent sudden and unexpected bursts of rain. When he reached the site of the German excavations, he stood atop Mesa Vouno, surrounded by ancient ruins, to watch the sunset over the caldera, and repeated this ritual every night, finding he took more delight in digging at Thera than he had even at Troy. He would always remember his first season on Santorini as something almost magical.

Although he primarily credited the beauty of the island for this, the fact that his scheme had worked so far played no small part in his newfound contentment. He saw no sign of Demir or anyone connected to him. When the season ended, and the archaeologists packed up, Philip decided not to return to Athens for the winter, instead buying — for an obscenely cheap sum — a small house outside Mesa Gonia, a village in the foothills of the mountains, famous for its wine. He loved walking through the barren vineyards in the winter, amused that this habit led his new neighbors to believe he was not entirely sound of mind. This did not stop them from inviting him to dine and welcoming them into the fold, and before the first signs of spring, he had adapted so well to island life it was as if he had never lived anywhere else.

The satisfaction he felt was very nearly complete. All he needed now was to find a way to draw Kallista to him. He had been patient long enough. The time had come for him to get what he truly wanted.

19

Adelphos was speaking so quickly I was not certain I understood his accented — though very good — English. "Σταματα τωρα!" I shouted at him — "Stop now!" — unconvinced I was using the imperative correctly. I would have done better in Ancient Greek. Fortunately, the rising register and tone of my voice had the desired effect regardless of my grammar, and Adelphos, who was still gripping my arms, snapped his mouth shut and stood, quiet.

"Tell us again, more slowly," I said.

"There is no time for slow," he said, immediately becoming once again agitated. "The man you seek, I have him. He is in the barn."

"What man?" I asked. "The drawing I gave you is of the man recovering downstairs —"

"Yes, yes, Lady Kallista, but I have found the man who sent him to the ruins."

"You have?" I had not dared hoped he would accomplish so much. Perhaps I had employed a certain genius in comparing him to the ancient heroes.

"Take us to him at once, my good man," Philip said.

"Margaret, you come with me," I said. "The rest of you stay here. I do not want to overwhelm him."

Philip scowled. "If you think we shall stand by and let two unaccompanied ladies —"

I interrupted him. "Adelphos is more than capable of looking after us." That settled the matter — as Philip was evidently coming around to the idea that it is best not to stand in my way — and Margaret and I followed Adelphos downstairs, pausing in the kitchen so he could tell us how he came to find his quarry. He explained that no one he queried knew the identity of the man in my drawing, but that a man who worked in the port at Oia admitted to having seen him arrive with a second stranger on a small fishing vessel two days before we spotted him at Thera. He could not speak as to the man's name or where he was from, and, unfortunately, the fishing boat that brought him to the island came from Cyprus, and had long since departed. He did not know the captain of the vessel. He did, however, point Adelphos to the boy who had guided the boat's passengers on donkeys from the pier to the village.

Adelphos convinced the boy — with a bribe for which I promised to reimburse him — to tell him the men's destination: a ramshackle house on the outskirts of Oia, a place long thought to be abandoned.

"And haunted," Adelphos added. "It is well known to be haunted, but this did not daunt me. I went there without delay, ready to face whatever dangers my foe could hurl at me."

I could almost picture him, bronze helmet covering his dark curls, sword in one hand, shield in the other. If only it were a different century!

"I watched from afar for a while, but there was no one in the vicinity, unless there was someone in the house."

"And was there someone in the house?" Margaret asked.

"Of course. How else do you think I caught the man?" His face was flushed pleasantly from exertion; he almost glowed.

"I had rather hoped you pursued him to an ancient cave," Margaret said, her voice taking on a dreamy quality. I knew she had formed as strong an image of Adelphos as ancient hero as I.

"Cave? No." He shook his head, confused. "I did not go straightaway to the house and knock on the door, as I know this man to be bad because he sent someone to hurt Lord Ashton, so instead I approach the building from the rear, and I look through windows until I see him."

"And then you charged him?" I asked. "Startling him into paralysis with a battle cry worthy of —"

"Achilles," Margaret finished. "I realize you object on principle, Emily, but it is the most fitting image. Adelphos is Greek. You cannot make him Hector."

"I was thinking more along the lines of Theseus slaying the Minotaur, if you must know," I said.

"My ladies, please." Adelphos grinned, enjoying our conversation. "It was not so difficult. He was sleeping. I climbed through the window and bound him with the rope I had brought with me. Just in case, you see."

"He must have woken up?" I asked.

"Yes, and he was most displeased, but I had no trouble keeping him under control. I am a strong man, Lady Kallista. You maybe should think of Heracles." He grinned again and motioned for us to follow him to the barn. There could be no doubt he was enjoying this immensely.

Once inside, I held up a lamp to illuminate the face of our prisoner, but saw only a dusty heap in the straw. Adelphos grunted at it. "If you want water you will sit up. And I know you want water."

The heap started to move, squirming in a most inelegant attempt to do as Adelphos suggested. Adelphos grunted again and as he tugged at it, its robes fell away, revealing the man's face, the lips pulled to reveal a particularly unattractive set of brown, jagged teeth. Margaret and I turned to each other, immediately recognizing him as the burlier of the men we had spied on at Nea Kameni.

"What is your name?" I asked.

"You may call me Savas." He spat the words.

"I do not have much Turkish," I said, crossing my arms and sitting on a convenient barrel, "but I know that word means 'war.' I do not suppose it is your real name, but that is of no consequence. I shall call you whatever you like."

"You are clever so I shall tell you. I am Batur."

"Thank you. What brings you to Santorini?"

"The view."

I laughed, softly. "I like you, Batur. Adelphos, give him some water." The Turk drank greedily when Adelphos lifted a cup to his mouth. "I am dealing with a great difficulty. Your . . . colleague, let us say, menaced a friend of mine at Ancient Thera some days back and was injured. As a caring woman, I of course wish to notify his family, as his condition is bleak."

"I am aware of his condition. You think I did not track him to this house when he did not return as arranged?"

"So you skulked around and eavesdropped and decided he was too ill to be worth further bother?" I asked. "Or rather, too ill to wake up and cause you any difficulties?"

"He could not cause me any difficulties even if he does wake up. He knows nothing."

"Ah, yes," I said. "You come to the matter at hand. You, Batur, do know something, and you are going to tell it all to me."

Now he laughed. "You are amusing. You think you come here, talk sweetly to me, give me water, and I will betray my master? You are naïve."

"I know about Demir."

"My lady, you do not," he said. "That I will tell you, but nothing else."

"I saw you at Nea Kameni with another

man. I know what you have come for: the Achilles bronze. The object is not Ashton's, you know. It is mine and has been in my possession for some time. So you may call off your dogs. If you want to negotiate, I will not do so with you. I will deal only with Demir." I paused, staring into his black eyes. "You may consider your options overnight. I will come to you in the morning." I stood up tall and tossed my head as I turned away from him and stalked out of the barn.

"Do you think that was wise?" Margaret asked. "What if the second man on Nea Kameni was Demir and what if he is here and has followed his minion to the house?"

"Adelphos, did anyone follow you?" I asked.

"No, Lady Kallista. I am certain of it."

"Well, then," I said, the confidence in my voice masking the deep concern gnawing at my insides.

"He could be dangerous," Margaret said.

"He certainly is, although I suspect it was Batur who shot at Philip and murdered poor Mr. Kallas, not Demir, who strikes me as the sort who leaves his dirty work to others." I turned to Adelphos. "The barn is not secure enough to risk leaving him there overnight. Take him to the storeroom. It has only one small window and a sturdy door that can be locked. He will have to remain tied up, and do please make sure he cannot free himself."

"I will see to it," Adelphos said.

"Thank you, Adelphos," I said. "You have done extremely well."

"Like Heracles." Pride beamed on his face and he gave us a little bow before heading back to the barn. Margaret and I watched him go.

"It is as if he stepped out of another millennium," she said. "How is it I never noticed until now? He is —"

"A perfect classical hero. Yes." We stood still, in silent appreciation, and then returned to the roof, where the gentlemen expressed their frustration at being able to see nothing of the scene but the roof of the barn.

"Well?" Jeremy demanded. "Tell us everything!"

"He would reveal nothing," I said, "but we ought not be deterred. Jeremy, I need you to ride with me to Oia, to the house where Adelphos found him. I want to search it."

"It is growing dark," Philip said. "Wait until morning."

"I will not risk it," I said. "I know this island like the back of my hand and will be

357

perfectly fine with Pyrois and a lantern."

I saw Jeremy hesitate, only slightly, but then he rallied himself. "So long as you can promise me that there will be no young ladies there trying to shoot me, we shall have no trouble at all."

"It is highly unlikely that a gentleman of your stature would be shot at by a young lady more than once in his life," I said, sorry the circumstances had brought to mind his former fiancée's attack on him. A glance in Margaret's direction told me she wanted to come to Oia as well, but I did not think this a good idea. I pulled her downstairs and into my room, where I changed into clothing suitable for a long ride.

"You aren't going to leave me here?" she asked. "Is it because I reacted so badly to poor Mr. Kallas's death?"

"Not at all," I said. "Philip, with his injury, is useless against attack. Furthermore, I am not altogether certain I trust him, and, hence, cannot be confident of Fritz's loyalties either. You and Adelphos will have to take charge of the house —"

"Along with Mrs. Katevatis." Margaret grinned. "She is an ally worth a hundred gentlemen."

"Yes," I said. "Colin won't be much longer, and I am almost tempted to wait for him and leave Jeremy with you, but I fear time could be of the essence."

"Is there any chance Demir could be in Oia?"

"No one reported to Adelphos having seen a third stranger. Batur and our unresponsive patient arrived on the island together. I would not be surprised if Demir, not having had any contact with one of his lackeys, reacts by either sending someone else or coming himself. I intend to sway the balance in a manner that will ensure he comes himself."

"Do not take any risks," she said. "Perhaps you should leave Jeremy and take Adelphos. He knows the island even better than you."

"A fair point," I said, "but he is also far more capable of managing our prisoner than Jeremy. Furthermore, I rather enjoy making the old boy do something useful. After all of this adventure he cannot possibly be anything but thoroughly distracted from the indignities heaped on him by Amity Wells." I tightened the laces of my sturdiest boots, ones I could rely on to be suitable not only for riding but for running, should it become necessary. Though we would have lanterns, I also put candles and a tin of matches in one of my jacket pockets and a small notebook and pencil in another.

Before going downstairs to meet Jeremy, whom I assumed would take less time than I to prepare, I went onto the balcony, straining my eyes for any sign of Colin returning along the cliff path. Seeing none, I knew I could delay no longer. I bade Margaret farewell and sent her back to the roof terrace to keep an eye on Philip and Fritz.

Jeremy was leaning elegantly against the wall next to the front door, dressed in tweeds and holding a riding crop. "Pith helmet, Em, really?" he asked. "There is no sun now and there won't be any until morning."

"I have seen too many people whacked over the head and am making an effort to avoid similar injuries," I said, taking him by the arm and pulling him to the back of the house. "Come now, we shall have to fetch the horses from the stable ourselves."

"Service falls utterly to pieces during your hideous investigations," he said. "Truly it is an indignity not to be borne. I shall have words with Adelphos when this is all over."

Philip
Santorini, 1897

No sooner had the volcanic landscape erupted with floral blooms than Reiner returned to the island, eager to check on his friend and prepare the site at Thera for another season of excavation. He had set off earlier than the rest of the archaeological party, wanting to see for himself that Philip had survived the winter unscathed by loneliness or a visit from Demir's henchmen.

"Truly, you are content here?" he asked. "I have brought you two more crates of books. I found everything you wanted except *Lady Audley's Secret*. It is not history, I assume?"

"No, far from it. Kallista read it on our wedding trip. It is the very worst sort of sensational novel, and tells a great deal about her character that she chose to bring it with her, do you not think?"

"I am afraid I cannot answer that, as I am not familiar with the story. Perhaps if I were to read it —"

"You would despise it." Philip laughed. "Kallista did not care what impression it made, she only wanted to read what she wanted to read. I gave her a first edition of *Pride and Prejudice* soon thereafter. I wonder which she preferred?"

"I spoke to someone in Fira today when I arrived. He said she is coming to the villa at the end of the month. She likes to spend time here in the spring. The servants are already preparing the house."

"How I wish I could see her, even from afar, but I cannot risk being spotted, not if I am to stay true to my oath to leave her undisturbed," Philip said.

"If we found out exactly when she was due to arrive, we could watch from a distance after the ship docked. The road to Fira is long and steep, and you know how slowly the donkeys move. We could find a spot on the cliff path and you could catch a glimpse of her through a spyglass without any danger of being spotted. We could be off and away before she reached town."

"It is tempting," Philip said. "So very tempting. I shall consider it."

If he were honest with himself, he knew even then there had never been anything to consider. He could not resist the tempta-

tion. And so, on the day she arrived —
Reiner, drinking with some locals in a taverna in Fira, had no trouble ascertaining
the date — they waited until a boat approached the dock far below where they
stood on the cliff path. Philip trained his
glass on it, and could see her, standing on
the deck, her fair hair spilling from its pins
and tumbling over her shoulders in the
wind, her hat in her hand, and her husband
close by her side. Philip watched as
Hargreaves helped her onto the dock and
then onto a waiting donkey. They were both
smiling and laughing, as if they had not a
care in the world.

An unexpected rage filled Philip. Kallista
he might be able to forgive, but Hargreaves?
That betrayal stung more, just as it had
when he observed the kiss at Berkeley
Square, and now the sight of his best friend
came near to inciting violence in him. He
lowered the spyglass and turned away from
the scene below.

"That is quite enough," he said to Reiner.
"This has very nearly cured me of my afflic-
tion. Come, let us to Thera. Our work
awaits!"

He may have put on a convincing show
for his friend — he very nearly persuaded
even himself he wanted nothing further to

do with that part of his life — but that all changed the day a party of visitors made the climb up Mesa Vouno to the ruins of the ancient city. He did not immediately recognize Kallista's laughter signaling her approach along the stone road skirting the edge of the cliff. It was another voice that drew his attention.

"Kallista!" a woman with a heavy French accent called. "You are going too fast. I will insist Monsieur Hargreaves scold you most severely if you do not slow down."

Kallista? Hargreaves? It had to be her, but how had this French woman known of his private nickname for his wife? Philip had been too reserved, even after their wedding, to use it to her face. Had Hargreaves commandeered it? Did he claim it to be an invention of his own?

"Colin would never scold me," came the reply in an angelic, silvery soprano. "He knows better than that."

Philip's heart raced. It was she, not that he had doubted it, and whatever happened, he could not let her see him. Very few tourists came to Thera, so few, in fact, that their presence did not irritate the archaeologists, the way they did at more popular sites, where their disruptive presence went beyond mere nuisance and frequently interfered with the excavations. On the rare occasions dilettantes made the trek up Mesa Vouno, Herr Professor Hiller von Gaertringen welcomed them, gave them a thorough tour of the site, and offered them the strong coffee he brewed in camp every day.

Philip edged his way along a wall that hid him from the main pavement leading through the ancient city to the stoa, where Reiner was supervising the reconstruction of a handful of Hellenistic columns. He pulled his friend aside, behind the safety of the wall, and explained to him, sotto voce, that he must disappear, quickly. Reiner offered to provide an excuse for his absence to their leader, and Philip climbed the narrow stairs that formed a street between rows of tightly packed buildings, or, rather, what remained of them. At the top, he walked along the ridge, crouching low, until he reached the end of the city nearest to the narrow path that led to the archaeologists' camp. Once certain Kallista and her party had made their way past him — aided by Reiner, who, as arranged, shouted a loud hail to them — Philip all but ran down the path, past the early Christian church, and back to camp, where he untied one of the donkeys and urged the surly beast down the mountainside.

He spent the rest of the day near Akrotiri on the red beach, whose sharp blood-colored cliffs offered him a background to match his anger. Much though he had longed to see Kallista, the manner of this near-encounter tormented him. Yet he could not go to her. He could not. He could not. Unless . . .

He began to formulate an idea.

20

The light had not yet altogether faded from the sky when Jeremy and I departed the villa for Oia. I knew the moon would rise soon, and while it would not be full — it was only just on the wane — its silver orb would provide ample light to supplement our lanterns. In fact, it shone so bright, especially when reflected by the island's white-washed buildings, we hardly needed the lanterns. The ride to Oia was so familiar to me I could have found my way blindfolded, and as we approached the cluster of its buildings, I urged Pyrois off the main road and up a narrow path.

Here the buildings were more scattered, with space between them, unlike in the more populated sections of the town. Soon Oia glowed below us in the moonlight, and we turned back onto a larger road, one that snaked past the town and north to the tip of the island.

"I suppose it would have been too much to ask for Batur to have taken a house on the outskirts of Oia on the side nearer to Imerovigli," Jeremy said.

"Are you tired?" I asked.

"Not at all," he replied. "A little anxious, though. Do try not to shoot me, whatever happens, will you? I still don't trust your aim entirely."

He was referring to the fact that I had shot his former fiancée when she had held him prisoner with the intent of murdering him. Despite any disparaging comments he might make about my skill (or lack thereof) with firearms, I had succeeded in stopping the malevolent woman with a single shot through the fleshy part of her shoulder and had, I still believe, handled the matter very neatly. She had suffered no serious injury, and I had been able to free Jeremy. "I have practiced since then, you know. I am quite confident I could shoot an apple off your head if the occasion called for it."

"Let us hope it never does."

"It should not be much further," I said. "Adelphos said to count six houses after that last turn we made. We are now at the fourth." We were well away from the lights of Oia. Insignificant though they were, the sight of them in the distance gave the illusion of assistance being fairly close at hand should we require it. I slowed Pyrois. These final houses stood along the top of the hill, giving their occupants a superb view of the island, Oia, and the caldera. More important, they were situated in a way that made approaching them by road impossible to do without being seen.

I dismounted between the fourth and fifth house and walked next to Pyrois. Behind the humble dwellings, I found a tree and tied my horse to it. Jeremy followed and did the same with his. We then continued on foot.

"There are no lights on," I whispered, once the house in question came into our field of vision. "We must proceed with extreme caution."

"You will let me go first," Jeremy said. I opened my mouth in protest, but the look on his face told me he would brook no argument. "Wait until I give you a sign that all is clear. I shall light my lantern when I am ready for you." He removed a pistol from his jacket and held it out, steady, in front of him as he started toward the house. I itched to follow, but knew taking insensible risks would not increase the odds of a successful mission, so I waited, moving closer to our target, but keeping a safe distance from him.

I had a pistol of my own, but hoped upon hope I would have no cause to use it.

I heard the creak of hinges and the groan of wood. He had opened the front door. Silence followed, but after what felt like an interval of ages, I saw the glow of his lantern. Moving as quietly as possible, I proceeded into the house. Once inside, I pulled the door shut behind me and latched it.

"I have checked every inch," he said. "There is no one here." He started bolting the shutters, giving us privacy and security for our search.

The small building contained only three rooms and was furnished very sparsely with old wooden pieces of rough quality. Batur had not traveled with much; I found his meager possessions in a bundle next to the bed. The only item of significance was a small bronze statue of Hermes identical to the one I had found in Philip's possession. I slipped it into my pocket. Feeling frustrated, I went through each room again, methodically searching every cupboard and every drawer.

"Nothing," Jeremy said. "I am afraid we have wasted our time."

"Not quite," I said. I went back to the bedroom and looked again at Batur's clothing. He had a spare robe with him, a grimy piece of cloth of indeterminate color — it might once have been white — that smelled strongly of goat. I shook it out and laid it flat on the dirt floor of the room. "There must be pockets somewhere." Its voluminous folds had revealed nothing when I searched it before, but that time I had left it hanging on a hook. Attacking it spread out proved easier and more effective. Sure enough, there were pockets. In one, I found a handkerchief in a state even worse than that of the robe. From the other, I pulled a grubby scrap of paper with the name of a hotel on the nearby island of Naxos written in Greek beneath what appeared to be its name in Turkish.

"This may be all we need," I said. "Come, let's go back to Oia. I want to send a telegram without delay. It must have been Demir whom I saw with Batur at Nea Kameni. He's convinced Philip has the bronze, and has sent his thugs to take care of ferreting it out, but doesn't want to go too far away so that he may get his hands on the object as quickly as possible. Naxos is the perfect location for him — a short boat ride away, but distant enough to keep himself from being implicated in whatever happens on Santorini."

"You can't be certain of any of that," Jeremy said.

"You have done very well tonight, my friend," I said, "and I am most grateful for your assistance. You are correct that I cannot be certain, but it is a reasonable deduction given what we know. If he is at this hotel in Naxos, he will reply to my message. If not, we have lost nothing. My instinct tells me this is the best next step."

"Far be it from me to side against a lady's instinct." He clasped my hand and we made our way through the night back to the horses. Once we were finished in Oia, the ride back to Imerovigli flashed by in an instant. When we reached the villa, I made Jeremy wait in the courtyard while I looked in on Batur.

"I am already in contact with Demir," I said, bluffing with a confidence that would have impressed even Colin. I dangled the statue of Hermes in front of our prisoner. "I expect his response at any time."

His black eyes flashed. "How did you —"

"Do you think you are the only one who knows about Hermes?" I was fishing now, having speculated the statue must have something to do with Demir and his nefarious associates. "You should have told me where he was when I asked. Now I have taken matters into my own hands. How long is the trip from Naxos to Santorini?" I gave him what I hoped was a menacing grin and stalked out of his makeshift cell, heading to the roof terrace, where I found the rest of my friends, as well as my husband, who had returned from his errand in Fira. I pulled him aside.

"Very well done," he said after I had related to him the events of the evening. "We must prepare ourselves. It is unlikely Demir will descend upon us in the night, but if he is on Naxos, and if he has the means to secure a ship — which we must assume he does — he could be here in the space of six hours or so. I suggest we get ourselves off the roof and do everything we can to secure the house."

"I do not think we should expect attack," I said. "I made it clear in my telegram I wanted a meeting and am willing to sell him the Achilles bronze. Furthermore, I told him I am staying in Fira."

"We know he and his thugs are capable of violence," Colin said. "It would be foolish not to prepare for the worst. You may have told him Fira, but it would not prove difficult for him to learn where we live."

"I did not give him my actual name," I said. "I signed the message 'Athena.'"

"Athena?"

"Yes," I said. "I considered 'Artemis,' but upon reflection came to the conclusion 'Athena' is preferable in this situation. I made sure to include for him enough details about both the bronze and Philip that he cannot doubt I am a force with which to be reckoned."

"You are a constant revelation, my dear. Regardless, it is best we take defensive action," he said, and kissed me before going downstairs and disappearing into the courtyard. The rest of us removed ourselves to a sitting room — one whose traditional Cycladic windows, small and high up on the wall, made us less vulnerable to invasion. I sent Jeremy and Fritz to close and lock all the shutters in the house, but did not let Philip out of my sight.

"You should let me help," he said.

"You are the one Demir wants," I said. "I will not make it easy for him to get to you. I may have failed you as a wife, but I will not fail you here."

Margaret emitted a sound akin to a low growl and rolled her eyes at me.

"Margaret —" I started.

"Your friend is correct to object," Philip said. "You did not fail me, Kallista. I suppose I had imagined you to be Penelope, and I your Odysseus."

"Penelope did not have every reason on earth to believe Odysseus was dead," I said. "She thought the gods were keeping them apart. Furthermore, I have no interest in weaving."

This made him smile. "My expectations — no, my hopes, as I expected nothing — were unreasonable, and I would not have you believe you failed me by not making them real. It is I who failed you, first by not returning to England sooner, and then by not immediately making my presence known once I was there. I have no one to blame for my loneliness but myself."

I met his eyes. "Philip, even if you had made your presence known in London, I already loved Colin. You might have legally got me back as your wife, but we would not have gone on to live the way you picture in your dreams. I would have been heartbroken and sad every day for the rest of my life. You speak of Penelope? I would have become like her. I would have learned how to weave. I might even have told you that when I finished my tapestry I would abandon my affection for Colin and give my heart to you. But like Penelope, I would have unwoven my day's work every night, and the tapestry would never be finished."

"I have loved you so very dearly for so long." Sadness filled his voice.

"You love the idea of me," I said. "That is all you have ever known. We were barely acquaintances when you proposed."

"I did know you then, and came to know you even better during the time — short though it was — of our marriage. Do you discount entirely our wedding trip? Why, I even decided to read *Lady Audley's Secret* after you spoke so highly of it. I have never had a passion for sensational fiction, but already knew I could trust your opinion on the subject."

"Did you read it?" I asked.

"I purchased a copy en route to Africa, but I am afraid I never got the chance to finish it."

"Regardless," I said, "we cannot claim there was a deep connection of souls between us. How could there have been? You were infatuated, I did not object. Like most couples of our class, we had no reason to believe we would bring each other happiness once your infatuation wore off. You are sad because you believe you have lost something, and perhaps you have, but it is not what you think. You mourn a dream, not something that was ever real. The Fates were never on our side. They brought Colin to me, and now all is as it should be."

I spoke with a passion so consuming I hardly noticed anything around me, but when I stopped I saw that Margaret had moved to sit closer to Philip, and had put her hand tentatively on his arm. She looked uncomfortable, but I am certain he appreciated the gesture. Behind them stood my husband, immobile, leaning against the doorjamb, looking like a perfect Praxiteles Apollo, his dark eyes sparkling.

"I do hate to break up this scene, but our patient has awakened," he said. "Furthermore" — he held up the two identical statues of Hermes, the one I had given him that I had found in Oia and the one I knew he must have taken from Philip's bag after I told him I had seen it there — "Ashton and I are long overdue for a little chat. Given what you told me about our prisoner's reaction to seeing this, it's clear they are significant to anyone dealing with Demir. It's time Ashton explains."

PHILIP
SANTORINI, 1899
A FEW WEEKS EARLIER

This year, when his colleagues had returned from their winters abroad, Philip felt not the slightest temptation to watch for Kallista's ship pulling into the port at Thera. This year would be different. This year, he would take matters into his own hands and no longer be a mere spectator in what ought to have been his life. All the years he had spent being patient would at last come to fruition. He knew she would be arriving soon. Last year, Reiner had done reconnaissance for him; this year Philip himself had shared drinks with the villagers in a taverna in Fira, and had learned from a boy employed to work in the stables at the villa that the English holidaymakers were expected at the end of the week.

He would not watch for her, but neither would he keep away, not any longer, and he felt confident his plan would work. When she saw him, apparently near death from an illness he could readily feign, the feelings she had long ago buried would begin to resurface, and her love for him would return. Hargreaves was bound to prove problematic, of that he had no doubt, and although he once would have believed himself incapable of harming his dearest friend, he found the idea not so unpalatable anymore. All that remained was to set his plan in motion.

On that count, the unexpected storm proved a bit of good fortune, as if Zeus himself had come to his aid, ready to return to him his lawful wife. The downpour had started suddenly, with a flash of lightning and a clap of thunder following without delay. The rain, coming hard and in sheets, blown in every direction by the strong winds high on the mountain, had bashed at the sides of his tent, but it did not blow over his cozy — if now damp — domicile. Nonetheless, it would be simple enough to convince his friends, once they believed him to be dangerously ill, to remove him from the wet and battered camp. When Kallista reached the villa tomorrow, she would find him already there, in desperate need of care. He was convinced the dramatic accounts — they would be dramatic — of his arrival during the storm would further endear him to her.

Reiner, drenched, stuck his head into Philip's tent.

"Friedrich invites us to come to his tent. It's the largest and the sturdiest of all of ours, and he has a fine bottle of schnapps. Bohn is finishing up some work and then will be along. You will come?"

"In a moment," Philip said. "I have some notes from today's work to complete first. I will join you shortly." Once the faint glow of Reiner's lantern had disappeared, Philip realized the time had come for action. Or inaction, such as it was. He would not go to the professor's tent, and when, after enough time had passed, his friends became worried, someone would come looking for him, only to find him on his cot, delirious. Heaven knows he had enough experience with illness to be able to feign delirium with skill.

First, though, he had to bide some time, and continued to work on his notes. No more than a quarter of an hour had gone by when someone again pulled back the flap of his tent. This time, Gerhard Bohn stuck his head in.

"Could you help me, Chapman? The storm has managed to blow hard enough to dislodge one of the stakes of my tent, and I fear the whole thing will be lost to the wind if I don't replace it. I don't have a hammer."

"I've got one," Philip said, removing from under his cot a wooden box of tools. "Will your lantern be enough?"

"May as well bring yours," Bohn said. "I can pull the tent back into place while you deal with the stake. Together we can make short work of it."

And they would have, except that when they reached the tent, they could not locate the missing stake, and were forced to search for it, their lanterns barely illuminating the rain-filled darkness. Philip, moving away from the camp, thought he caught a glimpse of something shiny, and headed for it. Before he could reach it, he lost his balance when he stepped on a slick rock and careened forward. He had not realized how close he was standing to the edge of the plateau on which they had set their camp, and he cried out as he tried to break his momentum, grabbing for anything that might give him purchase.

Somehow, Bohn had heard his call, and in the flash of an instant, he reached his fallen colleague. Simultaneously, Philip had started to roll onto his side, an act that enabled him, in one swift movement, to come to his feet. But the force of motion he mustered in order to stand knocked over Bohn, whom he could not see in the dark, and sent his rescuer tumbling down the side of the hill.

"Bohn!" Philip scrambled to catch him, but failed. Keeping low to the ground so as not to fall again himself, he made his way down the steep slope, until he came upon his friend. He held his lantern to reveal a grisly scene: Bohn was lying on his back, a bloody gash at the base of his skull. He was unresponsive, but breathing, though only shallowly. Not knowing what else to do, Philip picked him up and somehow got him back to the top of the hill. He set him down gently, then peeled off his jacket and put it over the injured man in a vain attempt to insulate him from the weather, and rushed to the professor's tent.

His head throbbed. Now he had a legitimate excuse to go to the villa. Bohn needed medical attention and to be somewhere clean and dry, and although the villagers in Kamari would gladly offer their assistance, they would not be able to provide what his friend needed. There was an English-speaking doctor in Oia, at the northern tip of the island. He would take Bohn to the villa and then go for the physician on one of the horses he knew Hargreaves kept in the stables. He had never felt so sick in his life, convinced his scheme had somehow brought about his friend's injury.

Not wanting to risk further injuring Bohn, who remained unconscious, he, Reiner, and the professor carried him, balancing him carefully between the three of them, down the slick cobbled road. When they reached the bottom, Reiner ran to the village, rousing one of their workers to bring a wagon to the road. Philip was hardly aware of the trip across the island to Imerovigli, only feeling alive again when they clattered into the courtyard behind the house. He leapt from the wagon and banged on the back door, shouting.

A maid, one of the local girls, opened it, looking annoyed at being disturbed. He started to speak, but she was not listening. She raised her lantern and murmured what sounded like a desperate prayer.

"Can it really be you?" she asked. "Lord Ashton?"

21

Philip's shoulders slumped when he saw the statues of Hermes my husband was holding. "I should have been more forthright with you," he said.

"This is not the time for apologies and regrets," Colin said. "I need you to tell me everything you can about Demir. Emily, Margaret, will you leave us, please?"

"Why don't we stay —" I started.

"No, Kallista," Philip said. "Leave us be. It is time for Hargreaves and me to face each other."

I would have given nearly anything to hear the conversation between them, but could hardly deny them privacy. Margaret and I went to see our patient, who was, as Colin had said, awake, but not coherent. Unable to extract any useful information from him, we found Jeremy in the sitting room. He and Fritz had alerted Mrs. Katevatis to the situation, and she insisted on going to the village to summon assistance. Not wanting her to go on her own, Fritz had accompanied her, as Adelphos insisted on guarding our prisoner. Barely an hour had passed before they returned, accompanied by every able-bodied man in the village, armed with old rifles, sticks, and a few pitchforks.

By this time Colin and Philip, both looking grim, had rejoined us, and Colin set about stationing the villagers around the perimeter of the house, a task not so easy, as in Santorini buildings are constructed almost one on top of the other. The walls on the sides of the villa abutted directly against those of our neighbors, and a person of malicious intent could climb from rooftop to rooftop until he reached ours. Fortunately, we had the manpower to place someone at the door of each house and on each roof. In front of us stood only the cliff path and the sheer drop to the caldera, and behind us, because Philip had purchased enough land to construct the barn and courtyard, there were no houses near enough to offer our enemies a good vantage point for attack.

Despite our best efforts, Margaret and I did not manage to convince the gentlemen that we, too, ought to be armed and standing guard. Instead, we had no choice but to reluctantly accept a forced retreat into an interior room, where we sat, waiting.

"Have you ever experienced something more tedious?" I asked.

"I had great hopes for the experience of being pursued by a maniac," Margaret said, sighing. "One expects it would be exciting, yet I have never been more bored in my life."

"He might not be a maniac, just a vicious criminal without remorse," I said. "But I do agree with you about our current plight — it can induce nothing save ennui. Colin tells me his work is often like this: high stakes, but seemingly endless time in a prolonged state of expectancy."

Mrs. Katevatis entered the room, bringing cups of steaming mountain tea, and sat with us. "Adelphos is in the courtyard," she reported. "Nico is on the roof. The men argued about what to do with the viscount, but in the end agreed to allow him to assist them, as what Nico called a 'fallback.' He is in the drawing room."

"It would be too risky to let him outside, given he is Demir's target," I said. "Not to mention he is injured and unlikely to be much use in a fight."

"He was not happy about it," Mrs. Katevatis said, "but his friend the German said many harsh words to him about putting the ladies in danger, and then the viscount relented."

We passed the entire night in that small room without any sign of disturbance. Once the sun had risen, Colin reorganized our forces, sending most of them back home to sleep, as we would need them again when darkness fell; in daylight, it would be easy enough for a handful of observers to raise the alarm if need be. We breakfasted inside rather than on the terrace, and so began a most wearisome day.

"You ought to nap," I said to my husband, who had come inside to gulp down a dish of tangy yogurt, as an accompaniment to a full English breakfast. No matter where we were in the world, he always managed to have something that reminded him of home. "You have been up all night."

"I do not require rest when I am working. I can go days without it when necessary. But you and Margaret must not have slept well," he said, "her on a chair and you wrapped in blankets on the floor. Look at how she is already yawning."

"It was an adventure," Margaret said. "Emily and I both felt strongly that Mrs. Katevatis ought to have the settee."

"That was good of you," he said.

"A telegram has come," Mrs. Katevatis

said, entering the room and handing the envelope to me. I ripped it open and read it through.

"Demir will arrive tomorrow morning and will be waiting for me in the taverna in Fira at noon."

"Well done, my dear," Colin said.

"It was only just sent from Naxos," I said, studying it, "but we cannot assume that means Demir is still there."

"Quite right. There are very few strangers on this island and it would be easy enough for him to locate us, just as it was easy for us to locate him on Naxos. Furthermore, everyone knows the archaeologists came to us after the attack. I am afraid we must resume our defensive posture," he said, blotting his mouth with a napkin before kissing me and heading back up to the roof, from whence he could watch for any approaching marauders.

Margaret and I returned with little joy to the small room that had begun to feel like a prison, where we both tried to read. Our minds were too unsettled to make sense of words on paper. Midway through the afternoon, we visited our patient, who was sleeping soundly and still had not uttered a single intelligible word in the brief moments he spent awake. Adelphos, who, like my husband, refused to nap, was dividing his time between patient and prisoner, keeping a close eye on both.

Back inside, we stopped in the kitchen when Mrs. Katevatis, who had started to prepare dinner, called, urging us to help her. "It is no good for a lady to know how to cook nothing," she said. "You are too competent to be useless, so I will show you." Soon she had us with our sleeves up, seasoning feta for tyropita, then rolling out the thin phyllo dough, and finally supervising us as we formed the delicate cheese pies. Our first several efforts were disastrous, as we kept tearing the fragile dough, but eventually we met with success.

"They are not pretty, perhaps," I said, brushing melted butter on the triangular tops of the pastry before we slid them into the hot oven, "but they will taste good."

"They are an absolute scandal," Margaret said. "Mine especially. Yours at least aspire to be triangles. Mine gave up altogether." The pan in front of her was covered with an assortment of shapes, most a variety of odd-looking lumps without any of the sides required by a triangle.

Mrs. Katevatis shook her head. "This is very bad, Mrs. Michaels," she said. "You shall try again tomorrow. I will not permit you to leave the island until you can prepare these well. Then you can go back to England and make them for your husband."

"You know, Mrs. Katevatis, Mr. Michaels might well enjoy that. May I make another batch now?"

This request was immediately denied, with a lack of dough cited as the reason, but I suspected Mrs. Katevatis could take only so much of our incompetence at a time, and I pulled Margaret back into the main part of the house before she could protest. We were both covered with flour and in dire need of baths. When the time for dinner came, we again ate inside, and the gentlemen were vastly amused by our culinary efforts.

"It is good to cook," Fritz said. "My mother is excellent in the kitchen and rarely allows the servants to prepare meals. I am impressed you ladies have made the effort when so few of your peers are willing to even try."

I had insisted Colin take a break for nourishment, and he reluctantly agreed we might all dine together while one set of villagers stood guard outside the house, but insisted he would return to his post as soon as we had finished. The other gentlemen would do the same.

"After I meet with Demir tomorrow, I

propose we return to the mainland as soon as possible," I said.

"I agree," Margaret said. "Regardless of what happens when you see him, we know he is not a man to be trusted, and we cannot remain holed up here indefinitely. He might follow us to Athens, but we would be in a much stronger position there."

Colin nodded. "It is a worthy proposition," he said. "I will go to Fira in the morning and arrange for a boat."

As had become his habit, Philip helped Mrs. Katevatis bring our coffee and baklava to the drawing room after dinner. Try though he might, she resisted all of his efforts to win over her goodwill. It was not, she had explained to me, that she found him unpleasant, but she believed he considered himself the master of the house, when that role by rights belonged to Colin — or Nico, as she called him, her voice warming whenever she uttered the name. Tonight, given his injury, Philip could not carry the heavy coffee tray as he normally did, and was instead relegated to being baklava-bearer.

I filled all of the cups with coffee, taking only a small amount for myself as I did not much care for it, while Margaret placed pieces of rich walnut baklava on plates. The sparse conversation as we sat in the sitting room reflected everyone's somber mood. Jeremy barely picked at his pastry, and Colin would not stop pacing. I poured him a second cup of coffee and pressed it into his hands.

"You will need this if you mean to stay up all night," I said. He accepted it with a grunt.

Philip, too, kept rising to his feet, starting for the door whenever he thought he heard a sound. Only Fritz, cool and imperious, polished off his baklava and his coffee without distraction.

"Are you ladies ready to retire?" Colin asked. "You will be safe in your bedrooms tonight. I have had no reports of anyone matching Demir's description from my lookouts on the island. That does not mean he is not here, but I am confident we have matters well in hand. I would, however, implore you to keep your shutters closed and locked."

We did as he instructed, but the lack of air flowing through my room stifled me. I expected to have difficulty sleeping, between the hot, heavy stillness and my general unease at our situation, but my lids grew heavy quickly, and I fell fast asleep before I had a chance to close my volume of Sophocles and blow out the lamp next to my bed.

When I awoke the next morning it had already passed nine o'clock. The lamp had burned itself out, and my Sophocles was crumpled beneath me on the mattress. Ordinarily I am immediately alert upon waking, but today even the act of getting out of bed took considerable effort. The anticipation of my meeting with Demir should have caused me to rise before the sun, and I ought to have been filled with impatient energy the moment I opened my eyes. I cracked the door to my room, expecting to find the mountain tea Mrs. Katevatis always left for me, but it was not there. Something was amiss. I dressed as quickly as possible and went downstairs without delay.

PHILIP
SANTORINI
A FEW WEEKS AGO

The storm was still pummeling the island as the maid who answered the door helped the three archaeologists get Bohn into the house. A second servant girl, coming at the sound of commotion, nearly fainted when she saw him. Once they had put him on a bed, Philip asked the housekeeper, a woman who had never worked for him when he had owned the villa, if he might borrow one of Lady Emily's horses.

"I understand she keeps several on the island," he said. "They will be much faster than our donkeys, and I must get to Oia as quickly as possible to fetch the doctor."

"Of course," she said. "I am rather confused about your identity, though, sir. How can you be Lord Ashton? We all know him to have died years ago. Yet —"

"Yet both of the maids recognized me," Philip said. "I will be more than happy to explain when I return, but right now I am afraid I must be on my way."

"I recognize you as well, even if I did not work for you. Go. May God be with you."

With the assistance of a stable boy, Philip saddled one of the horses and raced toward Oia, as quickly as the foul weather would allow. He kept to the inland road, knowing the cliff path to be dangerous during a storm. By the time he reached the doctor's house — the men in the taverna directed him — he was soaked, mud-splattered, and exhausted. Or, he observed, in precisely the same condition as when he had arrived at the villa.

In the space of only a few moments, Dr. Liakos had his horse ready, and they thundered back to Imerovigli. The housekeeper opened the door and ushered them in, but winced when the doctor asked to see the patient.

"I am most very sorry, Lord Ashton," she said. "Your friend is dead."

22

When I got downstairs, Mrs. Katevatis apologized for not having my tea ready. She herself had risen only half an hour before and assured me that she had not slept so late in the past fifty years.

"We are all exhausted after the night before last," I said, not wanting to alarm her until absolutely necessary. "Do not trouble yourself about it. Perhaps we should put some coffee on. Even I must admit tea may not be strong enough this morning."

Philip was not at his post in the drawing room. I opened the front door and saw my husband leaning against the wall of the house, half asleep.

"You need coffee at once," I said. "Margaret is not yet awake and I have only just risen from bed. Everyone slept too much and too soundly."

"Coffee would be most welcome," he said. "I am pleased you are well despite my having failed at my duties last night. I could hardly keep my eyes open." His lids hung heavy over his red-rimmed orbs. It was not like him to appear so sleepy.

"I suspect we've all been drugged. Have you seen Philip this morning?" I asked. "He is not in the drawing room."

He was off before I could finish my sentence, and I followed close on his heels. Fritz and Jeremy were asleep on the roof, slumped in chairs. A quick look into the Etruscan room showed it to be empty, and Philip was nowhere to be found. Having had little or no rest the night before last, we were all vulnerable. Finding the laudanum missing from our medical kit confirmed what I suspected: Philip had used it to force us all into unwelcome slumber. He had not forgot the villagers standing guard, either, as a quick interrogation revealed he had given them several bottles of ouzo to help keep their spirits up during their vigil. They all admitted to having fallen asleep.

"He has not gone to Fira," Colin said after returning from a quick ride into town, "but he did take one of the donkeys."

"He must have gone back to the excavations," I said. "But why?"

"Probably to draw out Demir," Colin said. "I will go at once."

"I am coming with you."

"No, Emily."

"I shall brook no argument," I said. "If there is any sign of danger I shall turn around, but I will not stay behind."

He nodded. "Is the bronze still safe?"

"I have it tucked away between the pages of my *Iliad*," I said, "and I gave the book to Margaret, who will not let it out of her hands."

While Adelphos saddled the horses, Colin and I questioned our prisoner, but Batur would give up no information. In the end my husband felt further interrogation would be a waste of our time. So, together as equal partners, we mounted Pyrois and Aethon and set off for Ancient Thera. Colin had left Jeremy and Fritz in charge of the house, and implored Adelphos to continue to keep a close eye on Batur and the semi-conscious patient in our servants' quarters.

We rode in companionable silence, the sun approaching its midday peak in the bright blue sky. As we came to the turnoff for Kamari, my heart broke for the newly widowed young woman in the village, but this was not the time to stop and offer condolences.

"Did Philip convince you of the veracity of his story after you accused him of lying about his identity?" I asked as our path started to snake up the mountain. "Do you now believe he is who he says?"

"I was taken aback by what he knew about that" — he cleared his throat — "that evening when I ventured to the Sacher Hotel in search of torte, but I still find it inconceivable I would have told him the story, given the implications, in any circumstances. I cannot prove it, however. At the moment, I am not convinced it matters one way or the other. What about you?"

"Like you, I am not convinced it matters one way or the other."

We had reached another of the turns on the steep road, and Colin tugged on Aethon's reins. I closed my eyes, trusting Pyrois, and we continued along the vertigo-inducing ancient path. When we reached the archaeologists' camp, there was a donkey — I recognized it from its saddle blanket as the one Philip had ridden to the villa — and a horse I had not seen before tied to a post. A cold chill ran down my back as we fastened our steeds.

"Do any of the villagers have a horse?" I asked.

"I don't recall seeing one," Colin said.

"Demir is here," I said. "I am certain of it."

"If he is, we are prepared to face him. He

will not harm us so long as he does not have the bronze."

"He might harm Philip, though," I said.

"I am afraid Philip would have no one to blame but himself," Colin said. He took my hand and we started to hike the remaining way to the ruins. After passing the early Christian church on the mountaintop just outside the ancient city, we paused to survey the scene before us, but detected no sign of anyone.

"Ashton!" Colin called. "Are you here?"

There was no reply.

I started at every sound, imagined and real, terrified at what we might find. Colin gripped my hand tighter as we made our way along the marble pavement of the ancient road.

"I suggest we trace the perimeter of the city," he said. "We will have a better view at the top and can then decide how to proceed. They have to be here somewhere." He called out for Philip again, as did I, but still no response came. Then, as we approached the end of the plateau, where the road turned to the west, near the spot where so recently we had picnicked, we saw them.

Philip was standing near a group of sanctuaries that included carvings of Egyptian gods, his back to us, his hands raised in fists, his lean body blocking only part of our view of the tall, sinewy man opposite him. They ran at each other, neither showing any sign of being aware of our presence, and hit each other with a spectacular crash. I screamed as they both fell to the ground, not far from the edge of the ridge, and continued to shout as I moved toward them, begging them to stop.

They paid no heed, if they even heard me, so I moved closer and closer until Colin began shouting at me to stop. I ignored him and continued to press forward, determined to stop the fight, no matter what it took.

PHILIP
SANTORINI
THAT MORNING

He had waited until he was certain the laudanum had taken effect and they were all sleeping. He went to the barn and saddled the donkey he had ridden to the house, not wanting to impose on his hosts by commandeering one of their horses. He rode first to Fira, where he banged on the door of the sleeping man who operated the telegraph, sent an urgent cable to Naxos, and insisted on waiting until he received a reply. Fortunately for the telegraph man, it came with little delay. As Philip had expected, Demir had not planned to leave Naxos until morning, and now he agreed to an earlier departure so he might see Philip before meeting with Kallista in Fira.

That settled, and the telegraph man paid an exorbitant sum, Philip weighed his options. He did not want to return to the house and risk being discovered leaving early in the morning; the laudanum's effects might not last that long. So instead, he made his way back to Ancient Thera, his donkey plodding slowly along the moonlit trail, and spent the remaining hours of the night back in his tent. He slept very little, and had already prepared himself to meet his nemesis by the time the first rays of the sun peeked above the horizon.

He had decided his best option was to seek the highest ground possible in order to watch the man's approach. He climbed up the path to the ruins, but stopped before he reached the main section, choosing instead to set up watch just beyond the Christian church, from where he had a clear view of the road up Mesa Vouno. Demir's telegram had said he would be there at ten o'clock, but Philip expected him to be early, and on this count, he was correct. Before nine, Philip saw a lone figure on horseback approaching the road, and he followed its progress up the side of the mountain.

The man stopped in the camp, and called out. Philip, unwilling to come down to his adversary, replied from above.

"You shall have to come up here, Hakan," he called.

23

I ran in the direction of the two men, who were pounding each other with blows that turned my stomach with every sickening thud, and I stopped only when I saw how close they were to the edge of the ridge. "Please!" I cried, feeling Colin come up from behind, grabbing me and restraining me from going any nearer to them. "You must stop!" I called again, so loudly that my voice started to break. The sound must have caught Philip's attention, for he turned his head in my direction, giving his enemy the chance to land a swift punch to his face. I struggled against Colin's strong arms — futilely, as he was not about to let me go — realizing only too late the catastrophic error of my decision to yell that final time. I had given his enemy the chance to topple Philip.

"You should never have taken what was not yours, Chapman," said the man. I recognized him as the tall man I had seen on Nea Kameni. Philip was swaying dangerously on his feet, trying to shake off the effect of the blow, which had left him visibly dazed. In a flash, Colin dropped his hold on me as the Turk lunged at his adversary, sending Philip sprawling backward over the ridge. In that same instant, Colin pulled out a pistol and fired it. The man, who had started in my direction, crumpled to the ground.

I rushed to the edge of the cliff and looked over. Philip's fall had been stopped by a large rock. His body contorted grotesquely, but his eyes were open, and he looked at me, pleading. Trembling and moving with extreme care, I slowly made my way to him, crouching down low to the ground, not wanting to risk taking a fall of my own. By the time I reached his side, his breathing was shallow and rough.

"I should never have troubled you," he said.

"Quiet," I said, pushing his sandy hair back from his forehead. "None of that matters now." Blood spattered his lips as he started to cough. "You must focus on breathing and taking care not to move. Colin will go for help, and before you know it you'll be on your way to recovery." The words sounded inane, and I knew them to be a lie, but I did not know what else to say.

"You don't understand, Kallista," he said. "I had no right. I — I am not —"

"I know," I said. "You are not he. I knew yesterday when you said you hadn't read *Lady Audley's Secret*. Nothing pleased me more on my wedding trip than learning Philip had read it even before I had. And yet, even after realizing you are an impostor, I still chose to come after you today, because I want to help you. I will hold your hand while you tell me your story, and you will see everything is going to be fine." I had heard Colin approaching from behind and looked back at him.

"The man is injured, but not so severely that I can't question him," he said. "I aimed carefully to make sure he would be able to stand up to interrogation. I have secured him, but should go back and get him to talk. I will not be out of sight. Call for me if you require any assistance."

I blinked back tears. "Mr. Chapman is telling me a story." The look in my husband's eyes told me that, like me, he knew the poor man was not long for the world. Nothing mattered now other than making him as comfortable as possible through these last minutes. "Though if there's any champagne to be had . . . I understand our adversary is finished. Did you hear that, Mr. Chapman? You need not worry any longer. You are safe." Colin slipped off to return to the man he had captured.

"I am most grateful. But you should leave me be," he said. "I am not worthy of —"

"I shall be the judge of that," I said. "Now tell me, friend, how all this came to be."

"I knew Philip quite well," he said. "I worked in an antiquities store in London that he frequented, and over the years we came to be close. We shared a passion for Greece and Homer, and he respected my opinions and analysis. I read classics at Oxford, you see." He paused to cough. "I had distinguished myself at Harrow. My mother always insisted I receive a top-notch education and my father ran a shop successful enough to ensure I could get one."

"So you and Philip were intellectual equals and enjoyed a lively discussion," I said. "I can see why you were friends."

"I thought we were friends, Kallista — but I should not call you that any longer, Lady Emily."

"You may call me Kallista." His hair had tumbled back over his brow. I brushed it away from his eyes.

"We spent a great deal of time together when he was in London. One day he came into the shop and we got embroiled in a discussion about Alexander the Great and Achilles —" He coughed again.

"A favorite topic of his," I said.

"Quite. It was time for me to close up, and he suggested we go to the pub for a pint so we might continue our conversation. From that day on, we met there regularly when he was in town. In general, the only topic we addressed was classics. He told me everything about how he came to love the subject, from his boyhood when his grandfather gave him a copy of *The Iliad* to his approach to learning Greek and the topics of his essays at Cambridge. One day, he was sitting at our usual table, beaming, and I asked him what had caused this joy — I expected it to be a frieze, at least — and he surprised me by saying he had fallen in love. He told me all about you, down to the details of what you were wearing and whom you'd spurned that night at Lady Elliott's."

"How very indiscreet," I said.

"It was not that way, madam, truly. He waxed enthusiastic about you like nothing I'd ever seen. I promise, he did adore you, no matter what you think about infatuation and the rest."

"I believe you," I said.

"As I said, I considered him a friend. I

even sent the two of you a wedding gift — a small sculpture of Hera, goddess of marriage."

"I remember the piece," I said. "Philip told me it came from an old friend. I have it in my gallery in our country house."

"He told me of his plan to give a photograph of you to the artist Renoir and have him paint a portrait from it. He showed me the ivory brooch he purchased for you as a wedding gift," he said. "He thought its beauty to be as delicate as yours. I agreed, which is why I chose a similar one to give you here on Santorini. I do hope you will keep it, although I have no rights to ask."

"Of course I will keep it."

"At hearing the news of my friend's death, I was terribly grieved. When the time was appropriate, I came to Berkeley Square to see you — to make a call of condolence. The butler brought me inside, but your mother refused to let me see you. An education alone does not a gentleman make, and I suppose she saw me for the shopkeeper I was."

"She is a dreadful woman," I said. "You ought not to have taken it personally."

"I did not, I assure you," he said. "I might have forgot about it altogether had I not seen you, later, in the British Museum,

409

engaged in a lively conversation with the Keeper of Greek and Roman antiquities. I confess I fell in love with you on the spot. You made such intelligent observations about the differences between Praxiteles and Polycleitus, stating in no uncertain terms that Praxiteles' wit made Polycleitus' sculptures look more like academic studies than passionate works of art. How could one not fall in love?"

"Indeed," Colin said, returning from his post. "Emily is constantly drawing in unsuspecting classicists. It is one of her most charming characteristics."

"I am most sorry, Hargreaves. I have behaved abominably toward you."

"Think nothing of it, old boy." Colin said. "Might I have a quick word, Emily?" He pulled me a few feet away and spoke in the barest whisper. "The man is not Demir, but admits that he killed Kallas. If he is not Demir —"

"Demir could be nearby and we are in danger," I said. "I cannot leave him alone here to die."

He looked at me, all seriousness, and I half expected him to argue, but he did not. "Very well," Colin said. "I shall do my best to keep watch for any unexpected visitors."

"Your husband is a very good man," Mr.

Chapman said after Colin had stepped away.

"Yes," I said. "But now you must take a little water." He could not raise his head, so I tipped my canteen to his lips.

"I did love you in that first moment, I confess," he said, "but I had no intention of declaring myself to you. Your mother had made it clear my attentions would not be welcome. But I kept coming across you in the museum — you spoke to me once. I was with one of the keepers. He introduced us and we discussed red figure vases."

"I am sorry I do not remember."

"There was no reason you should, particularly as I wore a beard then and looked quite different," he said. "Regardless, our conversation was enormously significant to me, because during it I realized that my soul longed for you, and I believed that we could be the sort of couple Shakespeare made immortal."

"Things didn't turn out well for most of his couples," I said.

"You are right, of course, but I felt certain we were intended for each other. At the same time, I knew I could not court you in any ordinary fashion. Earls' daughters don't marry shopkeepers, and what could I do to correct that injustice?"

I assumed the question to be rhetorical.

"I decided to take matters into my own hands. If I could not win your affection openly, I would try another approach. I cannot take credit for the initial inspiration. It came, one day, most unexpectedly, when I had gone back to Oxford to visit the Ashmolean Museum. While there, a gentleman I did not recognize approached me, calling me *Ashton.* Confused, I told him my name, and he apologized, saying I looked so much like someone he had known at Cambridge that he had assumed me to be him."

"And the man he thought you were was Philip," I said.

"Yes. We laughed about it, reminisced about him briefly, and went our separate ways. Almost immediately the seed of an idea took hold in me. I had all the time in the world before me, and I knew that with great care and patience, I would be able to realize my dreams. Twice before, when Lord Ashton was still alive, people who knew us both commented on how striking it was that our eyes were identical shades of blue."

"But Fritz — and his story of meeting you in Africa — he is nothing more than your accomplice?"

"No." He coughed again. "I am glad I will not be alive to see his reaction to my duplicity. I had managed to acquire a rather tidy sum of money from my shop over the years, and that, combined with what I acquired from selling it, enabled me to embark on my plan. First, I traveled to Africa, where I hunted with his favorite guide — I knew I would need firsthand experience in stalking big game if I were to convince anyone I was Ashton — and spent nearly a year there. I got the scar your husband recognized there, after convincing a group of Masai guides to take me on a lion hunt. I was so terrified standing there, as we encircled the thicket into which they had driven the beast, that I dropped my spear on my leg, injuring myself, not realizing how fortuitous the accident would prove. I knew Ashton had taken part in a lion hunt that resulted in him getting a scar, but I could never have anticipated being saved from exposure by having one of my own. I only regret that mine came from cowardice, unlike Ashton's."

His breath was becoming more ragged. "I did fall ill in Africa, though not seriously, and after I had more or less recovered, I went in search of a group of travelers whom I could convince to bring me to Cairo. My emaciated appearance brought veracity to my story."

"So Fritz knows nothing of this?" I asked,

pulling a handkerchief from my pocket. I moistened it with water from my canteen and wiped the dust and blood from his face.

"No. We had become close during our travels, sharing as we do an interest in Greece. From the first day we met on the Dark Continent, he has proven his sincere friendship time and time again. He even insisted I go with him to Munich, where I stayed in his parents' house. You know most of the story from there. Everything I told you about seeing you with Hargreaves at Berkeley Square and the rest was true. Reiner never suspected me to be anyone but Ashton, because I have lived as him for all these years."

"The story you told me — surely Philip was not so indiscreet as to have discussed our wedding night?"

"No, not at all," he said. "You told me the story, Kallista. All I did was respond accordingly and pause long enough for you to fill in the details. I knew a gentleman would have had port after dinner. I apologize for having prompted you to reveal something so intimate."

"What could you have hoped to achieve by coming to me here?" I asked. "You knew I had married again."

"It was my dearest wish that you might

414

come to love me. Or rather, to reignite the love I firmly believed you had felt for your first husband. I removed myself from the villa deliberately, hoping my gentlemanly offer of keeping away would impress you, that you would see my nobility and start to think you ought to give me another chance. If that failed, I was prepared to pursue my legal options. Your second marriage would have been declared invalid if Ashton were still alive."

I wanted to shout recriminations at him, but the gray pallor of his skin and the bluish tint beginning to color his lips changed my mind. "I am here with you now, on Santorini, just as you always wished."

"Yes." He was struggling to keep his eyes open.

"Would you do me one kindness?" I asked. "Would you tell me your name? I do not want to know you, a man of such devotion and conviction, only by your nom de guerre."

"Alastair Jones," he said.

"Thank you." I stroked his forehead. "Would you like some more water?"

"No — I don't think I could swallow it. But there is more I have to tell you." He reached for my hand. His skin felt cold as he recounted several more things that had transpired in the course of his masquerade. That done, he turned to the subject of the man who had died the night the archaeologists arrived at the villa. "You must know I did not mean Bohn to be harmed in any of this. It is my fault he fell, though. He was trying to save me. I brought on all this horror. He came into my tent the very night I was planning to go to the villa. I was going to feign illness."

"He uncovered your plan?" I asked.

"No, nothing of the sort. He needed my help with his tent and in the course of trying to assist him, I tripped and fell. I went over the edge near our camp, and when he tried to help me, he fell, but further and with greater force. It was my fault. My fault."

"We will have no more of that," I said. "It does not matter now."

"Will you ever be able to forgive me?" His voice was growing weaker.

"I already have," I said, and kissed him on the forehead. He continued to give me the details of his subterfuge as long as he was physically able.

"He who dies in youth and vigor dies the best," he said, struggling to form the words as he quoted Homer's description of the death of the noble Hector. Tears smarted in

my eyes.

They were his last words. He was not unconscious, and opened his eyes intermittently, but he could no longer speak. I sat with him, holding his hand as his breathing grew increasingly ragged, and I felt a deep sadness when at last it stopped. I choked back a sob, closed his eyes, and pulled myself to my feet. Colin, who had been no more than thirty feet away the entire time, came to me.

"It is over?" he asked. I nodded. He looked at Mr. Jones's body and sighed. "I am more sorry for him than I would have expected. I do hate to rush you, but —"

"Demir will be expecting me in Fira," I said. "We can't just leave him here."

Colin fetched blankets from the camp, wrapped Mr. Jones in them, and then carried him into the stoa of the ancient city. "We cannot bring him any further now," he said. "I will ask the men in the village to send someone up for him and the injured Turk. They will be able to keep him secure until the authorities arrive. I am afraid we will have to rush to make it to Fira in time for your appointment. Would you like me to meet Demir in your place?"

"No," I said. "I will need you there, of course, but I would not dream of missing the opportunity to bring that horrible man to justice."

24

We rode hard and reached Fira in time to send a message to the others at the villa, telling them not to worry and to remain where they were. We gathered reinforcements in the form of a select handful of persons whom Colin had arranged to have present and took our places at the taverna, which was empty except for the members of our group, who were scattered casually amongst the tables. I chose a seat on the terrace, in a chair whose back was placed against the railing, and ordered mountain tea. Colin, next to me, consumed cup after cup of thick Greek coffee. I watched the others, whom my husband had coached to behave as if they did not know us, as we all waited. An hour later than our appointed time, a tall man approached, with the coloring of a Turk and the dapper elegance of an English gentleman. His pale linen suit, finely tailored, and his winning smile caught me off guard. There was no hint of menace in his appearance, and had I ever subscribed to the theories of physiognomy, I would have abandoned them on the spot.

He bowed to me as he approached and then took my hand and kissed it. "You are an unexpected Athena," he said. "I thought the goddess would be Greek."

"It is my nom de guerre," I said. "Much as I imagine Demir is yours."

"No, no," he said. "May I sit?" I nodded and he took the chair across from me — I had deliberately left for him the one with the best view — and perpendicular to Colin. "Is this your henchman?"

"No, I am her husband," Colin said. "I have a funny habit of not liking her to engage in transactions without me present. Your colleagues are not always polite. I do hope I can expect better from you."

"I apologize on their behalf," he said. "To answer your question, yes, Demir is my name. I have no reason to hide it. I am a man of honor who seeks only to connect people with objects they cannot find anywhere else."

Colin betrayed not the slightest emotion through all this, and I greatly admired his skillful subterfuge. I was having a difficult time sitting calmly instead of rising to my feet and giving a very stern lecture on the evils of murder and antiquities trading.

"Yes, yes," Colin said. "I see now there is no need for me to be here. Do you mind, darling? I might just go for a smoke and see if I can find a newspaper anywhere in this town."

"Of course," I said. We had discussed every contingency of our plan in advance. He would never be more than a few steps away, and we hoped Demir would speak more freely to me alone. Men, I have found, generally underestimate ladies.

"Your husband is a very trusting man," Demir said.

"That he is," I said, smiling. "He knows I prefer tending to business on my own, yet insists on accompanying me until, as he likes to say, he gets a handle on things. You are interested in my offer?"

"If you truly have the Achilles bronze —"

"Do you doubt me?" I asked.

"I understood it to have been in the possession of another of your countrymen."

"Yes, Chapman. Do you know him well?" I asked.

"Well enough to know better than to trust him," Demir said.

"It is irrelevant now. He is dead," I said, shrugging. "As is the unsavory individual you sent to deal with him. I do not like messes, Demir. They trouble me. I do not like to do business with someone who causes them."

"That is not my usual manner, I assure you." His English was very good. "Unfortunately, in my line of work, there are times when my suppliers begin to make unreasonable demands and I must discourage them, but you need not worry about that."

"I am willing to sell you the bronze, for the price I sent you, but only if you agree to offer me your best pieces before they go to anyone else."

"The price you ask is already too high," he said. "Why should I agree to further terms as well?"

"So you are agreeing to my price?" I asked.

"I am confident we will agree on a price," he said, "but these things take time. You have the item in question with you?"

"What sort of amateur do you take me for?" I asked. "I will invite you to see it only after we have reached an agreement." I waved for service. "I assume you would like a libation?" I asked the waiter to bring him tea without allowing Demir to answer. "I understand the customs of your country, so you shall have your tea, and we shall sit and talk, but I warn you I will not change my terms."

"I do not object to your terms, only your price," he said. "I will sell nothing before first giving you the chance to buy it."

"Excellent," I said. "Now tell me what I can expect you to have on offer soon."

He leaned forward. "I do not like to discuss such things. It is bad luck."

"Then tell me what you have now."

"I have much coming out of Cyprus, from a site where no Westerners are currently digging. I have a new connection at Ephesus who sends me enough for you to feel it is like your Christmas, and my men in Delos and Macedonia are most reliable. What do you like? Pots? Jewelry? Statues? Friezes? I have them all."

"It sounds like quite an inventory," I said. "Where is your gallery? I should like to visit."

He laughed, but did not answer until the waiter, who had just brought his tea, was gone. "You know I cannot have a gallery. You will have to come to my home, in Constantinople."

"You keep everything there?" I asked. "How cunning. No one suspects you are running what is, if I may state my own opinion on the matter, the greatest illegal antiquities operation in the western hemisphere?"

"No one ever has," he said. "But I do not like the word *illegal.*"

"Quite. It sounds so harsh," I said. "The Achilles bronze is extremely valuable. It would be a worthy addition to your collection. I am certain any houseguests you entertain would admire it."

"I agree, if we can settle on a mutually acceptable price."

"When can I visit your home? I plan to be in Constantinople next month. May I call on you?"

"I will look forward to it with pleasure. Only tell me where you are staying, and I shall send my driver to fetch you."

"Very good," I said. "How can I reach you once I am there?"

"Go to my brother's shop. He sells spices in the Grand Bazaar. Give him this statue" — he pulled out of his jacket a small bronze Hermes identical to the ones I had already seen — "and he will take care of everything. The messenger god will tell him you are someone I trust."

"And the location of the shop? I know the bazaar can prove more daunting than Minos' labyrinth," I said. He passed me a card with the information, including a small map, printed on it. "I am grateful. Grateful enough to lower my price for you by twenty percent."

"Thirty?" he asked.

"Twenty-five. I must, after all, keep my husband in cigars."

He laughed. "You are a delight. Twenty-five it is. I will have to verify the authenticity of the piece, of course."

"I don't think that will be necessary," Colin said, taking advantage of my having left Demir the chair facing the caldera, and coming upon him from behind. "We already have everything we need."

"It is nothing but a formality, I assure you," Demir said. He stopped talking and rose from his seat as the men at the tables surrounding ours gathered close around.

The tallest — and broadest — who served as a policeman of sorts on the island, gripped Demir's hands and twisted them behind his back. "You can talk more in prison," he said. "For now, as you have already been told, we have everything we need."

"I have been tricked," Demir said. "This woman is a charlatan. I have not even taken possession of the item we were discussing."

"I am the mayor of this town," said the man who had shared a table with the police-

425

man. "We heard enough, and I can promise you my testimony will be held in high regard. No more will you steal our cultural treasures."

Demir made one attempt to break away, but was quickly — and thoroughly — subdued. Along with the mayor, police officials from Athens, the Keeper of the Ministry of Religion and Education, who oversaw the Acropolis and other archaeological sites in Greece, and several people from the Antiquities Department witnessed our conversation. My husband had summoned them all via telegram the night before when he had gone to Fira, believing at the time he would need them to deal with Philip, and had chartered a ship to bring them to Santorini overnight.

"A good day's work," Colin said, once Demir was in custody and on the vessel that would transport him to Athens. We walked along the cliff path, hand in hand, back to the villa. "You are very persuasive, my dear, and by encouraging Demir to reveal what he did, have no doubt made a significant contribution to preserving the cultural heritage of the Greeks."

"Now if I could only persuade my own countrymen to return the Parthenon Marbles to their rightful owners," I said.

426

"You know full well Elgin obtained them legally," Colin said. "He should not be held accountable for the decisions of the Turks, whom I need not remind you ruled Greece at the time."

"So if occupying forces take over Britain, you would not object to them selling off the contents of the National Gallery?"

"The Elgin Marbles were not in a museum, Emily," he said. "They were crumbling on the Acropolis. No one was looking after them, no one objected to their removal —"

"Ah, I see. You consider it a crime only when priceless treasures are removed from museums? And you assume the Greeks, who as you already pointed out were not in charge of the country, did not value the marbles? I can assure you that is not true. First, there is continuous evidence of people — Greeks included — visiting the Acropolis —"

"Not now, Emily," he said, and stopped me from continuing with a kiss, taking advantage of our arrival on a stretch of the cliff path devoid of all buildings and, hence, people. "I do love your passion, and if you want Elgin's marbles returned to the Greeks, I would gladly bring them here myself were it possible. For now, though, I fear you must content yourself with what you have already accomplished today."

"It is not simply a matter of what I want," I said. "The marbles should be returned because they belong to the Greeks. We would not have even the beginnings of our civilization without them. We —"

He kissed me again, this time with an intensity fierce enough to drive all thoughts of the marbles out of my head. I did, however, make him promise we would continue the discussion later. After a pleasant interlude, we continued, hand in hand, along the path toward Imerovigli.

"Why didn't you tell me you knew Jones wasn't Ashton?" Colin asked.

"I would have last night if we had been together."

"We were together all morning, alone, on the ride to Thera," he said. "You even asked me if I believed him."

"I suppose I hated the thought of being the person who caused you, once again, to lose your friend. I overheard a certain amount of the conversation between the two of you the night you sat outside talking."

"A certain amount?" he asked.

"I am not proud of my actions, but you must try to imagine what it is like, believing your two husbands are discussing you."

"I assure you we did nothing of the sort," he said, "but I should have been more cautious with him."

"As should I. He made it awfully easy for us both to believe what we wanted to. He really did look like Philip, at least as far as I remember, broken nose notwithstanding."

"Can anyone remember details clearly after a decade?" Colin asked.

"I was primed almost to expect him," I said. "First, there was the picture of the Parthenon addressed to *The Viscountess Ashton*. The next day, when we came home from the zoo, I found Philip's journal open on my desk in the library. I knew I hadn't left it there. I suspected Margaret, but Mr. Jones confessed that over the winter he had bribed one of the housemaids to bring it to him to read — easily enough done, as we weren't in residence — and then he studied it carefully. He paid even more for her to place it in the library, on my desk, shortly before we were to make our annual trip to Greece this spring."

"And the picture of the Parthenon?"

"She mailed it for him."

"I should like to think our servants are above such actions," Colin said. "We shall have to dismiss her."

"Do not rush to judgment," I said. "Let

429

me speak with her when we return to Park Lane and then we can decide."

"How did the maid know about the journal?"

"Really, my dear man, you are naïve when it comes to servants. Half of our current staff came with me from Berkeley Square, and everyone there knew I had read and reread the journal. I am not the least shocked to learn the fact is still, on occasion, discussed in the servants' hall."

"They ought not," Colin said.

"Yes, well, there is much all of us ought not. Seeing the journal put Philip into my head, especially as we were about to leave for Greece, and then when I thought I saw him on the ship —"

"Was it Jones?"

"Yes. The maid also alerted him to the date we planned to leave England, enabling him to put into action the final phase of his plan. Do you remember when I heard someone calling out to Philip Ashton at the zoo in London? Mr. Jones had hired an investigator to trail us while we were in town and to stage the scene whenever he felt it would be most appropriate. Jones himself traveled to Italy and followed us from there, boarding the same ship we did. And then, in Athens, I saw him at the Acropolis — no, do not interrupt: I would have told you, but hesitated to make such an outlandish and impossible claim. Would you have believed me?"

"I would not have accused you of fabricating the story, any more than I did on the ship," Colin said.

"Jeremy came upon me moments after it happened, and I confessed to him. He convinced me it was nothing more than me thinking about Philip because of being in Greece, and that I ought not say anything lest doing so dredge up those complex emotions with which you and I both struggled when we first fell in love."

"Bainbridge." Colin frowned. "You should know better than to listen to him."

"He made a fair point," I said. "The past ought to be left in the past. Then, when we reached the villa and Mrs. Katevatis told us who had arrived, I found myself all but expecting her to say Philip's name. Mr. Jones planned extremely well. I had all but accepted him before even laying eyes on him, and when he did present himself, all of his careful preparations slid into place. How could I not have believed I recognized him?"

"I may have received him with more initial skepticism than you, but he made neat work of convincing me when we spoke alone. He knew so many details — some of them with greater recall than I."

"That recall made me ever so slightly suspicious of him," I said. "He described the night Philip fell in love with me in such detail it sounded more like a studied recitation than a cherished memory, but I could not be sure, particularly as the night in question had made very little impression on me at the time."

Colin squeezed my hand. "You had no reason to be impressed by it at the time."

"As for his knowledge of the past you and Philip shared, he confided in me before he died that he knew about Kristiana not from something Philip told him — Philip would never have betrayed such a confidence — but from the lady herself. He ran into her in Vienna, of course having no idea who she was, and she hailed him under his adopted name."

"Philip had met her on more than one occasion."

"Apparently this meeting occurred shortly before she was killed," I said. "She spoke very openly with him about her relationship with you, only because she believed him to be your dearest friend."

"Whom she knew to be dead," Colin said.

"Evidently, she accepted his story almost

without question, even telling him that in her line of work it often behooved individuals to let the world believe they were dead before —" I stopped. "Good heavens, you don't think she might still be alive? Mr. Jones might have given her the idea to stage —"

"No, Emily, there is absolutely no question. She is dead."

"Yes, but you said the same thing about Philip, and —"

"And he, too, was dead."

"Right. Right. Of course." I frowned. "Mr. Jones did make it easy to believe him, didn't he?"

"Indubitably," Colin said. "Particularly as he did not act as if he wanted anything from us. The past, however, must stay in the past."

"Which neatly brings us back to the topic of the Parthenon Marbles —"

"It most certainly does not," he said.

We argued, each with a fervor normally seen only in religious zealots, about the subject all the way back to the villa.

25

Our argument, refreshing and stimulating as only intellectual debate can be, came to a crashing end when we reached the house. We stood outside for a moment, our mood bleak and somber as we considered the task before us. "I feel terribly sorry for Fritz. It will hurt to learn the truth about his friend." It could not be avoided, however, particularly as Margaret, having heard our approach, flung open the door.

"You took long enough to get here," she scolded. Jeremy and Fritz crowded into the doorway with her.

"Where is Ashton?" Fritz asked. Colin took him aside, as we had both agreed that on this occasion he ought to deliver the tragic news, while I ushered Margaret and Jeremy to the roof terrace, wanting to give Fritz as much privacy as possible for the difficult conversation he faced. Once we were settled around the table, I recounted everything that had transpired.

"Dreadful. Perfectly dreadful," Jeremy said. "So he went back to camp in that awful storm after Bohn died and destroyed his tent, just to ensure your sympathy?"

"Apparently," I said.

"Hideous that his friend lost his life in an accident that could have so easily been prevented," Margaret said.

"It is a terrible tragedy, from beginning to end." I clenched my hands in my lap.

"My dear girl, are you quite all right? You did seem a bit fond of the poor bloke — not in an inappropriate way, of course, but —"

"I did come to enjoy his company, initially because I felt guilty at not having taken the opportunity to do so when Philip — the real Philip, that is — was alive. But I have moved past abusing myself over long-ago sins. I am sad Mr. Jones was unable to find satisfaction in his own life and chose instead to try to steal someone else's."

"It is most tragic," Margaret said. "Reiner tells me he was an excellent archaeologist."

"And what about the Achilles bronze?" Jeremy asked.

"It shall go to the archaeology museum in either Athens or Constantinople," I said. "The authorities will sort it out. Personally,

I should like to see it in Constantinople, as Troy is in Turkey."

"Fair enough," Margaret said, "although I would rather see it in Athens. Achilles, after all, was Greek."

We did not debate the point, as Colin had come up the stairs, his expression clouded. "Reiner will be here shortly. He asked to have a moment to compose himself."

"The poor man," Margaret said.

"Quite." Colin turned to me. "One of the men from the Antiquities Department has arrived to collect the bronze. I thought you would want to be the one to give it to him."

"Of course," I said. "I will go at once."

"I'm coming with you," Margaret said. "I want to see it one more time before it's put behind glass."

"I was glad I did not have it with me this morning," I said as the two of us examined it in my bedroom before bringing it downstairs. "I would have had to turn it over on the spot."

"I know you despise Achilles, but no one could deny the magic of this bit of bronze," Margaret said, holding it gently on her palm.

"I console myself with the idea that it may once have been in Hector's presence," I said. "I wish they had not come quite so quickly to collect it, but I suppose they couldn't hold the ship much longer. They will want to get Demir settled into a nice, comfy cell as quickly as possible."

Mr. Dimitriou, a short but dignified man with a spectacular pair of mustaches, greeted us with a neat bow. I remembered seeing him sitting in the taverna at the mayor's table. "I did not get to speak with you at the taverna," he said, "as I arrived only a bit before our quarry. It is a pleasure to meet you now."

I handed him the bronze. He accepted the object with his thanks on behalf of his government and, as he added, all decent people on the planet. "You have done a great service for mankind by giving this to us," he said, wrapping the bronze in a spotless square of soft flannel before packing it in a small wooden box.

"I am delighted to be of assistance," I said, "and look forward to seeing it in whatever museum comes to be its home." Margaret and I watched as he and the two burly guards who accompanied him collected Batur and his colleague, whom they were confident was recovered more or less enough to travel. They would both stand trial.

"I wonder if we should have had Dr. Liakos look in on him one more time before letting them take him," I said after they had gone. "He is a criminal, but that does not mean we should treat him inhumanely."

"This morning he was lively enough to force me to have Adelphos tie him up," Margaret said. "You need not worry." Adelphos, who had supervised the removal of the prisoners, seconded her position, with great enthusiasm, and told me if, in the future, I planned to hold more criminals in the house, he could construct a more reliable cell. I assured him I did not expect to do any such thing, and am certain I caught a glimpse of disappointment in his eyes.

By the time we returned to the roof, Fritz had joined the gentlemen. I went to him at once, and offered my condolences. "I am most heartily sorry for your loss. Mr. Jones considered you a true friend and I can tell you without doubt that lying to you did not come easily to him. Guilt tormented him over it until his very last moments."

"Thank you," the German murmured. "It would be best if I beg my leave now. I should see to his body and take stock of things at the excavations. Hiller von Gaertringen will arrive soon."

"That can wait," I said. "Colin spoke to the men in the village and they will bring him here so you can arrange for whatever burial you think fitting. It does not appear Mr. Jones had any family to consider — his parents died long ago — and as you were his closest friend —"

"Yes, thank you. He should be buried on the island. I suppose it is too much to ask that you attend the service."

"We will be there," Colin said. "We would not leave you to stand alone." I beamed with pride at my husband's goodwill. To be sure, he did it out of respect for Herr Reiner, not Mr. Jones, but his motive did not diminish the gesture. That settled, we sat quietly for a while, no one certain what to say until Jeremy broached the subject of the remainder of our trip.

"I am of the mind that I have suffered through enough distraction for a lifetime," he said. "Can we not return home? Even the ballrooms of London would provide a respite after this trip."

I started to reply, but Mrs. Katevatis appeared at the top of the stairs. "There is another gentleman — a Mr. Marinos — here from the Antiquities Department, Lady Emily. Should I send him up or would you prefer to meet him downstairs?" I instructed her to bring him to us, deciding there might be merit to his seeing us all in full support of Fritz. I worried that his close association with Mr. Jones might unjustly taint him.

Mr. Marinos crossed to me with haste after his ascent to the roof. I recognized him from the taverna; the Greek flags embroidered on the band on his hat would be hard to forget. He thanked me, most graciously, for my assistance and Colin for his. He was not as well put together as his colleague Mr. Dimitriou had been, but something in his rumpled appearance, suggesting he would be more comfortable in a museum than an island villa, appealed to me.

"Do please sit down," I said. "May I offer you refreshment of any kind? We have fresh pomegranate juice and mint tea, or Mrs. Katevatis can rustle up anything else you desire."

"No, I thank you, Lady Emily. I cannot stay and have come only to collect the Achilles bronze."

"The bronze?" I could feel the color draining from my face as Colin rose to his feet and Margaret let out a little squeak. "I already gave it to one of your colleagues, Mr. Dimitriou."

"There is no one by that name in my department," Mr. Marinos said. "Are you quite certain —"

Colin did not wait to hear the rest of the sentence. He grabbed Fritz and Jeremy and ran downstairs. Not wanting to be excluded from the chase, I turned to Margaret. "Margaret, would you be so good as to describe for Mr. Marinos precisely what happened while I join the gentlemen in pursuit?"

"I want to come, too," she said.

"There is only one more horse," I said. She acquiesced, as I knew she would, and I rushed to the courtyard, where the gentlemen were already mounting their steeds. "Which direction?" I shouted to my husband.

"Bainbridge to Oia, Reiner to Perissa. I shall go toward Akrotiri and the southwestern tip of the island. We must try anywhere a boat could be put in water."

"Then I shall cover Fira," I said. They were gone before I had saddled Pyrois. Mine was the shortest ride, and I reached town in barely a quarter of an hour. Once there, I paid a donkey boy to hold my horse while I mounted his beast and rode it down to the port, where quick consultations with the motley assortment of sailors and fishermen loitering on the dock, confirmed my fears. Five men, one well dressed and the other four clearly his servants — although one had appeared to be injured — had boarded a large sailing yacht and left port more than an hour earlier. Several members of the contingent from the Antiquities Department, who had stood waiting on the deck of their own ship for Mr. Marinos' return, came ashore when they saw me and groaned when I told them about Mr. Dimitriou.

"I saw them from the railing," one of them said. "The well-dressed one with the large mustaches had the audacity to wave at me."

"I cannot apologize enough for my mistake," I said. "I thought I recognized him from the taverna. I thought everyone there to be part of our scheme."

"As did we all," he replied. "I met two of the men from Santorini who accompanied the mayor, but the third . . ."

"The third came in late, when you and your husband had already started your meeting with Demir," one of his colleagues said. "I only noticed because he made a show of greeting the mayor."

Without delay, I returned up the steep path to Fira and found the mayor, who was still at the taverna. When I asked him about the identity of the latecomer, he told me he did not know the man.

"I assumed he came from Athens," he said.

"But he hailed you directly and with great enthusiasm," I said.

442

"Yes, which made me think I ought to know him, and I did not want to insult him by admitting to not remember his name."

When I explained the situation, he blanched, but I told him not to blame himself. It was I, after all, who handed the priceless artifact over to the reprobate. I marched straight onto the ship and demanded to speak with Demir.

"Not bad for a brig," I said, surveying the comfortable cabin which served as his cell.

"This vessel not having one is my last stroke of good fortune," Demir said.

"Who did you send to my house for the bronze?" I asked.

"I sent no one to your house. You told me in your telegram you would bring it to our meeting."

"So I am to believe you came to Santorini alone?"

"I came with the man your husband shot at Ancient Thera."

"And no one else?" I asked.

"No."

"A man, accompanied by two guards, came to the villa identifying himself as a member of the Antiquities Department, come to collect the bronze. Later, another man arrived with the same purpose. The first was a fraud. Your cronies have the bronze, and I have come to tell you I will find it and take it to a museum."

He laughed. "What did this first man look like?" I described him and he laughed again. "The irony of this does not escape me. You handed the piece over to my most serious rival, who no doubt has already taken steps to acquire the people in my employ. I can tell you or the police or anyone you like everything I know about him, but it will make no difference. We dealers are like the Hydra, Lady Emily. You cut off my head and two more grow in its place. You will never find the bronze again."

"You cannot be sure of that," I said.

"I can," he said. "Why do think I spent so many years tracking it down? I do not care about Achilles or *The Iliad.* I heard the story of the execution of the worker who attacked Chapman — a simple example of tribal justice — and along with it the tale of the bronze fragment. When word of the piece spread, a buyer contacted me, a man who is convinced possessing any piece of the Greek hero's armor will make him, and his armies, should he ever manage to raise them, invincible. He is obsessed with the bronze, and I knew if I did not get it for him, someone else would. Logic told me the archaeologist was either lying or had kept the thing for himself, as it never turned up on the black market. Observation of Chapman led me to believe the latter theory. I knew eventually I could get it from him and sell it to my client."

"Who is your client?"

Demir laughed again. "I will not be tricked into telling you anything else. I may go to prison now, but I will be out eventually, and I would like to keep him as a client. The Hydra, remember. No one will eradicate us."

With a heavy heart, I returned to the villa and informed Mr. Marinos the bronze would likely not be recovered.

"It is a blow," he said. "My colleagues in Constantinople will be exceedingly disappointed. But remember, Lady Emily, no true scholar has verified the object. It may be that nothing of value was lost. Achilles would not have been able to dedicate his helmet to Zeus — he was killed in battle, and his armor was eventually given to his son, Neoptolemus, who would have taken it with him back to Greece. He would not have left the helmet behind."

"Do you really believe that?" I asked. "Doesn't history tell us Alexander the Great saw the armor in Turkey?"

He shrugged. "It is impossible to know

what happened so many thousands of years ago. I must focus on preserving what we can, and having Demir and information about his network will go a long way in preventing many more thefts in the future."

He was taking the news far better than I. After he departed, Margaret and I sat in despair. Her horror at what we had done — for she insisted on sharing the burden of culpability — equaled mine, and when Colin, Jeremy, and Fritz had each straggled back to the villa over the course of the next few hours, they'd found us mired in melancholy. My husband understood my distress and did his best to console me, but with little result.

Two days later, after Mr. Jones's funeral, I rose early, feeling considerably better. I had decided I would convince Colin to find a way to persuade the palace that he and his colleagues should be assigned to do whatever necessary to bring down the illegal antiquities trade. He did not react to the suggestion as I had hoped.

"I admire your convictions," he said, "but this problem plagues all corners of the globe. Only look at what goes on in Egypt — those sites are constantly in danger of being looted. Unfortunately, the world is content to let it happen, because collectors have nearly unlimited resources to buy whatever they want. So long as there is demand, there will be a market for these illegal sales. Buckingham Palace is unlikely to take up the banner and lead the charge to stop it."

"Is not the British Empire supposed to be a force for good in the world?" I asked. "Should we not guard the cultural heritage of Western civilization?"

"Of course, but one must be realistic, my dear. You object to the museum's having the Elgin Marbles, and they were acquired legally. I have heard scores of scandalous stories about Wallis Budge, assistant keeper at your beloved British Museum, himself removing things from Egypt under dubious circumstances. These issues are more complicated than they appear at first glance. That said, I shall make the suggestion to my superiors and volunteer for the service myself."

"Nothing will come of it, though?"

"I am afraid not, but I promise to do all I can." He took my hands in his. "You have uncovered the identity of an impostor who was interfering in our lives. You have removed the head of one of the most notorious antiquities gangs in the world. You have delivered into the hands of justice not only him, but also the man who murdered two innocent people. I think, Emily, you must content yourself with that."

"It does not satisfy," I said.

"Are you ever satisfied, Em?" Jeremy asked, strolling onto the terrace. "I do hope you are pleased with how well you have distracted me. Margaret tells me I ought to marry an island girl, renounce my title, and live out the rest of my days here, but I find myself beginning to miss home."

"He knows he can't go back to London," Margaret said, flopping into a chair. "Not until the season is over."

"By Jove, Hargreaves, I believe they mean to kidnap me," Jeremy said.

"By Zeus, you ought to say," Colin replied. "If, that is, you are to have any hope of Emily listening to you."

"We are not returning to England," Margaret said.

"Absolutely not." I said, shaking my head to agree. "What about Olympia?"

"And onward from there to Sicily," Margaret said.

"A brilliant suggestion," I said. "The perfect compromise between the Greeks and the Romans. We will start at the Valle dei Templi —"

"And then make our way north, where we

448

will commence our study of the Romans. I shall give you all volumes of Livy, Tacitus, and Suetonius to read on the boat so you are prepared. I shall not conduct formal examinations, of course, but shall expect you all to make an effort . . ."

She kept speaking, but had long since lost her audience.

"She can't be serious, can she?" Jeremy asked, a look of horror on his face. "I am not reading Latin. I can't read Latin."

"And you thought I was bad," I said, rising from my seat and grabbing my husband by the hand. "I am certain she would be willing to let you use an English translation. Perhaps you should ask her about it."

"Em, do not leave me here alone with her. Hargreaves! My good man! You cannot walk away from me. I —"

We did walk away, far along the cliff path to our favorite spot, where we stood, the sapphire seas of the Aegean churning below us. "Next year," Colin said, "we are coming here alone. No distractions. Just the two of us."

"Not even the boys?" I asked.

"They can come when they have turned five," he said. "Not a moment sooner."

"As disastrous as most of this trip has been, I would not trade it for the world," I said. "Mr. Jones somehow managed to purge from me any remaining shreds of guilt I felt about Philip."

"Tell me, though, did you ever wish he really were Philip?" Colin asked, not looking at me as he posed the question.

"No, not for a second," I said.

"So you didn't secretly long to be dragged back to Berkeley Square?"

"Never. Although I would not object to you dragging me back to our room."

"Dragging?" he said. "It is terribly uncomfortable and has a deleterious effect on one's clothing. Might I throw you over my shoulder instead?"

"One must do it without asking permission. It rather dilutes the excitement."

"Is that so?" he asked, his dark eyes lingering deliciously on mine.

"Quite," I said, all but trembling with anticipation. He took my hand and started to walk, continuing in the direction away from the villa. I will confess to being somewhat disappointed.

That is, until half an hour later, when he interrupted my finest discourse yet on the subject of the Elgin Marbles. He picked me up and, yes, threw me across his shoulder, refusing to put me down until he lowered me onto our bed in the villa. I am certain

Margaret and Jeremy were scandalized when we passed them on the terrace. I am also certain I did not care in the least.

AUTHOR'S NOTE

One of the most well-known stories of stolen identity is that of the sixteenth-century French peasant, Martin Guerre. Plagued by a disappointing marriage and an accusation of theft by his father, he fled from his home in Artigat, abandoning his wife and small child. Eight years later, he returned, as unexpectedly as he had departed.

Guerre's absence appeared to have changed him. He looked a bit different — as we all do after nearly a decade — but his friends and family recognized him, and they were delighted to find him a kinder, more affectionate man. His travels had improved his character.

What no one knew was that this man was not Guerre but an impostor who had carefully planned his subterfuge. After being mistaken for Guerre in a tavern, Arnaud du Tilh (known as Pansette) decided he would take on Guerre's identity. He spent three years learning everything he could about Guerre, and his studying paid off. The villagers, including his wife, accepted him. Eventually, Bertrande uncovered the truth, but by then she had decided she preferred Pansette to her actual husband, and did not reveal his scheme.

Trouble came when he pressed Guerre's brother, Pierre, for part of his inheritance. The case went to court and was settled in Pansette's favor; this made Pierre furious, and he began to say — no doubt because it was to his financial advantage — that this supposed Martin Guerre was an impostor. Eventually, Pansette was charged and had to try to prove his identity in court. And he might have been able to do so, had the actual Martin Guerre not suddenly appeared out of the blue, twelve years after he had left his village.

Guerre's story served as the initial inspiration for this book.

Greece — its history, art, and culture — have been critical to this series from the beginning. When I visited Greece for the first time in the summer of 1998, I stayed in a small hotel in Imerovigli on Santorini and fell in love with the village. The first image I had of Emily came to me on the cliff path, where I pictured her standing and taking in the view of the caldera below. When I walked the path then, there were still sections of it that were undeveloped. Going back in 2015 to do research for this book, I discovered those to be all but gone. Now there are more crowds and less open space, but the spectacular views over the caldera have not changed. Given the immense popularity of the island and its famous sunsets today, it is difficult to imagine that in the nineteenth century it had almost no tourism. Emily's island retreat would feel very different to Santorini today.

They might not have traveled to Greece in search of island beach resorts, but nineteenth-century Britons, ladies included, found the ancient world fascinating. Despite the differences in the education given to men and women, the latter could and did study Ancient Greek, although they were taught "lady's Greek" (the astute reader will recognize the phrase from Elizabeth Barrett Browning's poem "Aurora Leigh"), a version which left out the diacritical marks — which in and of itself proves the inequalities of the system. Byron popularized Greece in his poetry, giving legions of readers a set of expectations for what they would see when they visited. Although he and his compatriots were passionate supporters of Greek independence, subsequent English tourists were less interested in peasants and present-day Greek politics than they were in romantic ancient ruins, and for the rest of the century, Hellenistic ideals set the standards for English views of culture and beauty.

Friedrich Hiller von Gaertringen, Carl Humann, Wilhelm Dörpfeld, and Heinrich Schliemann were all archaeologists working at the sites I have described in the book. Jane Harrison, born in 1850, was one of the first female classicists (she studied at Newnham College, Cambridge), giving many popular lectures, and Dörpfeld included her on many of his trips to Greece and Ephesus. She wrote extensively about her experiences, as well as about Ancient Greek religion.

The maps of the archaelogical sites found in the front of this book are in keeping with those Emily would have found in her trusty Baedekers. It was assumed educated travelers could decipher them in French or German as necessary.

I took my epigraph from Robert Fagles, whose translations of Homer are my personal favorites. Emily is limited to what was available in her century, but I (fortunately!)

am not. She would adore his gorgeous command of language.

Miltiades' helmet, inscribed to Zeus, is on display at the museum in Olympia. Nothing belonging to Achilles has ever been discovered. Like Emily, I would prefer archaeologists uncover something of Hector's.

The employees of Thorndike Press hope you have enjoyed this Large Print book. All our Thorndike, Wheeler, and Kennebec Large Print titles are designed for easy reading, and all our books are made to last. Other Thorndike Press Large Print books are available at your library, through selected bookstores, or directly from us.

For information about titles, please call:
(800) 223-1244

or visit our Web site at:
http://gale.cengage.com/thorndike

To share your comments, please write:
Publisher
Thorndike Press
10 Water St., Suite 310
Waterville, ME 04901